Maybe This Time

MAYBE THIS TIME

Daoma Winston

CENTURY
LONDON MELBOURNE SYDNEY JOHANNESBURG

First published in Great Britain in 1988 by
Century Hutchinson Ltd, Brookmount House,
62–65 Chandos Place, London WC2N 4NW

Century Hutchinson South Africa (Pty) Ltd
PO Box 337, Bergvlei, 2012 South Africa

Century Hutchinson Australia Pty Ltd
PO Box 496, 16–22 Church Street, Hawthorn,
Victoria 3122, Australia

Century Hutchinson New Zealand Limited
PO Box 40–086, Glenfield, Auckland 10,
New Zealand

ISBN 0 7126 1782 5

British Library Cataloguing in Publication Data

Winston, Daoma
Maybe this time.
I. Title
813'.54[F]   PS3545.I7612

ISBN 0-7126-1782-5

Typeset by Input Typesetting Ltd, London SW19 8DR
Printed and Bound in Great Britain by
Anchor Brendon Ltd., Tiptree, Essex

Acknowledgements

With special thanks to Ruth Leon, who provided me with the technical background necessary for the writing of this novel, and to Charles Eldridge for additional information.

1

On a misty night in mid October the dark Manhattan streets glistened like black satin. Blurred halos encircled the traffic lights. Inside the cab the air was sour with rotting floor mats.

Sarah Morehouse wrinkled her nose and pressed closer to the window. It was cracked just enough to allow a narrow ribbon of cold to blow against her cheeks. It felt good, clean.

Beside her Daniel Clermont sighed. His hand lay on her knee, fingers curled, caressing either her or the silken mink of her coat. She wasn't sure which, but gave it no thought. He said, 'I'm glad you wanted to get away early. I've been anxious to talk to you ever since I got in.'

'Yes,' she said absently, her eyes fixed on the blinking signals from the cars ahead.

'You don't like the Roysters, do you?'

She didn't reply. They were *his* friends. If he cared for them, it was his business. She wouldn't tell him what to feel. But she had already decided that she wouldn't see them again. She had been taken aback by the small dish of white powder openly offered on the coffee table. Perhaps she oughtn't to have been. It was known, at least in the trade, that Edie Royster had had an operation on her nose to repair cocaine damage, although she claimed the surgery was for a deviated septum. Sarah didn't care what the Roysters did, but she wasn't going to risk everything she had built for herself by ending up in a drug bust, with her picture in the newspapers and her name endlessly repeated on the evening television news.

Daniel pressed against her. 'They're really very good people. And talented too. Everybody says so.'

Edie wrote TV commercials. Ralph acted in them. Sarah had seen their work often. 'Solid professionals,' she

7

agreed. But there was irritation in her voice. She didn't want to think about the Roysters. In fact she didn't want to think about anything but the day's taping. Something about it had been wrong. She didn't know what, but she had to find out. The long-running series, called *Oakview Valley*, was her baby and every episode had to be perfect for the midday market. It was her job as producer to be certain it was.

She held her breath as the cab driver suddenly jockeyed from the middle lane to the kerbside and then shot through a small opening into the far left lane, skidding past a red light to make an illegal left turn off Broadway on to her one-way street. Briefly he was heading in the wrong direction. Then, with a wild swing of the wheel, he lurched in a half-circle and managed to right himself to brake before her apartment house, grinning triumphantly in the rearview mirror.

Sarah was accustomed to such driving and was usually amused by it. But tonight she sighed in relief when the doorman opened the cab door and greeted her. The whole evening had seemed nothing but one long delay. She was impatient to put it behind her.

The cab driver told Daniel, 'I saved you a dollar and a half, at least, by not cutting over to Amsterdam.'

She didn't wait to hear what Daniel would say. She hurried into the lobby, anxious to see if her production manager, Robin Denver, was waiting for her. If he'd been able to get the tape, he'd be here by now.

But the green leather couch was empty. She bit her lip. She missed Rob when she needed him and he wasn't there. Because he so rarely failed her, the feeling was even worse. It was going to be a long night if she couldn't figure out what was wrong with the show. The only way to do it was to sit down with the tape, and play it and play it and play it, until she spotted the fault.

'The damn fool,' Daniel said, coming up behind her and taking her arm.

'Who?' she said vaguely. Daniel couldn't be referring to Rob.

8

'The cab driver. Thinking he was doing us a favour. He could have gotten us killed.' The heat in Daniel's voice surprised her. He was the most even-tempered man she had ever known. It bothered her sometimes. She wondered what he concealed behind that laid-back façade.

But she didn't answer him. There were times when she didn't feel like talking. This was one of the drawbacks of having Daniel in from Boston for the weekend. But the pattern had been established when they'd begun their affair two years before. There was no polite way to tell him that tonight she'd rather be alone.

Something must have gone wrong at the studio. Otherwise Rob would have been here, waiting for her. Her strong right arm. He never failed her. She knew she could always call on him, even for an errand like this which wasn't really part of his job. If he hadn't got the tape it was because it hadn't been ready. Just as it hadn't been ready this afternoon, although she had asked that it be delivered to her desk no later than five-thirty.

The elevator glided upward with a whisper. The indicator silently blinked each floor number. Twenty-five. Twenty-six. Twenty-seven.

Daniel said something. Sarah heard the sound of it but she was concentrating so intensely she didn't understand the words. She didn't ask him to repeat them. She was remembering that morning in the control room, watching the monitors while the episode was taped.

Thirty-two. Thirty-four. Almost home. Home, the penthouse. It was still hard for her to believe that she'd really done it; the best investment she could ever have made, although it frightened her to think what she had borrowed to pay for it, the size of the mortgage. And while she was still paying off for her mother's Connecticut Avenue condo in Washington.

The indicator blinked at thirty-five, and the door slid back. The mirrored wall reflected three Sarahs as she stepped out, all tall, very slender, with narrow hips and long shapely legs.

There was something about Sarah that made people

9

turn to look when she entered a room. They looked at the short, honey-coloured hair and at the deep-set green eyes, the tilt of her head, the slowness of her smile, and they didn't forget.

Daniel loomed over her. He was over six feet tall and very thin, with narrow bones and a knobby face. He had straight sandy hair and brown eyes set in a map of wrinkles. He was the assistant to the station manager at Station WZBT in Boston. They met at a dinner party soon after she became producer of *Oakview Valley*. He came to New York often, buying movie packages from one of the syndicates. He'd called her frequently, and finally they slid into an easygoing relationship, which was exactly what she wanted.

Now she glanced at the reflection they made, suddenly realizing that they were an odd couple. She had a quick confident swinging walk, sure-footed and smooth. He shambled along – that was the only word for it – with a hitch in his stride, as if he were perpetually off balance and fighting to keep from falling.

Daniel said, 'The thing I've been thinking about . . .'

'Yes?' she cut in, hurrying down the short hallway and around the corner. But she didn't give him time to go on. For there, leaning against her door, was Rob.

'Oh, darling,' she cried. 'Have I been a terrible bitch? Did I spoil your Friday night?'

A momentary look of pain tightened his face before he could control it. She didn't have any idea how he felt about her, how he hated the weekends because that was when he usually didn't see her. But he said only, 'You haven't been such a terrible bitch that I can't forgive you.'

She glanced at the book-sized cassette he held. 'You got it.'

'Of course. You said you'd need it tonight.' Rob grinned at her. 'The thing is, do you need me too?'

Daniel cleared his throat.

Sarah heard, but ignored it. She unlocked the door. 'I don't know. Let's have a look. Meanwhile, let's get you

10

a beer.' She led the way inside. 'Why didn't you ring for Laylie? Surely she's still up.'

'I didn't want to bother her. Besides, I haven't been waiting long.'

'Sarah . . .' Daniel cleared his throat again. 'If I'll be in the way . . .'

'Oh no. Of course not. Why don't you get Rob a beer? And one for yourself. This won't take long.'

'Couldn't it wait until tomorrow?'

'Daniel.' She smiled at him. 'You know better.'

He went into the kitchen after taking off his coat. She hung it, along with her mink, in the foyer cupboard.

Rob took the cassette into the living room. 'I'll set it up for you.'

Sarah went down the hall, paused to listen before the door to her daughter's room, then gently turned the knob. 'Laylie? Is that you?' the young voice asked sleepily.

'It's Mama, Peg.'

'Oh, okay.' A sigh. A yawn.

Sarah backed from the room, closed the door. *Laylie, is that you?* Peg had asked. Not Mama first. Laylie. Sarah winced, but told herself quickly that she'd been willing to settle for that all along. What did she expect? Laylie's always here. Mama isn't. So what? Peg was doing fine, a pretty, bright twelve-year-old. So was Tim, Sarah's fourteen-year-old son away at school in Washington.

Sarah hurried back to the living room.

Rob grinned at her. He was twenty-eight, ten years her junior. His smile made him seem younger. He had a shock of dark curly hair, always just a little too long. His eyes were blue, and changeable, sometimes light, sometimes almost black. He had the office next door to hers, and was involved with the logistics of the show, and the technical negotiations, so they were together a great deal.

But suddenly, for an instant, she saw him as if he were a stranger. He was handsome enough to work in front of the camera instead of behind it. He had a strong straight nose, chiselled lips. His jaw was square. It all added up to a man's face, powerful, but sensitive. Sexy too. As

11

suddenly as it had come that instant's vision was gone. He became her Rob again, no longer a handsome and sexy stranger, but the boy who worked with her and for her, and on whom she depended.

'Okay,' he was saying. 'Ready to go.'

She sat down.

The cassette was in the three-quarter-inch U-Matic. He handed her the remote control.

She tensed, leaned forward. In the control room, pulling it all together, watching everything and everybody at once, and still staring at both the line monitor and the preview monitor, she'd seen something she didn't like, but it hadn't quite registered. She'd said nothing to her director, Hy Berge, because she couldn't pinpoint the trouble. Now, without the shuffling, breathing, rustling, of the full staff, the network's Standards and Practices man, the executive producer, the account executive from Georgiana – *Oakview Valley*'s sponsor – and his various hangers-on, and whoever else had been there in addition to her own people, without that bunch, she'd instantly identify the problem.

Daniel gave Rob a glass of beer, sank into the sofa beside her and thrust out his long legs. She heard his deep sigh. This wasn't the way he'd expected to end his Friday evening with her. She understood, flashed him a quick absent smile, then pressed the switch.

The first frame appeared. The burn-in time code, which was the number of each frame, was clearly marked at the bottom. At about twelve minutes in, she murmured, 'Okay, okay, we're getting there.' And then, 'Oh, no!' She reversed to twelve minutes, began again. Davey, who in real life was Hart Carow, walked slowly across the room. 'I love you. I love you. Don't you understand?' He pulled Nella, played by Rita Porter, up from the edge of the bed and into his arms. 'Damn you, I love you!' He kissed her, the camera at centre. The side of his face, the side of her face, each clear. Unmoving. Unmoving as if dead. 'Got it!' Sarah cried, clutching the joy stick. 'Why

12

did it take me so long? Why didn't I see it right away? And more important even, why didn't Hy see it?'

'See what?' Rob asked. 'It looked okay to me.'

'Okay? It was awful! *Awful!* Rita looks dead. I want to see something happen. They're kissing. They're reunited. It's passion. And they look . . .'

'Dead,' Daniel said softly.

'What?' Sarah asked, without looking at him.

'Dead. That's what you said.' Daniel rose, disappeared in the direction of the kitchen.

'Passion. Sexual excitement. That's what we need,' she told Rob. 'I want to see something besides tinted skin, for God's sake.'

Rob looked at her. 'It's delicate, Sarah,' he said quietly.

'Delicate?'

'Kissing.' Rob shrugged. 'You know. These days.'

'These days,' Sarah repeated slowly. 'You're right. Everybody's thinking about AIDS. They can't help it, can they? But Rita's kissed Hart hundreds of times since she came on the show. And always made it look good.'

'Before it sank in,' Rob said. And added, 'Either about AIDS or about Hart.'

Sarah ignored that. She said, 'I just want to see movement. In the cheeks, the throat. They don't have to make it real as long as it looks real.'

Rob remained silent.

From the doorway Daniel said, 'You can't push that too far, Sarah. It isn't fair to the actors.' He held a glass filled, it seemed to Sarah, with a lot of Scotch and a little ice. That was unusual. He rarely drank more than a glass or two of white wine. Tonight at the Roysters' he'd had three. It was the kind of thing that Sarah always noticed.

'And you must be fair to the actors,' Daniel went on.

'The show comes first,' Sarah said.

Rob asked, 'Want to see more?'

'Yes. I'll go through it. But I won't need you.'

'What'll you do?'

She knew she wouldn't ask for a re-shoot. It was too late. And it would be too expensive. There was no room in her budget for repeating scenes. They were right the first time. Or else. All she asked was that actors act. It seemed completely reasonable to her. She wondered if Hy had seen what was happening.

Her impulse was to go in on Monday, raise Cain with Hy, jump on Rita – to do something fast. Fast. But she knew she had to move more slowly than that. First a few words to Hy. Then give him time to work with Rita, to bring her along. And then, if that didn't help . . .

Rob left, relieved to be getting away because it was hard on him to see Sarah with Daniel, hard to keep from imagining a time later, with Sarah in Daniel's arms.

Once, Daniel had been Rob's friend, his mentor. But now Rob couldn't stand him. He wasn't worthy of Sarah. Rob had seen that as soon as he'd gone to work for her. He'd realized he was in love with her only weeks after that. Nothing had changed in the time since.

When she and Daniel were alone, Sarah remained curled on the sofa, the joy stick in her hand, looking at the blank screen.

Daniel went to the hearth, and kneeling, lit the gas. Small blue-red flames licked at the logs. He said, 'Let me tell you what I've been thinking about.'

'Not now,' Sarah said.

'Now, damn it!'

She turned to look at him. There had been an unaccustomed roughness in his voice. Red spots burned in his usually pale cheeks. His hand shook so that the ice rattled in his drink.

'Daniel,' she said softly. 'What's the matter?'

'I've been trying to talk to you . . .'

'We've had a busy evening.'

'Don't speak that way to me, Sarah. You sound as if you're talking to one of the kids on your crew. To Rob, maybe. Mothering. Soothing. I'm not a child to be indulged.'

She sat up, leaned back against the dark green cushions, and crossed her legs. 'Okay, Daniel. What's this about?'

'You. And you and me.'

14

'Yes.' She drew the word out. 'And . . . ?'

He set the glass on the mantel, and leaned there. 'You're a wonderfully talented woman, Sarah. You don't have to waste your time on the kind of thing you're doing now.'

'Waste?'

'Oh, don't play dumb. You know what I mean. And you know you agree with me. You should be doing night-time TV. Mini-series. Full-length movies. Not daytime soaps.'

'I'll think about that,' she told him. As if she hadn't. As if she didn't think about it night and day. 'But meanwhile explain what you meant about "you and me".'

Daniel ran his fingers through his hair, took a few steps back and forth in front of the hearth, then turned to face her. 'Look, Sarah, what we should do is pool our resources and our talents. We could set up our own production company. You do your own shows. I'll sell them for you.'

'And what do we do for financing?'

'I'll put in whatever I have. I'll move down to New York.'

'And what do you think I ought to put in?' she asked.

'Whatever you feel you can.'

'I don't have anything, Daniel.'

'You don't have anything?' he said blankly. 'What's that supposed to mean?'

'Just what I said. I don't have anything I'd dare use as security. And there's very little that I *could* use. Oh, maybe I could realize a few hundred on the Honda. And perhaps I could sell my mink. But . . .' She watched the colour fade from his cheeks. Her heart was beating furiously. She wasn't frightened and she wasn't angry. At least not yet. She thought that soon she might become very angry indeed. She went on, 'But I doubt the mink would bring me very much either. No, Daniel, your idea just isn't practical. Unless you have half a million you can spare.'

His lips, pale now in his suddenly pale face, writhed as he said, 'I don't. You know I don't. Why are you mocking me? You have this apartment. Surely, Sarah . . .'

15

'The apartment is mortgaged,' she said quietly. 'And I wouldn't dare risk it further.'

'Risk it? With your talent? With my knowhow and contacts.'

'No,' she said bluntly.

'Okay, okay.' He shrugged. 'But what I really wanted to talk about is our future.'

'Daniel . . .'

'Where are we going, Sarah? What do you think we mean together?' When she said nothing, he rushed on, 'We *do* belong together. The two of us. And I don't mean just for weekends.'

She said softly, 'I thought it was what we both wanted.'

'It was, Sarah. But now . . . now we ought to have more. I want to marry you. I'll move down. We'll be a family.'

'But Daniel, we've never even considered that.'

'We haven't? You mean that you haven't. I have.'

'Marriage.' She drew a deep breath, smiled. 'I guess I'm a little surprised.'

'I don't see why. When two people are in love they usually want to live together, don't they?'

She thought of the scene she had just watched so many times. Rita and Hart. No passion, she'd thought, troubled, disappointed, frightened even. If passion didn't come across then there'd be nothing there for the audience. It was the same now. She said regretfully, 'I don't think we're in love, Daniel.' She went on quickly, 'I know that I'm very fond of you. And you're fond of me. In fact, we like each other very much, and have a lot in common. But, for marriage . . .' She let the words trail away. Even as she spoke them, she had begun to wonder. Was she fond of him, and he of her? *Did* they like each other?

'Is it because I suggested a business arrangement?'

'It's because I don't want to get married.' She smiled wryly. 'Remember that I've tried it once. And it didn't work out. I'm not sure I'll ever want to try it again.'

'It *is* because of that, isn't it?'

'I just don't want to get married, Daniel.' She smiled at him. 'But thank you for asking.'

'Thank you, and that's all?'

She didn't answer.

'Okay,' he said. 'That's it, I guess. I'll be on my way.'

Her heart had stopped its furious pounding. A sudden relief swept her. She said, 'Oh, you needn't. You can stay the night.' But she hoped he wouldn't. She hoped he'd leave now and that she'd never see him again.

He took his coat from the cupboard, pulled it on. 'You're very special to me. You always will be.'

She nodded, a faint forced smile on her lips. It faded after he closed the door behind him. A moment later she remembered that he had accumulated drawers full of possessions in two years of weekends here. She hurried out to call him back. But the elevator door had already closed. The indicator was blinking thirty-two.

She shrugged, went inside. No doubt he'd think of his belongings by the next day. He'd telephone with instructions. She would tell Laylie to deal with him. Laylie was going to be disappointed. She'd harboured hopes for Daniel and Sarah. A pity. Both Laylie's disappointment, and Daniel's.

Sarah herself, she was surprised to discover, felt nothing more than a growing relief. Perhaps she had sensed this was coming and had hardened herself. Perhaps she was shocked, and would, tomorrow, suddenly learn how much she missed Daniel. But she doubted that. She suspected that convenience and habit had hidden the emptiness in what there had been between them. And right now she was sleepy. She yawned, went into her bedroom.

It was a pleasant place. The rug was a rosy beige, and soft underfoot. There was a white spread on the queen-sized bed, and white drapes hung at the window. The furniture was teak, well polished and smooth. Near the bed was a stack of *Broadcasting*, the weekly everybody in television read and complained about.

Daniel had a suit in the wardrobe. A little worn at the elbows. In one of the dressers he kept a few shirts. She had the momentary impulse to take scissors to the stuff just to get it out of the way. To rend the shirts, rip the suit. The idea passed as soon as she became aware of it. If he didn't collect his stuff tomorrow, she'd call and remind him. The whole thing now seemed unreal. Daniel sitting there quietly while she and Rob watched the screen. Then, once Rob had gone, his proposing a production company, and then proposing marriage. In that order. *In that order*. How revealing. At least it was done now. Over.

She went to the mirror over the dresser, and leaned close to it, studying her face. Were there new wrinkles around her eyes? She wasn't sure. Was her complexion darkening? No. She was as fair as she'd ever been. And her eyes were still the same familiar cool green. She ran her fingers through her hair. It was soft and thick. But there did seem to be a slight sag below her jaw. She'd better watch that. In an industry in which so many were chosen for being beautiful and handsome, looks were all important. But even more, it was a commonplace that a woman was finished in television when she hit forty. Well, Sarah Morehouse was thirty-eight. That gave her two more years. Only she didn't plan to be finished. She was going to be doing a new job by then. She'd be producing night-time shows. Just as Daniel had said she should. A mini-series, maybe. But better yet, full-length television movies. She'd be the best-known woman producer in the business.

With that in her mind, she got ready for bed. But after she had turned the covers back and switched off the lamp, she found that she was too restless to lie down. She threw a quilted robe around her shoulders and went out to the terrace.

The concrete canyons were bejewelled with lights. An occasional flake of snow drifted by, melting before it reached the street below.

On the other side of the hedges that separated her terrace from the one belonging to the adjacent penthouse, a faint glow spread through the draped glass doors. That meant that Tony Statler had come in from Los Angeles for a few days. He was subletting from the apartment owner, an elderly man who had made a fortune in the movies, so it was no coincidence that Tony was a communications type too.

They'd been introduced soon after he took over the place, but she'd known who he was even before them. He looked exactly like his photographs in *Broadcasting*. Flashing eyes, even white teeth, a well-shaped head. He was part-owner of Stell-Stat, an independent TV production company. He was an attractive man, and she'd been curious about him. And: Stell-Stat was important. He'd said they ought to get together some time, and she had agreed. But that was as far as it had gone.

Perhaps one of these days, she'd arrange something. There was no rush. She turned away to lean on the parapet, her face raised to the cold wind.

It was a month later, a grey Saturday morning. The sky beyond the window was leaden when Laylie pulled back the drapes, saying, 'It sure is different without Mr Clermont here for the weekend.'

Sarah drew on her robe. She didn't answer.

Laylie looked at Sarah. 'It must have been a pretty bad fight.'

'It's all over, Laylie.'

'Oh, he'll be back,' Laylie said. She was a handsome black woman, with very dark skin and snapping black eyes. Her hair was straight, wrapped in heavy braids around her head. She was a few days older than Sarah.

Sarah said, 'He still might come for his things, and I hope he does. It would save us the trouble of sending them to him eventually.'

'I know you don't want him back,' Laylie said. 'But maybe you're taking it too seriously. A man walks out once in a while. It doesn't have to mean anything.'

It was something Laylie knew about. She'd been

19

married twice. Both of her husbands had walked out on her several times before they'd left her for good.

'I don't care what it means.' Sarah hadn't explained about the proposal that had been all business before the proposal that had supposedly been all heart. She wasn't going to explain now.

She went into the kitchen, Laylie following her. Automatically she turned on the TV set. It was what she nearly always did when she entered a room. Television wasn't just her job. She lived and breathed it. It was her life. Laylie handed her a cup of coffee, and as she sipped at it, she looked at John Carmody's *The TV Column*, in the Washington *Post*. It was because of his column that she had the *Post* delivered daily, and swore when it didn't arrive. There was nothing like it in the New York papers, and television people in both New York and Washington read it avidly for news of the business.

The phone rang. Laylie took the call, then covered the mouthpiece and whispered, 'It's Mr Bradford.'

Sarah sighed. Her ex-husband. He had a particular instinct for calling when she didn't want to talk to him. But she took the phone from Laylie. 'Hello, John.'

'Sarah? Am I calling at the wrong time? Did I get you up?'

It was his response to her impatience. They'd been divorced six years but there were times when he acted as if they were still married. Especially when he wanted to talk about Peg or Tim.

'What do you want?' she asked.

It had to be something. He never called except when he was in the mood to annoy her. Which meant when things weren't going well for himself. She refused to ask him what was bothering him. He might tell her. And she didn't care. It had been quite a long time since she had.

'I'm going to be in New York this afternoon. I'd like to see Peg. Carla's busy.'

Carla had once been Sarah's closest friend. She was now John's wife. It still hurt to remember that. Carla had done a lot for Sarah, and they had meant a lot to each other. But when Carla had married John, Sarah had felt betrayed. As if Carla had rejected her, their friendship. There was no way to go back to what they had been before.

Sarah said, 'I think Peg's occupied this afternoon.'

'Oh, come on. Whatever it is can be changed. I can't get in to see her that often these days.'

'Let's let her decide, shall we?'

John didn't answer immediately. She supposed he was counting to ten. 'Okay,' he said finally. 'Put her on.'

Peg was brushing her long blonde hair. She gave it two last swipes before she smiled at her mother and picked up the cordless phone on her vanity. 'Hi, Daddy. How are you?'

Sarah went into the kitchen. In a few minutes Peg stuck her head in the door. 'It's all right, isn't it? I told Daddy I'd go with him.'

'Sure,' Sarah said. 'Whatever you want.'

John was still frowning when he hung up. Sarah hadn't given him a chance to say anything. She ought to realize that occasionally they had things to talk over. Peg and Tim were *his* kids too, after all.

His wife, Carla, saw his face, and wished, as she had many times before, that Sarah and the kids lived halfway around the world instead of only thirty miles away. They were close enough to make him feel obligated to see the kids, be involved with them. Maybe a greater distance would have made the separation easier for him. But she said, smiling, 'Did you tell her you want to talk to her?'

'When I pick up Peg,' he said shortly. 'Then I'll do it.'

Her voice was sweet with sympathy. 'I know you miss Tim. It really would be better for Sarah too.'

'It's Tim I'm thinking about. He should be with his family. It's ridiculous for him to be away at school when he doesn't need to be any more.'

Carla patted her already smooth hair. 'I'm sure Sarah will agree when you put it to her.'

'You won't mind having him here with us? You're sure?'

'Really, John, how many times do I have to tell you? I'm very fond of Tim. I know it would work out.'

'Okay. I'll see what Sarah says,' John told Carla.

Smiling still, Carla repressed a sigh. Sarah Morehouse remained a continuing presence in her life. Even six years after John and Sarah were divorced, a certain note came into John's voice when he said Sarah's name. But, Carla reminded herself, *she* was now John's wife. He loved *her*. He'd married *her*.

As for Sarah . . . well, Sarah pretended that she and Carla had never been friends. It was Sarah's choice. But Carla had not forgotten how close they'd once been. She, and Sarah, and the two kids. It had been very special for Carla. And she hadn't intended to hurt Sarah when she started to go out with John. It had just happened. She'd been lonely. So had John. Their falling in love had nothing to do with Sarah. It would all be so much easier, Carla suddenly thought, if she and Sarah hadn't known each other before.

Carla picked up her car keys, linked her arm through John's. 'Come on, let's get the shopping done.'

2

In mid morning Laylie came into the bedroom.

Sarah was sitting at her desk in black jeans and a black turtleneck sweater. Her hair was tousled. It was a little while before she acknowledged the housekeeper with an impatient 'What is it, Laylie? I told you, I'm not at home for anybody. Can't you handle it on your own?'

'Me? I wouldn't even try to handle Ms Stinkowitz, as she likes to call herself sometimes. And that's who's coming right now.'

Sarah's head jerked up. 'You mean Glory Ann's here?' Only her friend Glory Ann would use that self-deprecating slangy nickname.

'Very nearly,' Laylie said. 'I calculate her at floor twenty-six, going on twenty-seven this minute.'

Sarah smiled. It was disconcerting that Laylie suddenly seemed to think she was a character in a situation comedy. Maybe the maid with all the good lines. But Sarah had always said television was a disease, and as contagious as measles.

Soon there was a hammering at the door. The chimes rang out. Laylie hurried to answer, with Sarah rising to follow.

Shouts, shrill cries, and Laylie's giggles filled the apartment.

At the threshold of her bedroom Sarah was enveloped in bunches of roses, in fur-covered arms, in a spicy scent.

'Glory Ann! What are you doing?' Laughing, Sarah pulled away.

'I'm trying to love you up, but you won't stand still for it.'

Glory Ann Champion had become a household word in the past two years. Daily her comings and goings were mentioned in the newspapers. Television columnists spoke

23

of her as many times a week as they could find, or make up, something to say. Her face, framed in silver-blonde curls, was known all over the world. Her voluptuous body was the envy of every woman in the country.

Now she wore baggy patched trousers, a blue waistcoat over a faded red shirt. And over both, a mangy fur coat. It was what she liked to call her bag lady disguise. She raised her dark glasses, revealing velvety brown eyes, jerked a scarf from her head and danced into the living room, where she flung herself on the sofa.

Sarah followed her, carrying the big shopping bag Glory Ann had dropped with a thump. 'I'm so surprised. I didn't know you were coming in. How are things on the Coast?'

Glory Ann sprawled on her shoulders, her long legs thrust out, her arms wide. 'All in good time. Meanwhile, shall we have some champagne?'

'Now? It's only ten-thirty!'

'On a lovely Saturday morning, when two good friends get together for the first time in six months, there ought to be a toast.' With that, Glory Ann took the shopping bag from Sarah and carefully drew out a bottle of Dom Perignon. 'I just happen to have it here.'

'What's going on?' Sarah asked suspiciously.

'We're celebrating.'

'Celebrating what?'

'Ralph left me three days ago, Sarah.'

'What?' Sarah asked.

Glory Ann raised her velvety brown eyes to the ceiling, to the heavens beyond it, and to the Being beyond both. 'Ralph's left me,' she repeated. 'And I must say, it was just as difficult to say the first time around.'

'I see,' Sarah said slowly, thinking of Daniel.

'And if it's okay, I'll stay here with you.' She added after a pause, 'Ralph knows your phone number. So just in case . . .'

'Of course you can stay here. You can have Tim's room.'

'I can?' Glory Ann's perfect brows rose. She leaned

24

forward, almost falling off the sofa, to look under the coffee table. 'Come to think of it – it's Saturday, where's Daniel?'

'Daniel is no more,' Sarah said dryly, and went on to explain what had happened a month before.

Glory Ann leaped up, flung herself at Sarah, hugged her tightly. 'We both got dumped!'

'It seems so.'

'And you're just a little sad still. Not heartbroken or anything. Just a little sad.'

'I suppose,' Sarah agreed.

'*I'm* surprised,' Glory Ann said. 'I mean . . . he knew what it would be like. Being married to me. I told him. He could see it beforehand. So how come he starts complaining now? I mean, I think he's got his nerve.' Her voice shook. She threw herself on the sofa and stretched out, wriggling and squirming until her every curve was comfortable. Then with a sigh she said, 'And I wish he'd call. But now I'm here, I *do* feel better.'

'I spent some time this morning wondering if I ought to consider a face lift. And now, looking at you, I realize it won't really help me.'

'Oh, Sarah . . .' It was a sorrowful reproach. Glory Ann didn't like people to compliment her on her looks, which were spectacular and always had been.

'Sorry, Glory Ann. I'm not myself.'

'If you're not, you will be in a minute.' Glory Ann took a deep breath. Her bosom rose, stretching the waistcoat and shirt that covered it. 'Laylie! Champagne! Can you help please?'

Laylie came on the run, took the bottle and offered to serve caviar and toast.

'Oh God, no!' Sarah groaned.

'I'm starved.' Glory Ann swung herself up. 'Laylie, you're going to spoil me.'

'There's nothing I'd rather do in this life than spoil you, Glory Ann.' Laylie giggled as she hurried out.

'You haven't told me what you're doing in New York,' Sarah said.

'Just getting away from it all. And besides, I have a publicity meeting later. And you're going with me.'

'I am? Forget it.'

'Sarah . . . please . . . I don't want to go through this on my own. Not now. Not with Ralph telling me that I'm impossible, and my life's impossible . . .'

'Well it is, Glory Ann.'

'*I* know that. But what am I supposed to do about it? Give up? Forget my contracts, and Hollywood. And my' – Glory Ann's voice dropped to a whisper edged with laughter – 'and my public?'

Sarah shook her head. Give up? Glory Ann didn't know the meaning of the words any more than Sarah herself did. That wasn't how they were made. The two of them were alike under the skin as peas in a pod. Determined. Tough. Focused. Each one set on being, in her own way, somebody. What else did Glory Ann want? What else did Sarah want? Love. Sure. Why not? They were entitled to love. They needed love. And that was the trouble. Or that made the trouble.

'First, though, I want a walk. You and me. On Fifth Avenue. Window shopping. Rodeo Drive's okay, but I've missed the real thing.'

'I have work to do, Glory Ann.' When Glory Ann had arrived Sarah had just decided that Rita Porter would have to be written out of the show. She'd been going over the bible, the master plan for *Oakview Valley*, looking for the most interesting and dramatic way to eliminate Nella without making Davey look bad. Sarah wanted to have suggestions to present to Bonnie Walker, her scriptwriter, when they met to talk about the change.

'You can work all night,' Glory Ann said. 'Now that Daniel's gone.'

It was easier to agree than to argue. But more important, Sarah had very little time with Glory Ann these days. She didn't want to miss out on what there was. 'Okay,' she said. 'We walk. When?'

'When we've finished the champagne.'

'The way you're dressed?'

'Why not?' Glory Ann said airily. But then, grinning, she patted her shopping bag. 'I have it all here. Wait and see.'

Laylie brought in the champagne, hurried out to get a tray, which she brought back laden with chilled goblets, small dishes with silver knives, a platter of black caviar, chopped hard-boiled eggs and slivered onions.

'Your glass, Laylie,' Glory Ann said.

'I'll get tiddly.'

'Just a sip then. To wish us all good luck,' Sarah told her.

'Then I'd better rinse good before Mr Bradford gets here.'

'Is John coming?' Glory Ann asked.

'To pick up Peg.'

'She's not back from her dancing lesson yet,' Laylie said. 'She ought to be along any minute.'

Sarah watched Laylie pour the champagne.

Glory Ann said, 'I haven't seen John for ages.'

'You've missed nothing. He's exactly the same.'

Glory Ann's sigh was eloquent. She cheered up when Laylie handed her the glass, served Sarah, then took a small sip of wine herself.

'To us,' Sarah said. And then, 'I'm glad you came, Glory Ann.'

'I'm glad too.' Then: 'I wish you'd move to LA.'

'One of these days . . .'

'Do you have anything cooking?'

'Not yet.'

'But you have an ear to the ground?'

'Oh, yes.'

'It'll happen.'

'I think so,' Sarah agreed.

'And soon. I want it to be soon.' Glory Ann emptied her glass, refilled it. 'Now I begin to feel better. Maybe it's the wine. Or maybe it's the thought of having a friend in LA.'

Laylie set her glass aside. 'You ladies enjoy yourselves.

27

I'd better get Peg's visiting clothes out, so she's ready when her dad gets here.'

When they were alone Sarah said, 'John and I are probably going to have a fight. You can referee.'

'I certainly do thank you for that,' Glory Ann answered.

Sarah grinned as she sipped her wine. She was beginning to feel good now. It wasn't just the drink. It was Glory Ann. It was having somebody to talk to who wanted to listen. But one small thing bothered her. Glory Ann had arrived before Sarah had had time to check what she called her day book, a big black leather notebook in which she kept memos to herself. Things she wanted to remember, such as birthdays of friends, business acquaintances, the people who worked with her. She included anniversaries, both good and bad ones. If she didn't take a look at the day book it would nag at her for the rest of the day.

She excused herself, went into the bedroom. As soon as she opened the notebook she saw Hy Berge's name. His birthday would be the next day. Sunday. She paused to think, then reached for the phone.

When she heard his grouchy greeting she said, 'Rob, dear, did I wake you?'

'Sarah? Good morning.' His voice warmed. It carried a smile to her over the wires. 'Everything okay?' He was imagining her sitting up in bed, a strap of her gown slipping down off her shoulder, her honey-coloured hair tousled over her shining green eyes.

She said, 'All's well.' Then: 'Listen, Rob, can you do a big favour? I have a friend in from the Coast, which is why I can't do it myself. But tomorrow's Hy's birthday. Could you go down to your favourite leather shop and pick up something you think he'd like to have? Make sure it's delivered tomorrow morning. And send the bill to me.'

'Okay,' he said. 'No problem.'

'You don't mind?'

'No. I'm not doing anything special.' Except that, when she called, he had been thinking of her. Which, since he

28

thought of her most of the time, couldn't be considered much of a coincidence.

'Thanks, Rob.' She made a kiss sound and put down the phone. Almost instantly it rang. She picked it up. 'Yes?'

'Oh Sarah, how are you? I'm so glad I caught you at home.'

The voice was immediately familiar. Sarah took a deep breath. 'Hello, Mother. How are you?'

'It's good to hear your voice. Do you feel good? How's Tim? Does he like school here? And what about Peg?'

'We're all fine. Just so busy. The time flies by.'

'Oh, I know. It's the same for me,' Katy Morehouse said. 'I have my volunteer work, and there's an aerobic class in the building now. And there's all the museums. I don't know what to do first.'

'I'm glad to hear it, Mother.'

'Your show, Sarah, I watch it every day. Religiously. I wouldn't miss it. And everybody in the building watches it too. They love it.'

'That's good.'

'When are you coming down? I'd like to see you. There's somebody I want you to meet, too.'

'Somebody you want me to meet?'

Her mother laughed. 'A friend. I'm not going to tell you more.'

'I'll be down as soon as I can,' Sarah said, laughing too.

They exchanged a few more words. Sarah hung up. Her mother had sounded so good. She'd always been a fighter, and somehow, in these last few years, she'd begun to make a life for herself. Now she wanted Sarah to meet a friend. It had to be a man friend. Nothing else could put that flirtatious sound into her mother's voice.

Sarah told herself she had to make time soon for a visit with her mother. When she last went to Washington to see Tim at school, she could have stopped by the apartment for a little while. Instead she'd set up a couple of business appointments. The trouble was that she didn't want to look back, and seeing her mother, even seeing

29

her as she was now, rather than as she had been, reminded Sarah of a lot she wanted to forget.

Now she shrugged. She didn't want to think about it.

She went into the living room.

The bottle was half empty. Glory Ann's eyes were shining. She sat cross-legged on the sofa.

Peg yelled from the hall, 'Glory Ann!' and came tearing in, her blonde hair flying. 'Laylie said . . .'

The actress was up in a single swoop. She grabbed the girl, pulled her close in a bone-crushing hug. 'My Peg! How I've missed you! I've been telling your mother she's got to come west! She can't come though, not if you aren't with her!'

'How are you? How long will you stay? What are you going to do next? Oh Glory Ann, I'm so glad to see you.'

'When I get my breath I'll tell all.' Glory Ann released Peg, looked her up and down. 'Wow, you're getting ready to be all grown up.' And to Sarah. 'Listen, lady, you'd better watch out. This one's going to knock them in the aisles.'

But the excitement was fading from Peg's face to be replaced with woe. 'Oh, I forgot. Dad's coming. We're going to spend the day together.'

'And you'd better get dressed,' Sarah said. 'Because you know who gets yelled at if you're not on time.'

'But Glory Ann's hardly ever here.'

'I'll be around,' Glory Ann said airily. 'We'll have plenty of time. And I tell you what, before I leave tomorrow, we'll have lunch together. Just you and me. I'll wear my bag lady outfit and we'll go to Rockefeller Center, and I'll show you . . .'

'They won't let you in in that rig,' Sarah said.

'They will,' Glory Ann retorted. 'I'll send Peg ahead. She'll get the table and then, when no one's looking . . .'

'It won't work,' Peg said. 'I'll fall all over myself laughing and looking guilty.'

'Don't worry. We'll figure something out. If worse comes to worst, I'll tell them who I am. Just go and get ready for your father now.'

A little later the door chimes sounded. Laylie let John in and he headed for the living room. At the threshold he stopped short.

'John,' Sarah said. 'You remember Glory Ann, don't you?'

He nodded stiffly. 'Of course. How are you? It's been a long time.' As far as he was concerned he could have waited for ever before seeing her again. Any friend of Sarah's was no friend of his.

'Hello, John,' she answered, smiling sweetly.

He turned to Sarah. 'Peg ready?'

'Just about.'

'I have tickets for a matinee.'

'She'll be pleased.'

'I have to talk to you about Tim.'

Sarah sighed. She supposed it wasn't very grown up of her to notice with glee that John's hair was thinning, that he was heavier than he'd ever been. She couldn't remember if Carla had been partial to fat, bald-headed men. She said, 'Tim was fine when I spoke to him.'

John didn't really want to talk about Tim. He wanted to keep still until Peg was ready, and then to get out of there. But Sarah got to him somehow. She made him mad. For years now everything about her had provoked him. He knew it was time to forget. But he couldn't. Her voice, the lift of her brow, the tilt of her head . . . they all made him feel like nothing, like less than nothing. From the beginning she'd made him see himself as dull, plodding, a tortoise to her dancing hare. Even when she lay between his legs, all silk and fire, moaning and clutching him, he knew that he would collapse emptied and panting, while she cried, 'More, John. Oh, please . . . more . . .'

Sarah was staring at him. He said, 'Tim hates that school. He hates Washington too.'

'Please don't start now.'

'But he does, Sarah.'

'He will if you keep talking him into it. He's at the age when he'll say anything he thinks you want him to say.'

'Sarah, I know what I'm talking about.'

It was John's fault that Tim was in a private school in the first place. He'd been an exceptionally bright child, reading by the time he was five, but with a bad stammer that had already showed itself. John's nagging attempts to correct his speech had made a nervous wreck of Tim. The local school couldn't handle him.

Now she could ignore John's angry old accusation, in which he ignored the obvious. Tim would have been in private school no matter what, just as Peg was. John had nothing against Beltraney Prep. He just wanted Tim closer to home. Closer to John's home, that is. She said to Glory Ann, 'Excuse me, will you? I'm going to dress.'

John said loudly, 'Sarah, listen, you can't keep running away from it.'

She didn't answer. She smiled at Glory Ann and went into the kitchen to ask Laylie to find out when John expected to bring Peg home. Then she stopped to tell Peg to have a good time.

Peg said, 'You don't mind my going, do you?'

'Of course not.'

'You look funny.'

'We were about to have words. I beat a retreat to avoid that.'

'It's my fault. If he wasn't here to pick me up you wouldn't fight.'

'Baloney. We'd find some way or other to fight.'

'Suppose Dad wants me tomorrow too?'

'It's up to you. But Glory Ann's planning on lunch with you, remember?'

'I don't know what to do.'

'He hasn't asked you about tomorrow yet. Why don't you wait and see?'

Peg grinned. 'That's just postponing it, Mama.'

'It's not worrying about something until you have to.'

'I hate having to decide.'

Sarah grinned. 'Don't we all.'

'Not you, Mama. You like it.'

'That's only how it seems, Peg. Not how it really is.'

Sarah went slowly down the hall. Was she wrong? Maybe it wasn't fair to Peg to tell her she had to choose for herself what she wanted to do. See her father. See Glory Ann. But it was the only way. At twelve, it was time Peg learned that. The more times you dealt with choices, and the sooner you started, the easier it became. Or did it?

Never mind. It was settled for now.

Sarah paused at the hall cupboard. One of these days she had to bestir herself and send Daniel his things.

But it was time to get ready for her walk with Glory Ann. Sarah chose a white silk shirt and dark woollen trousers, and put them on the bed.

In the shower she recalled how she and Glory Ann had met. It had been on the fifth floor of the old rented National Television Network low-rise on 67th Street. Glory Ann's agent had brought her in for a reading. She was twenty then, breathtakingly beautiful. The casting director was there, and Hy Berge too. Sarah was impressed with her from the moment she said hello, more impressed after she read a few pages from the script, and then, with no sign of nervousness, proceeded to do a scene. She was a natural one-take actress. A rare find. She didn't even seem to be reading from the teleprompter. The casting director had been uncertain. Hy Berge had promised auditions to two other actresses. But Sarah had been insistent. She'd drawn up the contracts the same day.

Two weeks later Ardette Dane had arrived in *Oakview Valley* and Davey had fallen in love with her at first sight. A week after that the letters began to come in. First a few, then stacks of them, quickly mounting into the hundreds. Very soon Glory Ann was well known in the industry, and then to nationwide viewers. The role of Ardette, conceived originally as a two-month character, began to take over the show. Sarah rewrote the contracts, and at the same time, rewrote the bible, huddling night after night with the scriptwriter, to move Ardette to centre stage and keep her there. It had meant reducing the role

33

of one actress, who hadn't liked it. She'd been bitchy to Glory Ann, vicious to Sarah. In the end, the actress had to go. Sarah saw to it that the bible wrote her into an auto accident. And offered to buy out her contract. She wouldn't have it. So she didn't work for six months. The same could happen with Rita Porter, if she didn't want to cooperate. Sarah hoped she would.

She stepped from the shower, stood before the full-length mirror to study her body. It wasn't bad for a thirty-eight-year-old woman. Narrow waist. High, round breasts. Long legs, thank God. It made her feel good. But of course it didn't matter. What mattered was in her head. The ability to hold ten thousand details in her mind, and sort them, file them, shift them around. A good memory, quick inspiration, fast decision-making. She supposed those were the three qualities most needed for her job. Plenty of people had them. But there was something else. It was what Glory Ann had, aside from her looks. It was what every person successful in television, maybe in anything, had to have. They had to be hungry for success. They had to need it. Need to be somebody. Without that, there was nothing. Neither skill, nor talent, nor experience meant a thing without the need that put steel into the backbone. Made sacrifice possible. Made not having everything okay, as long as you had what you wanted. To be somebody.

Sarah knew that Glory Ann understood. Not many did. Not many wanted to.

When she had dressed she went into the living room. Peg and John had gone. Glory Ann had changed into a pair of good-looking pants.

Laylie was clearing up the tray and champagne bucket. She asked, 'You forget about your Aunt Ida coming for lunch tomorrow at one?'

'Oh no!' Sarah cried.

'Relatives?' Glory Ann asked.

'My aunt. From Washington. I think you may have met her.'

'Maybe,' Glory Ann agreed. 'Remember I'm taking Peg out.'

'But if Peg has to go with John?'

'Then I'll be here. So what? If the aunt doesn't mind, then I won't either.'

'You're sure?' Sarah asked. Glory Ann hated to meet new people. She said they always stared at her.

But now she smiled. 'I'll hold it against you, of course. But if you're committed . . .'

'She's the one person in the world, besides you, that I don't want to cancel on.'

'Oh, what's a lunch for a relative between friends?' Glory Ann thrust her arm through Sarah's. 'Come on. Let's walk.'

Fifth Avenue. A watery sun glinting on shop windows. Bustling crowds. One tall man stood out, dark haired and wearing a dark moustache. Briefly she thought of Tony Statler. The man moved on. Tony faded from her thoughts. Vendors of Thai silk scarves, steaming chestnuts, umbrellas, berets and golden chains. Fleets of cabs, buses, cars roaring from red light to red light, stopping with squealing brakes. A babble of languages and accents. And Glory Ann's voice: 'Oh, I do like this. I need to do it more often. What do you say, Sarah? Shall I come home? Buy a co-op? Settle down? And live on my ill-gotten gains?'

Her trademark silver blonde hair was out of sight within a dark blue beret. She wore little make-up. The pants under her fur coat were conservative, and so was the coat. No one gave her a second glance. Which was what she wanted, but only for the moment, as Sarah knew well.

She asked, 'Would coming back to New York to retire satisfy you?'

'No, I guess not.' Glory Ann laughed. 'Would retiring satisfy you?'

'Certainly not.'

'We're not reasonable people, Sarah. When we get

35

there, we want to stay. We don't want to give up, or go backwards. We want to stay. And go on. And on.'

'Yes.'

'Only where?'

'In your case?' Sarah smiled. 'You've got a lot more roles to play.'

'And what about you?'

'I should feel I have everything. But I don't.' Sarah paused, unwilling to jinx her hopes by putting them into words. 'I know there's more. Only I'm not sure what.'

'You'll figure it out by and by,' Glory Ann told her.

By one o'clock the two women were in Sardi's, sitting with Andrew Reynolds.

Reynolds was a slim man with a narrow waspish face and hands that darted and danced and flapped in the air when he spoke. He was plainly at ease and enjoying himself, looking first at Glory Ann and then at Sarah.

As soon as they'd been introduced Sarah understood why Glory Ann wanted Sarah to meet him. His column, appearing four times a week, concerned itself with the professional and private doings of stage, movie and television personalities.

Glory Ann launched into a long and involved story about two ageing actresses.

Andrew listened, chortling. Then he told a story of his own. By then Sarah had her own tale to tell.

As she told it, she could already see Andrew's Sunday morning column in her mind. *Glam gal Glory Ann Champion in from the Coast, seen at Sardi's, with Sarah Morehouse, doyenne of NTN's best soap opera.* Soap opera! That's how he would write it, damn him! *Oakview Valley* was a show. It could hold its own at night, in prime time, with anything. And so could she!

Paragraphs below the mention of Glory Ann and Sarah there would be the lines, *Could be that AIDS will destroy certain actresses as well as actors. Fear's a killer too, isn't it?*

Sarah wondered if Rita Porter would read that and get the message.

3

Laylie said, 'If you're wondering about those flowers, they're from that man next door. Mr Statler. He brought them in, along with a note for you.'

Sarah had known he was back in town after an absence of several weeks, and she'd thought of him when walking on Fifth Avenue. It was an interesting coincidence that she was hearing from him just now.

She opened the note. It asked if she would join him at dinner that evening. She considered. Should she? Shouldn't she? Finally she shrugged. Why not? Glory Ann had already announced that she'd be going out. Laylie would be at home with Peg. She told the housekeeper, 'Say I can make it. But it'll have to be nine or so. I'm going to Gracie Mansion for cocktails. You can mention that too.'

It took only a little while for her to shower and dress. When she was ready she looked at her mail. There was a letter from Tim. She sat down to read it. He said he was fine, but complained about the three term papers he'd have to write. He asked if he could have new skis, and go skiing with Russ Bates, whoever he was. It was the usual. No sign of the malaise John was trying to create. She decided that she would take a weekend and visit Tim, try to figure out what John was up to. Then she remembered that Tim would be coming home for Thanksgiving only a week away.

Before she left she discussed Peg's role in the school play. Laylie was all for a gold lamé costume. Peg wasn't sure. Sarah suggested blue taffeta, thinking of her own personal budget, rather than the show's, this time.

Peg and Laylie were happily discussing the style when Sarah left the apartment.

*

That night, having returned home from the cocktail party at Gracie Mansion, Sarah was sorry that she'd accepted Tony Statler's invitation to dinner. She was tired, longing for a hot bath and bed. But it wouldn't do to cancel at the last minute so, sighing, she walked the few steps down the hall and tapped at his door.

Tony let her in. He didn't seem as tall as she remembered him from their previous meetings. He was closer to her own height, and with a wide stocky build, although he wasn't fat. He moved lightly on his feet, taking the shawl she had thrown around her shoulders, leading her to a comfortable chair. His face was square, his eyes deepset and dark. He wore a full black moustache that curved over his upper lip, and beneath it his teeth sparkled as he spoke.

Soon, drinking the white wine he gave her, she found that her fatigue had fallen away. There was no effort in being with him. It was as if they'd known each other for ever. They knew many people in common, both in New York and Los Angeles.

He said, 'I've been hearing your name for years. It's damn funny that we've never crossed paths before.'

'And I've heard about you.' It wasn't true that she'd heard about Tony Statler. It was Stell-Stat that she'd heard about.

'This business . . .' he said.

They grinned companionably at each other.

Then he said, 'I've brought you here under false pretences. I asked you to dinner. But I'm not a gourmet cook, so I hope you'll understand why our meal came from the deli down the block.'

'I don't care what we eat,' she told him.

'Good. Then maybe you'll enjoy the corned beef sandwiches and potato salad I've set up.'

She laughed. 'Two of my favourites. When I first came to New York I went berserk on deli foods.'

'When was that?'

'Oh, about fifteen years ago.'

That began a brief exchange of biographies. While they

39

spoke he brought in a tray of sandwiches, a bowl of potato salad, a dish of coleslaw. Still talking they settled down to eat. As they did, Sarah realized that she was hungry after all. They had more wine while he described how he had moved into television from radio, in Detroit, his home town, and how he had decided that the place to be was New York. 'So,' he said, laughing, 'I ended up in California, naturally.'

'Where most of the industry is these days.'

'Most, but not all. There's still a lot going on here.'

'Enough,' Sarah agreed, 'for a new production facility to be built uptown. It should be in operation in six months or so.'

'Which means even more'll be happening here,' Tony said. He went on, 'Actually that's why I've decided to spend as much time here as I can spare. It ought to work out five or six days every month. Sometimes more, maybe. It'll be a lot easier on me to have my own place.' He grinned at her. 'I didn't realize there'd be a bonus. This is very pleasant. I'm sorry it took us so long to get together. Now I don't like remembering that I'll have to go back to the Coast soon.'

There was a lot that he hadn't told her, but he didn't see why he should. It would be okay. And everybody loves a success. Just as everybody hates a failure. He'd been down for a while, but he was up again, feeling a good rush. It was Sarah Morehouse. He already wanted her. He was already determined to have her. It would be good. Good in every way. He knew it.

Sarah was saying, 'I may be out to the Coast one of these days,' thinking now of Glory Ann. Perhaps there'd be time for a weekend. And then: 'It's possible I'll be scouting a location for some *Oakview Valley* episodes.'

He rose, went to the sideboard, scribbled on a card. 'My unlisted number,' he said, handing it to her. 'Promise you'll call if and when you get there. And in case there's some way I can help you . . .' When she thanked him, he went on, 'I mean it, you know. I want to see you again, Sarah.'

Soon after, she excused herself, saying, 'I'd like to stay longer. But I had a big day today, and tomorrow's going to be another.'

He walked to the door with her, bent his head to kiss her lightly. His face was warm, his moustache silken. 'This was nice. Thanks for allowing me to be so informal.'

The brief touch of his lips had been sweet. She leaned against him, wanting more. His arms came around her, hard and strong. His stocky body pressed closer. His mouth came down on hers again, demanding now, swallowing her breath. She felt his muscles tensing, his heart beating against hers. For an instant she found herself giving way. She was curious about him, his effect on her. There was a sense of promise about him and their having gotten together now. But it was too soon for more than these few moments. She drew away, smiling at him. 'Until next time then.'

He hesitated, then nodded and turned away.

Inside her apartment she stepped out of her pumps, threw aside her wrap, thinking about Tony. He was a complicated man she suspected, although on the surface he seemed to be relaxed and straightforward. There had to be more to him than showed in a two-hour conversation. Deep burning funds of energy, perhaps anger even, had fuelled his drive to get where he was. She would have to ask Glory Ann about him. Perhaps she'd heard of him, even met him.

Sarah didn't realize that she wasn't alone until she heard the deep rasping voice.

It was Daniel, speaking from the shadows of the living room. 'So,' he said unpleasantly, 'you've already found my replacement.'

He was sprawled on the sofa, his best suit rumpled and stained with ash. His face was grey, his eyes glassy. The air was smoky and smelled of whisky.

'How did you get in, Daniel?'

'You forget, my lady. You yourself gave me a key.'

She *had* forgotten. She said, putting out her hand, 'Yes, thank you. And I'll have it back now.'

He rose, stood wavering. His long lean body seemed to hunch. His sandy head dipped between his raised shoulders.

She remembered that when she had first met him she had reminded herself never to trust a big man who hunches his shoulders. When he does that he wants you to think he's not dangerous. But that means he is, and knows it, and he wants to hide it from you. Just the same, he had been interesting, and they'd drifted into what she considered a comfortable relationship.

'You'll get your key back when I'm ready,' he told her now. When she didn't respond he asked, 'Who was that man?'

'That's none of your business, Daniel.'

He ignored that. 'I was listening.'

She shrugged.

'So who was it? The old goat that owns the place next door? Or one of the maintenance men? Or somebody you're putting up there?'

'What's wrong with you?' she asked softly. She was looking at a man she'd never seen before. She wondered how she could have known him for so long and never known him at all.

'I'm upset. I guess you could call it that.' His words were slurred, his voice thick. When he reached to refill his glass he went off balance, almost falling. 'Whoa,' he muttered to himself. He raised his glassy eyes to her. 'I've been thinking about you. The whole month since I last saw you . . . I've been remembering . . .'

'You should forget about me, Daniel.'

'Don't tell me what to do.'

She stood still, caught in a rare moment of uncertainty. She didn't know what to say, what to do. From the corner of her eye she saw that Laylie had appeared in the doorway, was motioning to her. Sarah went to her, her eyes still fixed on Daniel.

Laylie said, 'Be careful with him. He's drunk. I heard him come in. He said he wanted his things. The next thing is, he's into the whisky. You want me to call somebody?'

42

'I can handle him,' Sarah said. 'Go to bed.'

'Not until he's gone from here. I'm going to be on the other side of this door if it takes all night long, and it might do just that.'

'What about Peg? Glory Ann?'

'Not a peep out of them.'

'Ladies,' Daniel said, 'what's the whispering about? What's going on? Are you planning some sweet surprise for me?'

Without lowering her voice Sarah said to Laylie, 'Be sure it's not going to take all night.' She turned to Daniel. 'You'd better go now. You're making a fool of yourself. Tomorrow you'll regret it.'

'Thanks for the advice. But we have things to talk about. You and me. To talk about.' He filled his glass until the whisky ran over the rim. And when he saw Sarah's disgusted glance he said, 'Never mind. You can afford to buy yourself a new rug.' Then, with no change of tone he asked, 'Do you know, by any chance, what they call you in the trade?'

She didn't answer. He was drunk. Stupid, ugly drunk. She had never seen him that way before. She had trouble believing that this was the same man who drank only a glass or two of white wine, rarely more, and never anything stronger.

'Iron Tits,' he said with unpleasant satisfaction. 'Iron Tits. I'll bet nobody's dared say it to your face before. People are afraid of you, Sarah. Did you ever realize that? You can make a strong man shake. And not with passion either. Just shake. Because, maybe if he gets on the wrong side of you, you'll ruin him.' His narrowed eyes swept her up and down. 'I've always assured them that you do not have iron tits or an iron ass, but none of them believe me.'

Heat burned in her cheeks and behind her eyes, but she said coolly, 'Thanks for the endorsement. I appreciate it. And now . . .'

'Not yet, Sarah. Just tell me . . . tell me what's wrong

43

with me. How come you don't forgive and forget and smile at me the way you used to?'

'Daniel, you're not here for a reconciliation.'

'Don't tell me what I'm here for.' He emptied his glass, once again reached for the bottle.

That time she snatched it away. 'No! You've had enough. And so have I. I want you to take your things and get out.'

His grey face was glistening with sweat. His red-rimmed eyes glared at her. 'I've only just begun. I've been thinking for a long time of the things I wanted to say to you. I never did say them of course. So now I must take the chance I have.'

He lunged towards her, reaching, and her temper came up, hard, hot and uncontrollable, like her mother's, flashing like fire through her. She heard herself say, 'You son of a bitch! Don't you touch me. Don't say another word. Just pick up your stuff and get out of here. Do you hear me? Get out of here right now. I don't want to see your face again. Not as long as I live. Get out. Get out!'

She found herself pushing him, both hands against his chest. Pushing. Shoving. Kicking. Her voice loud, but even. Deadly. Her lips pursed, spitting the words at him as if they were stones. He was suddenly at the door. She had it open behind him. She thrust him into the hall and slammed the door. He yelled. She stood there, shaking, until her eyes finally fell on his suitcase, packed before he started on her whisky, and his coat folded on top of it. She couldn't bear to look at them. They were befouling the air. Her air. The air she needed to breathe. She caught them up, hurried back to the door. She didn't think about the danger. She swung the door open, threw suitcase and coat at him, and while he was struggling with them she slammed and double locked the door and slipped the chain into its slot. The key, if he remembered it now, would do him no good.

By then Laylie had run in. 'What's happening?'

'He's gone.' Sarah's voice was a dry whisper. Her throat

had tightened. It felt raw, as if she had been screaming for hours.

Fists thudded against the door. There were shouts. Sarah refused to hear the words. Laylie gasped, 'What should we do?'

'Nothing, Laylie.'

But there was no way to escape Daniel's yell. 'Damn you, Iron Tits. Open up. Listen to me. I've got to talk to you, Iron Tits.'

And now Sarah heard another voice, deep, calm. Tony Statler's. She shivered. Why hadn't he gone to sleep? Why did he have to be a part of this humiliating nightmare?

Tony said, 'You're making a disturbance. What's this about?'

'Who the hell are you?' Daniel cried.

'I live here,' Tony said reasonably. 'And you're keeping me from my night's sleep,' he went on, as he pressed the elevator button. He was thinking that Daniel was witless and gutless. What good would this behaviour do him? How would such an exhibition make Sarah want him?

'You're fixing to move into my place with Sarah, aren't you?' Daniel said bitterly.

Sarah squeezed her eyes shut, as if closing away the world would also protect her from hearing the exchange beyond her door.

'Animal!' Laylie groaned. 'What's the matter with him?'

Daniel went on, 'Listen, you don't know. But take it from me. Save yourself, bud. Old Iron Tits'll get you in the end. She's a user. She'll squeeze you dry and then you'll finish up like me. Like me. Ask anybody. They'll tell you. Sarah Morehouse is a man killer from way back. A ball breaker. Ask how she got to be a top producer. How she got to be little dictator of the world.'

'Calm down,' Tony said easily.

The elevator doors wheezed and opened. There were sounds of movement as Tony gently manoeuvred Daniel into the elevator and the doors closed behind them.

Sarah let out her breath in a long sigh. And suddenly thought of the key. Daniel must still have it. She had to

45

remember to change the lock. She must tell the superintendent, Harry Stowe.

A quick hard wave of nausea hit her. She ran for the bathroom and made it just in time to retch over the sink. Her one glass of wine at the mayor's party, her wine at Tony's, the meal she'd eaten, all came up, in great pounding surges.

Afterwards, shaking, sweating, she washed her face with a cold flannel, gargled, and brushed her teeth. Under the tousled curls her forehead and cheeks looked strangely colourless. Only then did she begin to feel the throbbing in her upper arm. When she looked she saw the dull red outline of four fingers, and on the underside, the mark of a thumb. By morning she'd have black and blue bruises. Daniel's signature.

How could he act like that? How could he say such things? Where had all that bitterness come from?

She thought of Tony Statler, listening. Good God, what the man must think of her!

Laylie called from beyond the door.

'I'm all right now,' Sarah said, coming into the hall and going towards the bedroom with Laylie at her heels.

'You better go to sleep,' the housekeeper said. 'Just forget you ever knew Daniel Clermont.'

Sarah nodded. 'What about Peg? Glory Ann?'

'Thank goodness those bedrooms are way to the back. They slept through the fuss like lambs. Though I don't see how they did. I thought that fool would wake the dead.'

'I was so . . . so paralysed, Laylie. I couldn't do a thing. I don't know what happened to me. How I could act like that. So helpless.'

'You didn't seem helpless to me, the way you shoved him out of here. I don't know how you did that, and I won't ever know.'

Sarah smiled faintly. 'I don't either. It just happened. I was angry enough. And he was drunk enough.'

There was the sound of the phone.

The two women looked at each other. Laylie said, 'Don't let's answer. Let it ring until it stops.'

But Sarah said, 'I'm afraid to ignore it. Maybe it's downstairs . . . Harry Stowe . . . You take it, see who it is.'

She watched as Laylie took up the receiver, then covered the mouthpiece. 'It's him. From next door. Wants to know are you all right?'

Sarah took the phone. 'Thanks for calling, Tony. And for coming out to see what you could do.'

'I put him in a cab. He probably won't be back.' Then: 'I need to see you, Sarah.'

'Not now.' With horror, she heard that her voice shook. She swallowed, drew a deep breath. 'Sorry. I couldn't . . .'

'Now,' Tony said firmly. 'It's very important. I'll be at your door. Open up for me.' There was a click, a hum. He was gone.

He'd known even as he talked that drunken fool out of the building what he would do. If he didn't go to her now, reassure her, he'd never see her again. She'd be too embarrassed to face him. He had to wipe that scene away. Otherwise it would always be between them. And he didn't want that. Already he knew that she was his kind of woman. He wouldn't let anything come between them.

Laylie was saying to Sarah, 'I'll tell him you don't want to see him.'

'I'll do it. You go to bed.' Sarah waited until Laylie had gone to her own room, then she unhooked the chain, unbolted the door. Again she thought of the door key. She must be sure to talk to Harry Stowe before she went out the next day.

As soon as she had the door open, Tony stepped in. He closed it quickly, put on the chain. Turning to her, he said softly, 'Don't say anything,' and took her into his arms.

Before, her voice had shaken. Now her body shook. He held her tightly, held her even as he led her to the sofa and sat down, still holding her.

It was very quiet. A clock hummed softly. The wind suddenly tapped its fingers at the terrace doors.

He touched the red marks on her arm, whispered a wordless curse. Gradually the warmth of his body enfolded her so that the deep inside chill she had felt began to thaw. Her trembling lessened, faded away.

Finally he said, 'I'm sorry our evening ended the way it did. I'm sorry if I had any part in it. But I have to tell you, I'm glad that man is out of your life.'

'*That* man was never part of my life,' she answered after a long moment. 'I never saw *that* man before.'

'I didn't suppose you had,' Tony said. 'He's not your style.'

Sarah remembered that Glory Ann had said the same thing after meeting Daniel for the second time. 'He's not your style, Sarah. What are you trying to do? Protect yourself against getting involved with a man you can take seriously?' Smart Glory Ann. She understood other women a great deal better than she understood herself.

Tony asked, 'Do you want me to go now, let you go to sleep?'

Sarah burrowed her head into his shoulder. It was warm in his arms. The cold inner chill had dissolved. The trembling was gone. She didn't want to move away lest both return. She clung to him, needing the comfort, the reassurance, of his embrace.

'Good,' he said. 'Just close your eyes.'

He held her for a long time. She drowsed. Daniel's words, his voice, the look on his face, came back in slowly fading echoes, until, at last, they were gone. Only Tony remained, one arm around her, the other across her chest, resting lightly on her breasts, a hand clasped loosely around her shoulder.

There was a prickling in her nipples. Small hot arrows flickered wherever his body touched hers. She turned her head and their eyes met. He smiled a little, bent his head. His lips settled on her mouth. She moved closer to him, pressing her lips to his, a sudden blooming of hunger

48

sweeping through her, tasting sweetness, and wanting more.

When, finally, he raised his head, he said, 'This sofa wasn't built for the likes of me, Sarah.' And waited.

She rose, took his hand, and they went together into her bedroom.

The lamps filled the room with a pale glow. The white drapes stirred on a faint breeze. Four red roses in a vase on the dresser scented the air.

He said, taking her face in his hands, and cupping her cheeks, 'I've wanted you since I first saw you. I asked to borrow a lemon, but I was thinking something else.'

She smiled, raising her lips to his, her arms going around him. He lifted her, laid her on the bed. Slowly, smiling down at her, he undressed her, his hands lingering at her throat, her breasts, moulding the curve of her hips, sliding along the length of her thighs. When he had taken off his own clothing he stretched out beside her and gathered her into his arms, belly to belly and breast to breast, so that she could feel the whole of him against her. And she clung to him as tightly as she could, drawing him closer and closer, their legs entwining, lips opening together to touch tongues. Closer and closer until they were joined, moving in a slow delicious excitement at first, then caught in swifter currents until with explosive suddenness she cried out. For an instant he paused, leaning over her. Then his body weight came down on her again. He moved in a slow rocking rhythm that enveloped them both. Just as she cried out again, she felt his long slow yielding breath on her throat. Then they were both still.

When she woke in the morning he was gone, but there was a note on the pillow in the place where his head had lain. *Appointments tonight and tomorrow. And must leave for LA. Will call you from there. Late. I'll be back as soon as I can. I love you. Tony.*

She smiled reading it, smiled holding it to her lips.

There was an ugly blur of memory in her mind. Her arm ached when she moved it. But she felt happy. She just felt happy.

4

Sarah read Andrew Reynolds' Sunday morning column. The mention of Glory Ann and herself was written almost as she had imagined it. The reference to AIDS possibly ruining an actress's career through fear was also there. Once again she wondered if Rita Porter would read it and know what it meant. Soon, though, she put the newspaper aside. She had things to do.

She wore a white silk shirt, narrow dark green silk trousers and a silk waistcoat in the same shade of green. There was a string of pearls at her throat, and small pearl drops on her ears.

Laylie was busy in the kitchen. Glory Ann and Peg had gone out earlier, having decided on breakfast together so they could have lunch with Aunt Ida.

Now Sarah turned on the TV, inserted a cassette into the VCR, and stood shielding the screen with her body. Anyone coming in unexpectedly wouldn't know what was showing there. Credit frames unreeled against a grey background. When she first went to NTN as producer of *Oakview Valley* she had made a cassette of those frames, just those, for herself. Executive Producer in Charge: Lyman Ogloe. He didn't really count because he was on the administrative side rather than the production side. Then: Sarah Morehouse, Producer. She played it back. Sarah Morehouse, Producer. She hit the off button and turned away, smiling faintly.

She checked the dining room. The table was set. White linen with a bowl of blue delphiniums as a centrepiece. Silver salt and pepper shakers. Silver sugar bowl and creamer, all well-polished. Not fashionable nowadays, but what she liked. And she knew why. The menu would be Eggs Rockefeller, a mixed melon and cress salad. Miniature napoleons for dessert. Small cups of filtered coffee.

There'd be Bloody Marys or screwdrivers for whoever wanted a drink. She touched the array of flatware. Small forks and large. Two teaspoons. Meat knife and butter knife.

She remembered her cousins' giggles. The two of them sitting across from her, watching. How old had Sarah been then. Four? Five? She was uncertain.

'Look,' said one of the cousins. 'She doesn't know which to use.'

Aunt Ida said, 'Hush, you silly. That's not polite.'

'How come she doesn't know?' the two chorused.

'I do so!' Sarah shouted belligerently, feeling heat in her cheeks and the sting of tears in her eyes. She reached blindly, spilled her glass of milk. The crystal rolled across the white of the cloth, leaving a long flooding stain. The maid ran for a towel. The girls giggled loudly. Sarah ran from the table in tears.

'I told you so!' her mother shouted that night, having prised the explanation for red eyes from Sarah. 'You don't listen to me, Mike, but I know I'm right. What good is it, sending her to visit your sister? Seeing what she'll never have. Teaching her what she won't ever need to know!'

'Look, Ida's my only relative,' her father said. 'Sarah's got to have somebody.'

The trips across town continued. Aunt Ida had a black uniformed chauffeur. In those days, in the fifties, he was called coloured or Negro. Aunt Ida made certain that Sarah knew that only guttersnipes like Sarah's mother, Katy, pronounced Negro in the Southern way. The man's name was Buckman. He was slender, with neat hands and feet, and close-cropped wiry hair. His grey cap sat square on his head, and his grey uniform fitted as if tailored to him. He was profoundly shocked when she asked to ride in the front seat with him rather than alone in the back. Years later, in the 1960s, she was just as profoundly shocked when she saw his picture on the front page of the Washington *Post*. By then he was chubby. He wore a large Afro and a full-length dashiki. The caption quoted him as saying, 'We got to get them honkies before they get us.'

Once a month, sometimes twice Sarah had ridden across town in the big black Buick. Buckman solemnly handing her into the car on Lebanon Street in Silver Spring, driving away from the brick garden apartment while the neighbourhood children stared. When they arrived six miles away, in the District, and stopped in the driveway of the big fieldstone house on Foxhall Road, he solemnly handed her out into a different world.

As she grew older she became more and more aware of just how different a world it was. She went to Merrimack, a public school not far from her apartment. Her cousins went to private schools. She wore clothes from Sears, along with a few hand-me-downs given her by Aunt Ida, and was humiliated when her cousins reminisced about when they had worn them. They had shrimp for lunch, and steak on toast. At home Sarah ate peanut butter and jelly sandwiches, and sometimes a hamburger.

In summer the big house was cool and smelled of flowers. In winter a fire burned on the hearth, and fresh roses stood on the mantel next to the silver-framed pictures of Aunt Ida and Uncle Steven. Sarah's home in the red-brick three-floor walk-up in Silver Spring was hot in the summer and cold in the winter. In all seasons, after dark, large black roaches stalked the kitchen, and silverfish scurried across the bathroom floor.

After each of her visits Sarah swore to herself that she'd show them all: Aunt Ida, the cousins, her own folks. She'd wear mink, own a limousine. She'd be somebody.

Then, when Sarah was sixteen, her father disappeared. It had been a cold November day; the windows were streaked with frost. Sarah sat in the kitchen trying to do her French homework: a fifteen-hundred-word essay on an imaginary summer vacation. If she'd been one of Aunt Ida's girls she could have written about a real holiday. A trip to Maine perhaps. A visit to Newport. But she'd been nowhere the past summer. So she pretended she had, and struggled with her French. Her brother, Jerry, just a year older, was at basketball practice.

Her parents had been arguing heatedly about money

for hours. It began with a pink tweed coat that Aunt Ida had sent home for Katy with Sarah. Her mother had looked at it, grumbled, 'What would I do with pink tweed?' She showed it to Mike when he got home. He said it was good-looking, and Katy said, 'I'll never wear it.' Mike asked, 'To spite Ida?' 'Damn your sister! And damn her rich husband,' Katy yelled. 'Just because she was smart enough to marry money doesn't mean she can lord it over me! I don't want that whore's second-hand clothes. I'll buy my own, thank you. Just give me the money and I'll find a coat as good as any of hers.' They went on that way, her mother finally screaming, weeping, her father yelling back.

Sarah tried not to listen, but couldn't help hearing. It had always been that way. Even when she was younger and threw herself under the bed to hide. Even when she covered her ears, or fled outside to stand, shivering, in the shadows of the alley. She could always hear them.

Now Katy was weeping. 'Seventeen years, and nothing to show for it! Seventeen years out of my life! Where did they go? What happened to them? And nothing, nothing to show for them.'

'I don't have anything to show for them either,' Mike said. 'But I want you to remember . . . you're the one who got yourself pregnant. I'll bet you even planned it.'

'Me? Me? Don't you dare say that! You should have known better. You should have been careful.'

'It was you insisted we go ahead, get married. You cried. Don't you remember? And threatened.'

'You wanted to marry me,' Katy screamed.

Sarah managed to unclench her hands. She banged the chair against the table. She cleared her throat loudly.

There was a brief silence. Then the outside door slammed shut.

Katy shouted, 'Damn you, come back here,' and began to weep again.

Sarah put her hands over her ears and whispered, 'God, God, let me out of here. Make them stop it.'

Over the years she had put it together from the bits and

pieces she'd listened to in their arguments. Mike had been discharged in Washington after World War II. He'd started courses at the George Washington University, and was living with Ida and her husband Steven. He'd wanted to get a degree in law. The GI Bill paid for his tuition and gave him a little to live on. Steven had already promised him a job with his real estate firm when Mike graduated. He knew exactly what he wanted and where he was going. And then he met Katy, and they'd fallen in love. Katy had become pregnant with Jerry in the same year. Ida was shocked, disappointed. She and Steven offered no help. Mike couldn't ask. He quit school, went to work in a clothing store on F Street. He planned to study at night, but he couldn't manage it. A year later Sarah was born. He'd been working ever since. Now he had a job at Hecht's in Silver Spring.

Over the years Ida and Steven had grown wealthy. They'd not forgiven Katy for what had happened, though they never spoke of it and tried to maintain a semblance of family contact by infrequent invitations to Mike and Katy, which were never accepted, and by keeping in touch with Sarah, which Katy allowed only at Mike's insistence . . .

When Mike didn't come home that night, or the next day, Sarah went looking for him. She stopped at the drug store where he often went for morning coffee, at Hecht's where he worked. No one had seen him. No one knew where he was. Jerry looked too. Finally Sarah called Aunt Ida. Her aunt hadn't seen Mike, hadn't heard from him.

After that there were daily, twice daily, calls from her. 'Is there anything new? Have you talked to him?'

Katy cursed him. And cursed Sarah too, for calling Ida. She sat in a chair at the window, murmuring, 'He's punishing me. I know it. I know him. We've been married for seventeen years. I know him. He's just trying to make me worry.'

Jerry wanted to go to the police, but she wouldn't let him. On the third day, without discussing it, he reported his father missing. When the desk sergeant heard that there'd been an argument, he said, 'He'll be back.'

On the fourth day, as Sarah was returning from school, a police car passed her, siren screaming, red lights flashing. It turned into her street, stopped before the next apartment building. Immediately after, an ambulance arrived. There were men running. Neighbours appeared. They stood in small groups, shivering in the November cold.

As Sarah approached one of them came to her, put a hand on her arm. 'You'd better go home, Sarah. Don't stay here.'

While she hesitated the building handyman came out on the steps. He sank down as if his legs had melted from under him. His face was grey – lips, cheeks and jowls; they looked as if sprayed with dirty flour. 'Hanging there,' he said unbelievingly. 'I went into the dark, and he was hanging in the storeroom.'

Sarah ran up the stairs, into the apartment. Her mother came out of the kitchen holding a damp dish towel. 'What's all the noise in the street?'

Sarah clung to the back of a chair, trembling. Her lips felt frozen shut.

'Sarah?' her mother asked. And then, on a high thin wail, 'Sarah, what's happened? Something's wrong!'

There was a knock at the open door. A policeman looked in at Katy. 'Are you Mrs Morehouse?'

Katy's face went ashen. She nodded.

He came in, spoke in a soft slow voice. He said the words that meant Mike Morehouse had hanged himself.

'No,' Katy said. 'He just went away for a few days. We had a fight. And he went away to cool off. He's done it before.'

'I'm sorry,' the policeman said.

Sarah saw the knowledge suddenly settle on her mother's face. Knowledge. Guilt. The woman shrank, shuddering, into a chair. She put her face in her hands, and from behind her shaking fingers a terrible keening sounded.

The next day, after the funeral, after Ida and Steven had left, she tore the pink tweed coat to shreds.

At the end of the week President John Kennedy was assassinated in Dallas. For ever after the two deaths were linked together in Sarah's mind.

The visits to Aunt Ida stopped. Buckman was gone. The cousins had entered college. Uncle Steven was no longer well.

But that June after her father's death, when Sarah graduated from high school, the youngest in her class, and was elected to the National Honor Society, her Aunt Ida came to see them. She sat stiffly on the edge of a straight chair and said into the rejecting silence, 'I want Sarah to go to college.'

Sarah had her notebook on her knees. She wrote Sarah Morehouse. Then again, Sarah Morehouse. She wrote it at the top of the page, at the bottom. She printed it in small letters and large ones. Straight. Diagonally. In wide margins and narrow ones. She wrote it in round and flowing curves. She printed it in double lines, blackening the straight legs and slanting the round ones. Sarah Morehouse. And while she wrote her name she listened to her mother and her aunt argue about what her future was to be.

Her mother said, 'We'll make out. Sarah can get a job.'

'But she's so bright. We want to send her to college. Steven and I, we feel that's what she should do.' Aunt Ida was sweetly determined. 'It's what Mike would want for her, Katy. You ought to remember that.'

'Mike! How can I forget? I know you blame me. I know what you're thinking! It's always been my fault. You've always blamed me. Always. From the beginning.'

Sarah risked a quick glance at her mother. Her face was scarlet. Tears glittered in her eyes. In a moment she would be crying.

Ida looked more calm. But her plump cheeks had a faint flush. Her pink lips were set, her jaw too. When she raised a hand to tighten a pin in her chignon, diamonds flashed from her fingers. 'Nobody's blaming you, or anybody. Let's forget the past and think of Sarah's future.'

'You want her to go to college. And I'll be alone.'

'Katy, listen. You have to think of what's best for her.'

'I'm her mother,' Katy said thinly. 'I know what's best for her.' And then the tears came, the sobs. And: 'You're always meddling. And always have been. Right from the first. If it hadn't been for you . . .'

Sarah wrote her name one more time. Sarah Morehouse. Large. Black. Determined. She pushed the paper into the notebook and rose. 'I'm going to do it, Mama.' Her voice was steady, matter of fact. 'Nothing you say will stop me.' Inside small tremors shook her. A quickening in her chest. A shaking in her knees. She turned to her aunt. 'Thank you. You won't be sorry.'

'And what about me?' her mother cried.

'I'm sorry, Mama. It's what I have to do,' Sarah said. To be somebody. Somebody . . .

Now the silver flatware glistened. The blue delphiniums hurt her eyes. She gave the table one last glance and turned away.

She was looking out of the window when Glory Ann came in, pulling the blue beret from her head.

'We had a good breakfast and a good walk. Peg's a joy to be with. In fact, she's an angel. Now she's in the kitchen, consulting with Laylie about her appearance at lunch. My judgement wasn't quite to be trusted.'

Sarah laughed. Peg too responded to these rare visits of Aunt Ida's as if they were a general's inspection. Peg had sensed Sarah's own feelings. *She* wouldn't spill milk on the tablecloth. *She* wouldn't worry about what forks to use either.

'Laylie's judgement is final in all things,' Sarah said.

'Does that bother you?'

'No. But I'm lucky that Laylie has such good judgement.' Sarah remembered Tony then, asked if Glory Ann knew him.

'Tony Statler?' Glory Ann repeated. 'I don't know him. Just Stell-Stat. It's doing pretty good stuff.'

The phone was ringing. Sarah let Laylie answer it in the kitchen. Soon the housekeeper came in, her face deadly serious, whispering. 'It's Daniel,' even as Glory Ann was saying excitedly, 'Maybe that's my Ralph,' with her velvety eyes suddenly afire. Then, as she understood, her face was suddenly shadowed, all the glow gone.

Sarah said, 'I'll take it in the bedroom.'

She walked slowly, reminding herself. First the business proposal. Then the marriage proposal. Then the scene last night. She couldn't believe that Daniel was calling her.

She picked up the phone. 'Daniel?'

'I feel such a fool,' he said, his voice deep and steady. 'Blame it on diminished responsibility. I'm sorry.'

'I am too.'

'I'd like to see you, Sarah.'

'That's not possible,' she said. 'I expect a guest for lunch in a little while. And Glory Ann is here.'

'So it's a full house,' he said slowly.

'I'm afraid so,' she said. She was thinking of Tony now, the silken touch of his moustache against her breast. He'd written that he'd call. Be back soon. When?

Daniel was saying, 'I have to talk to you, Sarah.'

'You've already done a lot of talking.'

'I know. I've said I'm sorry. If you'd just give me a little time . . .'

'I have a meeting the first thing in the morning. And I'll be in the studio most of the day. In the late afternoon . . .'

He cut in roughly, 'Never mind. I get the message. You don't even want to talk. That's okay. Now I know where I stand.'

Before she could answer she heard a loud click, followed by the dialling tone.

She looked at the phone, put it down, sighed. That was that. And just as well. She was on the way back to the living room when she heard the chimes at the front door.

Aunt Ida had gone. Peg was in her room watching television. Glory Ann had changed to her blue trousers, had packed her shopping bag. She glanced at Sarah over the top of it. 'Daniel wanted to make it up, didn't he?'

'I think so.'

'You wouldn't see him?'

'There wasn't any reason to.'

'Men!' Glory Ann muttered. 'We both know that Ralph wouldn't want me if I weren't *me*. Me. Glory Ann. With everything that means.' She looked at Sarah. 'And the same goes for you.'

'So I realized. Although Daniel didn't seem to want to put it that way.' Sarah's voice was dry.

'He's a jerk. And so is Ralph.' Glory Ann sighed, rose to her feet, stretching her fingertips towards the ceiling. 'I'm tired of trying to be two people. Me, what I want. And the me that he wants.' She let her arms flop to her sides. 'And I guess I don't have to any more.'

Soon after, wrapped in her fur coat, carrying the shopping bag, she set out for the airport, promising to call, to return as soon as she could.

As the cab swung into the driveway Glory Ann fumbled through the jumbled contents of her purse. Wallet. House keys. They had to be in there somewhere. She had taken them, hadn't she? The cab bumped up the hill, slowed at the levelled parking terrace.

The house was low, redwood and glass. The lower windows were bright with light. Ralph! He was here! He'd come back! Now, as the cab stopped, she saw his car, the Le Baron. Ralph!

She grabbed her shopping bag, threw bills at the cab driver. 'Ralph's here,' she cried excitedly.

She ran up the steps, flung the door open. 'Ralph!'

He appeared in the arch that led into the room he had used as a study. There was light behind him, a shadow over his face.

But she saw his stony expression. 'Hello, Glory Ann. I thought you'd be coming back later. I stopped by to get some books I need.'

60

'Oh,' she said. 'I see.'

'Was your trip okay?'

'Yes.' She dropped her shopping bag, held on to the wall beside her, and slowly let her body sink down on to the first step of the stairs that curved upward to the first floor.

'Where's your maid?' he asked.

'She quit to have a baby,' Glory Ann told him.

'Why didn't you hire a new one?'

She shrugged. 'I don't know.'

'You're going to have to figure out how to take care of yourself,' he said.

'I am.'

'You left the front door unlocked,' he told her.

'I did?'

'I walked in. Walked in, Glory Ann.' He went on, his voice softening, 'Look, you're going to need somebody around. You can't be here all by yourself. I'll get you a maid. Okay?'

She nodded. There wasn't any use arguing with him. He wasn't going to change his mind. Not about the maid. Not about coming back either. That's how he was. Stubborn. It was just like when they got married. It had been only weeks before Sarah auditioned her for *Oakview Valley*. Glory Ann's maiden name was Thatcher, and she'd always planned on using Glory Ann Thatcher for her career. It was what she was used to. She was sure she'd remember it. But when she told Ralph that, he'd said, 'You don't want to use my name, you don't want to be my wife,' with that same stony look. So she'd become Glory Ann Champion. He'd been an assistant producer at NTN at that time. When she'd come to Hollywood, he'd stayed behind for six months, waiting until he lined up an associate producer's job at Universal. He was very good, had a terrific reputation in the business, but producers didn't appear in front of the cameras, so they didn't get the kind of coverage that stars did. *They* had their own lives. They had privacy. And that was what Ralph wanted.

He was saying, 'I'll get you a driver too. Somebody reliable. You can't depend on cabs. You ought to know that.'

'All right,' she said wearily.

She leaned back, drooping inside her fur coat, looking like an abandoned rag doll, her legs sprawled, her arms limp. She supposed it was crazy for her to feel so let down. Ralph wasn't all that much. He was scrawny and underfed-looking. He had rumpled red hair and icy grey eyes. Every working day she spent her time with better-looking men, and even more powerful men. For, although he was very good at his job, he was still an associate producer at Universal. He was so damnably honest he sometimes turned people off.

'You're tired,' he was saying. 'You ought to go to bed. I'll finish packing up, and take off.' He disappeared into the study.

She remained on the steps. For a little while she heard him moving around. Then he returned, carrying a big canvas bag. 'Okay. I'm through. Take care of yourself.'

'I will,' she said.

He hesitated. Then: 'I'll see you.' The door closed softly behind him.

Soon she heard the car start, gravel spinning under its wheels as it drove away.

She flung her purse at the door as hard as she could. Its clasp broke. It burst open, spewing its contents all over the foyer.

'Oh fuck!' she said. 'Oh shit! Oh damn!' And then, as she drew her knees up, and hugged them, and put her head down and burst into tears, 'Oh gee whiz!'

A cloud hung over the street below, muting the distant lights. From somewhere between the steep ranks of buildings a siren wailed.

Sarah, a coat around her shoulders, leaned at the parapet, surveying the city.

'I'm so proud,' Aunt Ida had said at lunch today. 'You

62

have the world at your feet, Sarah. I feel . . . I feel as if I had a part of it. And your Uncle Steven . . . he did too. Before he died, he often . . . he always said . . .' She smiled tremulously. 'He was so proud of you too.'

The world at your feet . . .

A trite way of saying that Sarah was successful. That she'd done what she set out to do. And how had it happened? What had she done?

She was seventeen the September she started college. She had enough money for tuition, for clothes and bus fares, but her mother always wanted a little something extra from her. Within a month Sarah realized that she would need a job if she didn't tell her aunt what her mother was doing. Sarah didn't want to do that. Her first job was typing a manuscript for one of the professors in the English department. Her second job, one he found for her, was as a typist, part time, for television station WTOP, as it was then known. From the instant she walked into the Connecticut Avenue office, she knew she belonged there. She liked the sound and smell of the place. She liked the dingy corridors and the cubbyhole offices and the scarred desks, the control rooms with ranks of monitors, the cameras on their pedestals, the wires snaking along the floors. Here was the quick living heart-beat of the world, she thought.

And that was where she wanted to be. But within days she saw that she couldn't learn anything sitting at her typewriter. And she wanted to learn.

She made friends with an elderly man in the news department. She reminded him of his daughter when she was the same age, he said. She played up to that. He responded by trying to teach her everything she wanted to know. He took her with him to shoots. He introduced her to the cameramen. He showed her the inside workings of the station. She knew very quickly that she was interested in the production end, that she didn't want to be on camera. She wanted to design what *went* on camera. Of the dozens of people who worked on a show, any show, there were only six roles that were indispensable: the

63

actors, the director, the cameraman, the producer, the production designer, the writer. The producer was the most important of the these indispensable people. His was the ultimate responsibility for the success of the show, his the job to bring in the programme on time and within budget. Even then, when she was a lowly typist, that was what she aspired to be.

While others her age let their hair grow and climbed into blue jeans and went adventuring on the road or joined communes, while campus demonstrations against the Vietnam War heated up, Sarah was too busy with school and with her part-time job to notice. At the end of two years, when she was a Phi Beta Kappa junior, her elderly friend was fired. Soon after, his replacement let her go. By then, though, she'd made contacts in the city. She quickly found another job, this time as a production aide, the formal title which actually meant 'gofer'. It was just what she needed and could do. She learned quickly. She befriended the young son of the general manager. By the time she graduated from the university in 1968, she was engaged to him. She broke with him when she was offered a better-paying job, still as a production aide, at another station.

She met John soon after that. He was in Washington doing a three-week training course in connection with his stockbroker job. She continued to see him occasionally after he returned to his home in New York. She worked on several news programmes. She collected guests and delivered them for the station's daily magazine programme. She stood behind the cameramen, watching. She talked budgets with the producers, and story lines with the writers, and unions with the shop stewards. But at that point, she was stalled. Nothing was happening. She'd been in television for four years, but there were only a few women working behind the camera then. There weren't many jobs for them; Sarah began to fear she would be a gofer for the rest of her life. And she wasn't willing to settle for that.

It was then that John asked her to marry him, and she

said yes. Her mother wanted her to have a big wedding, even suggested that Ida would pay for it. Sarah refused. She and John were married by a justice of the peace, and she immediately moved to New York.

For nearly a year after that she made the rounds. She went from NBC to CBS to ABC. She covered every radio and television station to which public transport could take her. Finally she landed a job as a receptionist at a local radio station. She hated everything about the job, and was glad when she became pregnant. She had Tim. After a few months she went job-hunting again. But that time she had help.

She had discovered that her across-the-hall neighbour was Carla Janssen, an account executive with Halloran, Fox and Deerling, an advertising agency that specialized in television advertising. She cultivated Carla, whose already rocky marriage fell apart a few years later. Carla heard a good deal about Sarah's Washington career, and even more about Sarah's desire to go back to work. Within a few months Carla got her a job, this time as a production assistant. She had worked in it three months when she heard the producer telling the young man who was his associate producer, Gary Crane, that somebody was leaving a morning show, and that opening might be his chance out of commercials. She listened while Gary phoned for an appointment to see the person in charge.

Only a few days before, Gary had patted her on the rear end as she walked by him. She had given him a hard elbow to the ribs, said loudly, 'You keep your damned hands off me!'

Everybody had heard, sniggered. He turned red, and mumbled a non-apology. She was delighted to do him dirt if possible.

Half an hour after she heard Gary making his phone call she presented her résumé, and herself, at her very best, to the same person in charge. She got the job Gary Crane had applied for.

That was her start at ABC. But within the year she became pregnant. She went back to work after Peg was born, but John began to make old-fashioned husband noises. He wanted a full-time wife to look after their full-time children. He wanted a house in Connecticut. He wanted everything that she didn't want, and nothing that she did. She spent a lot of nights talking him out of what he wanted. Meanwhile she worked her way up the ladder. She went from ABC to CBS to NBC. With each change she had a new title. She was assistant producer, guest coordinator for a morning show, researcher, then head researcher. She did script editing for a while, then assisted the casting director before becoming casting director herself. From there she made the big step to associate producer. By the time she won the job of producer at NTN, she was divorced from John, and he was married to Carla Janssen.

Now six years after the divorce, four years since she went to work on *Oakview Valley*, she looked down at the blurred lights of the city. She was Sarah Morehouse. She had a lot, but it wasn't enough. She wanted more. She wanted it all . . .

5

Morning light filtered through the pale curtains at the kitchen window.

Laylie stirred oatmeal while Sarah, standing, gulped black coffee.

Peg came in, slammed her books on the table.

'Well, hello,' Sarah said.

Peg made a sound that was halfway between a grunt and a croak and flung herself into a chair.

'Cereal's almost ready,' Laylie told her.

'Cereal? Ugh! Just what I don't want.'

'You always want cereal,' Laylie said, laughing.

'Not today I don't.' Peg's voice was tart.

'Somebody get up on the wrong side of the bed?' Sarah asked.

'Oh Mom, honestly, do you have to say things like that?'

Sarah put down her cup, blinked. This wasn't the Peg she knew. Cranky, spoiling for a fight . . . Good God, what was wrong? 'Aren't you feeling well?' she asked.

'Mom! For Pete's sake . . .' Peg yelled.

'Hey, hang on,' Sarah said. 'We can do without the hollering. Something's bothering you. I can see that, so . . .'

Peg jumped up. 'I'm okay, I tell you. Just stop picking on me . . .'

'*Excuse me.* I didn't know I was picking on you.'

Peg grabbed her books, ran to the door. 'Well, you are,' she cried, her face scarlet. 'Why don't you just leave me alone?' With that she was gone. Her footsteps thudded down the hallway. The outer door slammed.

Laylie sighed. 'I wonder what's eating her.'

'I don't know,' Sarah said. 'She's certainly not acting

like herself, is she?' She glanced at her watch. It was time to go. She and Laylie would have to talk about Peg later.

There were sidewalk vendors at each side of the entrance to National Television Network's new building on 55th Street. One sold apples wrapped in green tissue paper. The other sold garish ties. One proprietor was a very old Korean. The other was a very young one.

The building guard stood between them, dividing his disapproving stare between the two. He greeted Sarah, held the door open. Inside the marble-floored lobby another guard waved her towards the elevator. Security had become more tight in the past few years, necessary to protect the place against the theft of expensive and easily-removed equipment, as well as to protect the personnel against the ever-increasing army of troubled people who had made the media the centres for their problems.

NTN'S front offices and reception areas, where sponsors and guests were welcomed, had been elegantly decorated. But beyond them, where the staff worked, the quarters were plain and cramped.

Upstairs Sarah passed by the long row of cubbyholes, each with its own fluorescent light, its small desk and word processor or typewriter.

She was lucky, she thought, to have her own office.

Robin's was next door. He was already at his desk, as unflappable as always. He was a part of her morning sense of wellbeing. Her shower, her coffee, and then Robin, here and ready to go to work. As she looked in, he raised blue eyes, brushed back a lock of dark hair.

A very good-looking boy, she thought briefly, waving at him as she went on to her own office. The kind that girls would go for. No doubt there were plenty of them in his life. But probably no one steady. At least not yet. He was too available to Sarah's calls, always prepared to work late. A steady girl would want more of his time to be hers.

Even before she put down her briefcase and purse Sarah

switched on the small television set in the corner, its volume turned low. It would play all day while she worked. Once in a while she would raise her eyes to look at the screen, or she would pause to listen to its soft mutter. When her own show came on she would watch moments at a time while going over scripts or answering mail.

Rob came in now. Smiling, he asked, 'A good weekend?'

She thought of Daniel. Ugh. Then she thought of Tony Statler. Would he call?

'Not bad,' she told Rob. 'Not bad at all.'

Some time later Rob sat at his desk listening to the murmur of voices from Sarah's office. Hers smooth, husky. Hy Berge's a deep rumbling growl.

Rob didn't care what they were saying. It pleased him just to hear Sarah speak, just as it pleased him to see her walk across the floor. He'd never felt that way about a woman before, although he'd been in love, or felt in love, several times. Now, though, his earlier affairs seemed to have been preludes. What he felt for Sarah was entirely different: deeper, more intense, somehow more real.

He wished that Daniel had stalked out on that Friday night, annoyed that Rob was there, so Rob and Sarah could have been left alone together. Not that anything would have happened. She'd have watched the tape until she saw what was wrong, and then she'd have sent him home. Still, for a while, there might have been just the two of them, in her apartment . . .

Inside Sarah's office Hy Berge was saying, 'Have I talked to Rita? What do you think?' He ran thick fingers through his sandy hair. 'Naturally I've talked to her. She says she doesn't know what I mean. She says she's doing the best she can. What do you want me to do? Grab her and throw her into Hart's arms?'

Sarah sat very straight. Her square shoulders under pink cashmere were braced against the back of the chair.

69

'Now, Hy, I don't care how we do it. But there's going to be more passion in our scenes. I want a better performance out of Rita. And that's that. She's had plenty of time to work herself around to understanding what we need. And I'm sure you've explained . . .'

Hy said tentatively, 'I have. Believe me. Maybe if you talked to her yourself . . .'

It was what Sarah had hoped he'd say. She knew him well enough to suspect that he had hemmed and hawed and stalled around, too concerned about Rita's feelings to say anything strong to her.

That wasn't Sarah's problem. She smiled at Hy. 'If you want me to, I'll be glad to talk to her. Ask her to come to my office when she gets in.' Sarah made it sound as if she were doing Hy a favour.

He reacted as if she were. 'Thanks. I know you'll be able to make her see what we need.' He turned away, then swung back. 'And Sarah, thanks for the birthday present.'

She smiled at him, watched him walk from the office.

Two hours later Rita Porter pouted over the rim of her coffee cup. Her violet eyes were dark with anger. Her long curly black hair seemed electric with it. She was slender, and even in the large white over-sized sweater she wore, her breasts seemed high, pointing, very sexy. 'Hy told me,' she said in a husky voice. 'You've been looking at the tapes, and you're worried. Worried about what? I don't understand. Sometimes Hy's like an old woman. He dithers and doesn't make sense. So what's he talking about? Do you want to tell me?'

So Hy *had* worn kid gloves, Sarah thought. Well, he'd had a month to get through to Rita, and he hadn't managed to do it. Now it was time to take the kid gloves off. 'Look, Rita, let's not beat around the bush. Every time Hart gets near you, you freeze up. It shows. When he puts his arms around you, you look like a corpse.' She smiled. 'A beautiful corpse, I must tell you. But a very dead one just the same.'

'Which is just what I'm thinking about. Dead bodies.

And me possibly being one of them very soon.' Rita's voice was louder. It came out of her like a shouted whisper. 'That fag! Hart Carow turns my stomach. How can you let him be Davey? Davey's a man. And Hart . . .'

Sarah said brusquely, 'Hart is gay. Fag isn't an acceptable word to use.'

'Use whatever word you want! My stomach turns over every time he touches me.'

'And that's just what it looks like,' Sarah said softly.

'I don't care,' Rita cried. 'I can't stand it any more. Ever since I first heard about AIDS it's been on my mind. What do you want from me? To die, so you can have a good sexy scene? To hell with it, and Hart, and you too. It's not worth it to me.'

It was odd, Sarah thought. Rita wasn't afraid of losing her job with *Oakview Valley*. If she were, she'd have said she was sorry; she'd have promised to do better. That she hadn't done so made Sarah even more determined. She said softly, 'You're not going to get AIDS by simulating a passionate kiss. You don't have to open your mouth, you know. You don't have to do anything except pretend, Rita.'

'And *you* don't know how AIDS spreads. I don't either. Nobody does. Just being next to Hart gives me the willies.'

'So you won't even try.' It was silent in the room except for the steam hiss of the radiator and the distant bleep-bleep of a telephone. 'I see, I see.' Sarah's brows rose. Her voice was silky, thoughtful on those words. There was a lot she could have said. The cast was a team. A family. What happened to one happened to all. She could ring the changes on what working together meant to the show, the ratings, the success of every one of them. But she didn't bother. Rita's reaction told her clearly it wouldn't be worth a single wasted breath.

'Oh, don't be like that,' Rita said, 'of course I'll *try*.'

There was no conviction in her voice, but Sarah said, 'Okay then. Just remember. All you have to do is make it look good.'

'We ought to write Hart Carow out. That's what we

ought to do.' Rita rose, paused. 'I guess you saw that item in Andrew Reynolds' column.'

Sarah didn't answer.

'It was a plant of course. Andrew Reynolds must have heard it from somebody.'

Still Sarah said nothing.

'Don't think I'm responsible. Because I'm not. And if anybody's career is going to suffer, it's not going to be mine.'

'I should hope not,' Sarah said, picking up a folder to signal the end of the meeting.

After a moment's hesitation Rita, swaying on high patent-leather heels, left the office.

Considering Rita's behaviour, the insincerity of her promise to do better, her haughty independence, Sarah decided that there must be something she didn't know.

She looked around, as if searching for the answer in the small office. It was a comfortable place with two moderately lumpy armchairs near the big old desk and a row of chipped yellow filing cabinets across one wall. Shelves, floor to ceiling, crammed with books and cassettes, covered another wall. The rug was clean and fluffy, but not luxurious. The potted plant on the windowsill was flourishing, largely because Rob made it part of his job to remind somebody to care for it.

The phone on her desk trilled. She touched the answer button and Robin said, 'I just saw Bonnie coming in, in case you want to see her.'

It was like him, knowing what she would want, and when. What a good kid he was. She thanked him, hung up and put in a call to Bonnie.

A few minutes later Bonnie stood in the office doorway. She was a short girl, just barely five feet tall, and stubby, with plump arms and legs, and a pale round-cheeked face. Her black hair was cropped short, her dark eyes encircled by dark rings under tiny rimless half glasses that rode the end of her nose. She wore black trousers, a white silk shirt and a narrow black tie. She sank into the easy chair near the desk, almost sliding away into its depths. 'I hope

72

there's no bad news, Sarah. I don't think I can take any stress this morning,' she said seriously.

'It's bad,' Sarah said, 'only if work is bad news.'

'There's times when it is.' Bonnie had been writing scripts for *Oakview Valley* for the past year and a half, and still hadn't come to realize her own skill and ingenuity at it. She also wasn't yet adult enough to know that it was her personal and not her professional life that was bothering her.

Sarah, on any other day, might have asked what was troubling Bonnie, but thought it best, today, not to inquire. She said, 'I've been thinking about Nella Rogoway as played by Rita. We've wrung about as much from Davey's affair with her as we can. I'd like to see us go off in a new direction.'

'And that's where I come in,' Bonnie muttered.

'Right.'

'And where Nella Rogoway goes out for ever.'

'Right again.'

Bonnie regarded Sarah intently, then asked, 'What's happened?'

'I think we need a new direction.'

'Or you need a new Nella Rogoway,' Bonnie said dryly. 'How much time do I have?'

'Plenty. Give me some rough ideas by the end of the week.'

'Plenty!' Bonnie groaned. 'Are you kidding? The end of the week!'

'Just suggestions,' Sarah said soothingly. 'We'll work them over with some things I have on the boil, and see what we come up with.'

Bonnie hesitated. Then in a tentative voice asked, 'Is this a good idea?'

'I think so.' Sarah took her day book from her briefcase. She looked up at Bonnie. 'I'm going to improve the show. With your help.'

'Does Hy Berge know?'

Sarah smiled. 'I think he might have got a slight hint.'

'And what about Lyman?'

Lyman Ogloe, as executive producer, worked for the network but was closely associated with the show's sponsor, Georgiana, and whoever was delegated to represent the soap company. Sarah was directly responsible to him for bringing in the show, within budget and on time and at the best quality she could achieve. How she did it, from his point of view, was supposed to be her business.

Sarah told Bonnie, 'Eventually he'll hear about it, of course. But I won't tell him the details until I know them myself.'

Bonnie shook her head from side to side, saying, 'No, no.' The small glasses flew off the end of her nose. She made a swipe at them and they sailed across the room. Swearing, she went after them.

While she collected her glasses and herself, Sarah looked into the day book. There it was, a page labelled Lyman Ogloe. His birthday. His wedding date. His wife's name. Their three children, with birthdays, and wedding dates too. There were also, in a code of her own design, a few other notes.

Bonnie, back in her chair, said, 'There was a rumour about a year back . . .'

Sarah closed the day book. 'Don't tell me . . . please . . .' But of course she'd heard the rumour. There was a note of it in the day book. Rita had been hired by Hy Berge, after an audition arranged by Lyman, who owed a favour to an executive at Georgiana.

Maybe it was true. Maybe not. Either way it didn't matter to Sarah. As long as the girl did her job well, how she got that job wasn't relevant. She was no longer doing the job well. She wasn't trying. She could be a source of damage to the show. So she was finished at *Oakview Valley*. She didn't know it yet, although if she were a little more clever she'd have guessed. But within a few weeks, when her air time grew shorter she'd have to face it. Soon she'd be referred to on the show in the past tense. If she were referred to at all. Sarah sighed. And that was when it would sink in, and the big scene would come. First

74

with Rita. Then with Lyman, who would have to deal with the possible Georgiana executive. Unless, Sarah suddenly wondered, Rita had been hired by Hy as a favour to Lyman himself, under the cover of a favour to someone else. It was something to think about. But it wouldn't change Sarah's mind.

'If you don't need me any more . . .' Bonnie said, getting up.

'Just find me some good angles.'

As Bonnie left, the phone on Sarah's desk trilled. She hit the button, picked up the receiver. 'Sarah?' Robin asked. 'Do you remember your lunch date?' In his voice there was the usual note of apology as he added, 'With Carla Bradford.' He'd still not recovered from the gaffe he made when he first came on Sarah's team, telling her, 'Carla Bradford's probably going to own Halloran, Fox and Deerling one of these days.'

He was so fresh on the job then that he didn't know that Carla had once been Sarah's closest friend, but had, by then, become Mrs John Bradford.

Soon after that Carla left her job and retired to the house in Connecticut, where she and John lived the life that John had wanted with Sarah but could never have.

It couldn't be easy on Carla. But it was hard on Sarah too. She hadn't wanted John, but her pride had been hurt when he asked for a divorce. His marriage to Carla had made that even worse.

'I hadn't remembered the appointment,' Sarah said dryly. 'Thank you, Robin.'

The Bradfords, Carla and John both, were beginning to be too much a part of her life, Sarah thought. She had just seen John last Saturday. That was enough Bradford for a while. Still, this lunch date had been made weeks ago when Carla phoned. Carla was determined to maintain the myth that John and Sarah had had a very amicable divorce and that the three of them remained the best of friends.

'Are you running on time?' Robin asked.

'Only a little late. It'll be a shorter lunch than Carla planned.'

'There's rehearsal at two.'

'Yes.'

'And . . . Rita's stalking around like a . . . well, I don't know what.'

Sarah laughed. 'It'll be okay. See you at two.'

Rob looked at the phone, frowned. He wanted to warn her to watch out. Maybe something was brewing that could spill over on her. Instead he asked, sounding more like a concerned parent than an assistant, 'Is there anything I can do for you while you're gone?'

She gave her notes a swift glance, then told him that there wasn't, and she'd get back to him later.

She went into the small washroom next to her office. The light was dim, which was the only good thing about the place. The mirror was too high. She strained to see her reflection before she washed off her make-up, then quickly applied fresh blusher and a dusting of powder and lipstick. She ran a comb through her hair, smiling faintly. The rivalry between Carla and her was long over, but some smidgen of habit made her want to look her best when they met.

'It's good to see you,' Carla said, not mentioning that Sarah was fifteen minutes late. 'You're looking well. I guess your schedule agrees with you.'

'I guess so,' Sarah said, smiling.

'John told me he saw you on Saturday but only for a minute.'

'Yes.' Sarah shrugged. 'We'd have had a fight if he'd stayed longer.'

'There's no reason for you two to fight any more,' Carla said. She'd been told once that she resembled Meryl Streep, and the comment had sunk into her so deeply that she'd begun to accentuate the very faint similarity between them. Hair, eyes and make-up were all modelled on the actress. Even the way she held her head on her long neck

76

seemed practised. There was, however, something just a little dowdy about her, Sarah decided.

The two women eyed each other. The waiter took their orders, then left. At last Carla said, 'John's been very worried about Tim.'

'A made-up problem. All in John's mind.'

'He only wants the best for Tim, for Peg too. He believes they need a real home life.'

'The kids are fine. Tim's doing well at school.'

'I rather think that Tim shows his best face for you. On the rare occasions when you see him.'

'I doubt it.'

'And boys,' Carla went on, 'at his age, do relate better to their fathers.'

Sarah took a deep breath. 'You seem to have forgotten that when you took over my husband, you did not take over my children.'

A blush shaded Carla's throat. 'Now Sarah, you mustn't dwell on the past. As I said, we just want what's good for the kids. And you know perfectly well that I've always loved them. Why, Sarah, don't you remember . . .'

'I remember,' Sarah said quickly. It was perfectly true. Carla had always doted on Tim and Peg. And, Sarah supposed, she still did.

That was the only reason Sarah permitted herself to engage in these periodic meetings. Carla was the children's stepmother, as well as long-time friend. They mustn't be made to feel that Sarah and Carla hated each other. Still, Sarah couldn't let everything go by. She said evenly, 'I'm so glad to hear how concerned you and John are. Shall we drop the subject?'

The waiter brought Carla a martini, and a cup of black coffee to Sarah. Carla took up her drink and with a sigh of relief began to ask about people they'd both known at Halloran, Fox and Deerling.

While she answered Carla's questions Sarah thought of another lunch she'd had with Carla. They'd been at Sardi's. A spring day more than six years before. Carla had

77

leaned across the table. 'Sarah, is there anything wrong between you and John?'

There had been a lot wrong, just about everything. In spite of their closeness, Sarah didn't intend to discuss that with Carla. She said, 'Only the usual things that go wrong between married people.'

'Are you sure?'

Sarah asked quietly, 'What are you leading up to?'

Carla looked uncomfortable. 'It's just that . . . well, I don't know how to say this . . . but I've been hearing . . .' She paused, looked into Sarah's eyes, then looked away. 'They always say the wife is the last one to know, don't they?'

'They said that fifty years ago. I don't know what they're saying now. Suppose you tell me.'

'There's nothing to tell, Sarah. Honestly. It's just that somebody said she'd seen John with somebody else.'

A few months later John told Sarah that he wanted a divorce. He needed a wife. A real wife. A woman at home who loved him, would entertain his friends, be what he needed her to be.

A few months after the divorce was final, Carla and he had married.

It was the dishonesty of it that Sarah so resented. She knew perfectly well that at the time of that lunch with Sarah, Carla hadn't been seeing John. It was only later that she'd begun sneaking around, going behind Sarah's back, making use of her knowledge of Sarah's feelings to ingratiate herself with John. She knew it, and it hurt.

Now Carla said, 'You're happy at NTN, aren't you?'

Sarah agreed that she was.

Carla sighed. 'It's good to come into the city once in a while. Although I admit I hardly ever do.'

'Then you're happy being a housewife.'

'Oh yes,' Carla said. But she shifted in her chair, and her narrowed eyes moved in a quick assessing way around the room. 'I'm glad I finally made the break.'

'You don't miss the job?'

'That rat race? Don't make me laugh.'

'Then all's well that ends well, isn't it?' Sarah said. As far as she was concerned it had ended very well indeed. She'd probably have killed John if he hadn't asked for a divorce. It was only after they were apart that she realized how much time she had wasted on him. And since she felt it wasted, it had been. She thought fleetingly of Daniel, and then Tony. It would probably have been the same with Daniel. Would it be the same with Tony?

Maybe there wasn't a man in the world who could understand her, be what she needed a man to be. Maybe she was asking for the impossible. Meanwhile she had more important things to think about.

'But about Tim . . .' Carla said. 'John and I have been talking. I know he didn't mention it to you, although he should have. We'd both be happy to have him. Instead of that expensive private school in Washington, he could be at home, live with us, have his father again.'

'No,' Sarah said quietly.

'Just no?'

'No, goddamn it! And that ends the discussion.'

'Do you have any plans for a vacation this year?' Carla asked immediately.

The waitress brought their food. They ate, speaking of Pleasant Cove, a resort in St Thomas they had both visited at different times. When they finished they parted, smiling. Sarah returned to her office, knowing she wouldn't be invited to lunch with Carla again for another six months, if then. And that was fine with her.

The set designer was waiting at Robin's desk. He followed her into her office. She looked over his new sketches quickly, okayed them, and then leaned back in her chair. 'There'll be some changes coming up. We'll be bringing a new character in, I think. We'll want a new work-up. I'll get back to you later in the week when I have more details.'

She was thinking of Rita's replacement. It would require new dimensions. That meant new sets possibly. She didn't mention Rita but of course, the grapevine being what it was, he already knew something was up.

79

He asked, 'Do you have any ideas yet?'

'Bonnie's working on them now. I'll give you plenty of time.'

'I hope so, Sarah. It seems to me that lately we've been doing nothing but crisis creation.' He grinned, plainly liking the phrase. 'It's not the best way to operate.'

'That's the business,' she told him.

'Sure. But it can be contained. At least I've always thought so.'

That was why, or one reason why, he was a set designer, planning the living rooms and bedrooms, and she was a producer. It amused her that everyone on the team considered he could do her job better than she could, but didn't know how to do more than his own job. But the set designer was good at his. When she set a budget he didn't try to expand it. He had a feel for what she wanted and seemed to know how to get it. So she said slowly, 'Maybe you're right. Thanks for the tip. Sometimes an outside view helps.'

She didn't believe a word of it, but he went away, smiling and happy, which was what she wanted.

By then it was time for the read-through, the reading rehearsal. She took the bible and the copies of the five scripts they would be shooting that week.

When she walked into the room she knew at once that it would be one of those days when everything went to hell.

Hart Carow was standing in a distant corner, alone. His handsome face was set in grim lines. Rita was giggling in another corner, surrounded by a group. Hy Berge had retreated from the palpable tension by bending his head over a script, acting as if he heard nothing, saw nothing, knew nothing. But his forehead glistened with sweat. Bonnie stood next to him, looking like an unhappy puppy waiting to be kicked.

Everyone turned to Sarah in hopeful and expectant silence. She ignored it, went to Hart. 'Hi. How're you doing?'

'Fine,' he said glumly.

80

'Fine? You sound like a very unhappy weekend.'

'No. The weekend was good. I went to Fire Island. It was relaxing. Restful.'

'And fun, I hope.' She linked an arm through his. 'Let's get going, shall we?' As she spoke she walked him to the long conference table. When he had seated himself Sarah sat down next to Hy. She pointed at the empty chair beside Hart. 'Rita? Ready for you.'

Rita ambled to the table, swinging her hips. She hesitated, then sat next to Hart.

Hy looked relieved. He said, 'Okay? Script one. From the top. Rita?'

She read smoothly, competently. But it was, Sarah thought, the part that had made her. And the part was Bonnie's work. Bonnie had written a bitch, the kind of character that the watching public seemed to find fascinating. That Rita and the part coincided was just that. Coincidence. But it helped her be convincing. Bonnie couldn't have played the part if her life depended on it.

Hart came in on cue. He was, himself, nothing like Davey, the role. But he was an actor. He read two lines and then stopped, looked up at Hy. 'That sounds wrong to me. Too many esses. I can hear myself lisping.'

There was a quick squeal of malicious laughter from Rita.

Sarah's voice cut through it sharply. 'We have these read-throughs just to find problems like that.' And to Bonnie, 'Can you fix it?'

Bonnie read the sentence aloud twice. Her voice shook when she offered word substitutions.

Hart began again. He nodded happily and went on.

The rest of the reading was uneventful.

'Okay,' Sarah said to Hy.

He waved at the cast. 'Okay then. Tomorrow.'

Sarah caught up with Bonnie in the hallway. 'It looks as if Rita's going to make a mess one way or another. We'll have to work fast. Conference tomorrow in the late afternoon?'

'I'll try to have something by then.'

Sarah grinned. 'So will I.'

She spent the last of the afternoon answering mail and thinking, at the back of her mind, of a smooth way to turn the show, eliminate Rita, and bring in someone new.

The bottle of white wine stood in the ice bucket. The canapes, John's favourite, sliced hard-boiled eggs with black caviar on rye toast, were close by. There was a vase of yellow roses on the windowsill. Carla had carried them back from the city because John particularly liked yellow roses.

She was planning what she would tell him of her lunch with Sarah but when he came in she forgot what she had earlier decided, and as she poured wine into his glass she said, 'I told Sarah we'd like to have Tim with us.'

'You called her?'

'Oh, no.' Carla was shocked. She'd told John she was having lunch with Sarah. Had he forgotten? Or was he pretending that he had? No matter. Carla went on smoothly, 'Why, no. We had a lunch date. So I decided it might be better if the suggestion came from me.'

'And?'

'I'm sure you'll be able to talk her around eventually. But of course she said no. She would at first. She wouldn't want to look eager to give Tim up, after all.'

'She wouldn't be giving Tim up.' John took a gulp of his wine. Then: 'Don't mix in, Carla. Leave the dealing with Sarah to me.' There was heat in his voice. His mouth had that tight look it got whenever they spoke of Sarah.

Carla said, 'Of course, John. Whatever you think. The thing to remember, though, is that Sarah's a very busy woman. Very. After all, she has her career. And as a single woman she also has a social life. And we both know that being a mother is a full-time job. Tim, and Peg too, really would be better off with us.'

If only she were younger, Carla thought. She and John could have a child. He'd be satisfied then. And so would she. But she was forty-two, and past it. And even if she weren't, she wasn't sure she wanted to have a baby now. Maybe it wouldn't solve the problem of John's feelings anyhow. If only he would forget the kids and Sarah. But he couldn't, and didn't. So having them here would be best. And it would save a great deal of money too. Carla was careful never to mention *that*, however.

John was saying, 'We'll see, Carla. Just don't butt in.'

That night Sarah sat at her desk in her bedroom, going over the messages Laylie had given her.

There was a small sound at the open door.

She looked up.

'May I come in?' Peg asked tentatively.

'Sure. I thought you were asleep.'

Peg shook her head. She came closer, but stopped just beyond the circle of light so that her face was in shadow.

She looked different, Sarah thought. Solemn, a little shy, uncertain maybe.

Sarah waited, remembering Peg's morning outburst. She'd realized during the day that it wasn't the first time. Peg had seemed edgy for nearly a week, her sweetness alternating with quick sarcasm. Maybe now she wanted to talk about what was bothering her.

Peg said quietly, 'Mom, you'll never guess what just happened.'

'What, Peg?'

'I've been feeling so funny. Like getting ready for a really important test. Kind of screwed up tight inside, and holding my breath until it was over with. It was making me nervous, I guess. But now, I understand what it was.' Her voice dropped to a whisper. 'It's happened, Mom. I just got my first period.'

Hormones, changing, increasing, racing through the blood. So that's what Peg's tantrums had been about. Thank God she'd explained the menstrual cycle to the girl six months ago. Later they would talk more about the practicalities. But now . . . now Sarah said, 'Peg! Oh Peg, honey. That's . . . that's wonderful . . .' She opened her arms and Peg came into them. They squeezed each other in reciprocating bear hugs. 'Time goes so fast,' Sarah said, feeling the sudden sting of tears in her eyes. 'It seems as if only the other day you were running around in diapers. And now here you are, on the way to being all grown up.'

She thought fleetingly of John and Carla, and hugged Peg even harder. Nobody was going to take this closeness, this reality, away from her. Nobody. Never.

6

Several days later Sarah slipped into her chair just before shooting began. The room was as crowded as usual. She hadn't had to travel far, just two floors down from her office, and through a long narrow hallway. A far cry from when she was at NBC. Then she had to take a cab to the low-rise building where a few floors had been rented as studio space. Now a lot of production was done on Long Island at Astoria. But NTN had adequate space in its own building, at least for the time being.

Hy Berge nodded at her, looked at his watch, and with his plump hand over the lapel mike he wore, growled, 'Everybody and his brother, along with a couple of cousins too, it looks like. This better be a good one.'

She smiled at him, thinking for an instant of Tony. He had called. It had been a good conversation, and he was coming in for the Thanksgiving weekend. She was fleetingly warmed by that thought. Then she forgot the holiday, Tony. The whole world fell away. There was only this place full of murmuring voices. The monitors overhead, the sound stage beyond the thick panel of glass that made it seem as distant as the moon. She became totally alert, all senses keyed to their highest. Her mind quickly working through the file cabinet of detail registered there weeks, days and hours before Hy murmured into his mike. The floor manager, his head bracketed by ear pieces called cans by the crew, stood waiting. Rita was on the set. Above her head, on the mantel, there was a book. It stood open, its cover showing clearly on the monitors. *The Gun-Runners*. Sarah had read enough of an indifferent review in the *Times* that past Sunday to gather that the novel struck the reviewer as phony from start to finish, and not very interesting either. Shields, the single named author, was known as a man about town, macho type, who wrote between bouts with women and cocaine. Briefly Sarah wondered why Max Hollis, the set dresser, had used that book. Probably because someone had given him a free copy, and it was handy when he was setting up.

Now the floor manager was looking around. Hy Berge suddenly rose. 'Where's Hart?'

Damn! A frown etched lines into Sarah's forehead under the blonde fringe she wore that day. What was the matter? Where was Hart? It was time to get started.

Hy was speaking into his mike, a sheen of sweat on his face.

'What's wrong?' she asked. 'What's happened to Hart?' But she already knew. She'd decided to do this scene first, had told Annette to change the cast schedule accordingly. There'd been a foul-up.

Hy sent someone to find Hart. He was in his dressing room. He looked startled when told he was holding up the shooting. 'But I'm not due for another hour and a half!' he protested. 'Look at the cast schedule.'

In the control room Hy's big bulk seemed to be shrinking within his clothes. He spoke into his mike. The brilliant lights went out. The cameras hung motionless. From beyond the glass panel, amplified by his mike, the floor manager's voice suddenly boomed, 'Okay. We have a wait!'

Word came back that Hart was changing for the scene. He'd get through make-up as quickly as he could.

The Standards and Practices man, responsible for every line, paragraph and even pause, shrugged and leaned back, a look of saintly patience on his face.

Lyman Ogloe, the executive producer, left his two guests and waddled to Sarah. Bald head pink, fat cheeks aquiver, he leaned over her. 'Better find out what happened,' he growled.

She gave him a grim look. It was like him to contribute the obvious suggestion. What did he think she was going to do?

She stepped over a nest of wires and opened the door

86

to the sound stage as Robin appeared at her elbow. 'Just hold on,' she told the floor manager. And to Robin, 'See if you can hurry Hart.' And as Annette Stone, her associate producer, appeared wordlessly at her side, 'Go with him, Annette. I'll talk to you later in my office.'

She went back to her seat, green eyes as cold as emeralds. She took out the casting schedule. There had been no accommodation made for the scene change. Hart was not listed as due for another hour and a half.

Robin and Annette had disappeared in the direction of the dressing rooms.

Annette was a short girl, pink cheeked and blue eyed, with a thick mane of dark hair that hung well below her shoulders. She was in her mid twenties but still dressed like a college girl of the early 1980s in over-sized sweaters, trailing scarves and low-heeled pumps. She had come to NTN from Washington, with enthusiastic letters of recommendation and a particularly urgent note from one of the congressmen from Illinois, who happened to be her uncle.

Sarah considered her associate producer while she waited, unconsciously tapping her foot, squeezing the script in her clenched hand. No one came near her. There was a rustling of paper. Movement. Voices. An expectant tension, which she ignored. She shut her eyes, seeing hundred-dollar bills floating away before her, seeing the carefully drawn and designed schedule she had set up and priced disappearing into shreds of paper.

Damn. Damn! Why had this dumb thing happened? How could it have happened? It was, in this case, a matter of robbing Peter to pay Paul. Of shifting figures from one account to another. When she figured the cost of a show, breaking it down into episodes, one of the numbers involved was rent of the studio, another was cameramen's time, another was editing time . . .

She made herself stop. What was the use? The delay would cost thousands. She'd have to find a way to make them up. Otherwise she'd run over budget. And she couldn't. It was a matter of pride with her. She never ran over budget. That's one reason why she was considered so good at her job.

It was not quite an hour before Hart appeared, dressed as Davey, made up, ready to go, and waving his copy of the casting schedule.

In a little while the floor manager was signalling. Rob and Annette returned to their seats before the monitors.

Hart came on the sound stage, then went to stand at the door, reaching to open it. Rita stood by the fireplace. The floor manager, out of camera range, raised his hand, pointed. He spoke into his mike. The lights blazed. Hy spoke again. The cameras swung into position. The monitors went on. Hart began to speak.

The scene went smoothly, but there was a telling stiffness between Hart and Rita, an unease that pervaded the roles they played. Nella and Davey were lovers, but what showed on the monitors was very different from love. It was closer to hate. Still, the segment was taped without overt event.

The Standards and Practices man followed every word, watched every movement, listened for every nuance. It was his job to be certain that NTN's code was followed in all respects. Nothing was to be allowed to show on screen that might provoke the ire of the watching and listening audience. If something got by him that brought angry letters to Georgiana or to the network, then he was in trouble.

When Hy said tiredly, 'Okay, folks. That's a wrap,' and they were finally alone, Sarah told him, 'It looks all right for the rest of this month and next. But there'll probably be changes coming up after that.'

'Rita, you mean?'

Sarah nodded.

'I'd hoped we could forget about it.'

'You know we can't, Hy.'

'Trouble,' he answered. 'But all right. I'll stock the aspirin.'

In a little while Sarah was back at her desk.

Annette came in, seated herself, looking like a fright-

88

ened schoolchild hoping for the best but expecting the worst. She swallowed a cough, choked, grew red with the effort to contain it.

A new surge of anger swept Sarah. There was no room for mistakes in this business. Apologies didn't repair the damage done.

'All right,' she said. 'We have to deal with this.' Her green eyes flashed. Her voice was low, but tight. 'Something happened that cost us thousands of dollars. We were delayed for close to an hour while Hart Carow got himself ready. And it's a miracle he managed it as fast as he did. He wasn't listed on the cast schedule because a change hadn't been made to conform to what I laid out. I did tell you, Annette, what we were going to do. You were supposed to alter the cast schedule. You know there's nothing, but nothing, more important than that. We can't shoot when the actors aren't there, can we? What happened? Why didn't you take care of it?'

'It was a . . . an accident,' Annette said.

'I know it wasn't deliberate,' Sarah retorted. 'But we have to figure out why it happened. And how. To make sure it won't happen again. Never.' On the 'never' her voice was a whispered scream.

'It won't happen again, Sarah,' Annette said fervently. 'You needn't worry about that.'

Sarah was silent, waiting.

At last Annette went on unhappily, 'It was because . . . well, I was just so busy. I was going to get the new call sheets made up, I knew I had to do it, but then it slipped my mind, I guess. Maybe I felt . . . overwhelmed . . . so many things to do at once, so many things to remember . . . anyway, I just forgot.'

'You forgot!' Sarah heard the shrill edge in her voice. She stopped, fighting back any more recriminations. There was in her mind, suddenly, an instant's replay of a scene years before.

Jimmy Carstairs. An assistant producer, working with her in Washington at WETA. Late for a taping, with eyes shining after a two– or three-martini lunch. She had told him just what she thought of him, with an embarrassed audience listening. Stupid. Slob. Incompetent. She had seen him turning white and then red. He finally walked out to escape her flailing tongue. It had been long ago, but it seemed as if it had happened yesterday. They'd never worked together again, and rarely met. But on the occasions when they had, she'd seen hatred in his face. Word had come back to her, and sometimes still did, that when her name was mentioned Jimmy Carstairs made a vomiting sound. She'd made a permanent enemy then. And in television that meant an enemy for ever inescapable. It was a small world in which the participants moved from station to station, city to city, network to network. They shifted from the East Coast to the West Coast and then back again. Always on the same track. Your friends were always your friends, and your enemies were always out to get you. She didn't need any more Jimmy Carstairs in her life. Just as she needed no more Daniels.

She said tiredly, 'All right, Annette. I wish it hadn't happened. But I hope you've learned from it. It was your job to do the cast schedule. If you were overloaded with work you should have said so, told me, got some help.'

'I know,' Annette said unhappily. 'I'm so sorry, Sarah.' But, although she sounded humble, there was a rouging of red on her cheekbones and a glint in her eyes that held no apology. 'I'm very sorry,' she went on, 'believe me, it won't happen again.'

'I know it won't,' Sarah agreed quietly. 'From now on, you won't forget to do what you're supposed to do, will you?'

Annette shook her head vehemently. Then, as Sarah reached for some papers, she rose and started out.

Watching as the associate producer walked from the room, Sarah saw the girl's swagger, subdued but still noticeable.

They were alike, Sarah thought then, she and Annette. The two of them were hungry and wanting. Sarah was further along than Annette; the younger girl was struggling to catch up. Sarah wondered briefly just how far

Annette was willing to go to make a place for herself. Had Annette's overlooking the cast schedule change been a deliberate ploy? It made herself look bad to Sarah, but if there was a big budget over-run, then it was Sarah who would look bad. Sarah remembered how she had beaten Gary Crane out of a job. Was Annette Stone using whatever chance she had to undercut Sarah?

There was an echo of Daniel's words in her mind. The young ones come up. They push. They're impatient. They'll do whatever they can to take your place. She sighed. Annette Stone would bear watching.

Sarah leaned back in her chair. Her temples throbbed. Her neck ached. She went next door to the washroom to wash her face. As she made up again she wondered if Tony would call that night too.

Still thinking of him, she phoned Bonnie to delay their meeting until the next morning. Early, she suggested, before the taping. Bonnie agreed, sounding pleased. It would give her more time for writing Nella Rogoway out of the show.

'Then you have an idea?' Sarah asked.

'Oh yes, but I'm not all that sure of it. Maybe, when we talk it over . . .'

'Tomorrow,' Sarah said firmly. 'I've got to run.' She smiled as she put down the phone. It would be okay. She knew by the sound of Bonnie's voice that something was coming. The problem of Rita Porter would soon be resolved.

'What I want is another drink,' Rita said, pouting. Her out-thrust lower lip glistened, and her eyes glistened, and even the points of her breasts seemed to glisten through the thin net of her blouse.

Lyman Ogloe ran his pudgy hand along the curve of her thigh, down quickly, then up slowly, and sliding around and in, between her legs, and then out and around. 'Let's go upstairs to the room,' he suggested. 'I'll have drinks brought in.'

'I want the drink now, Popsie. We have to talk. You have to tell me.'

'It's going to be okay.'

'How do I know? What're you going to do?'

'I'll take care of it.'

'Oh, Popsie . . . I can't believe it . . . the way she talked to me. To *me*. As if I was just nobody.'

'I told you, Rita.' Lyman was beginning to sound desperate now. 'I *will* take care of it.'

'But when?'

'I'm just waiting,' he said. 'For the right time.'

'There's a rumour. They say Bonnie's working on something. Changes in the bible. Sarah's helping her. They want to get rid of me. Just because I can't stand Hart.'

'Don't worry about it.'

'You'll stop her, Popsie?'

'I told you.' He rose, drew Rita to her feet. 'Come on. Let's go upstairs to the room.'

'You won't let her get rid of me?'

'Of course not.'

'You promise?'

'I promise, Rita.'

She gave him a quick open smile, her tongue flicking at her lips. 'Okay then. What are we waiting for?'

7

Thanksgiving was over. It had been a long, busy and, because of Tony, an exciting weekend. Sarah had spoken to her brother Jerry and her mother. Katy again mentioned 'the someone' she wanted Sarah to meet, and asked when they could get together. Sarah had promised that it would be soon, but avoided being specific about when.

Laylie had roasted turkey and made sage stuffing and marshmallow-topped sweet-potato pie. Tim came up from Washington, and Tony came in from the Coast. Everyone ate too much except Peg, who had chosen that particular time to start her first diet.

Tony was good with the kids. Peg responded by being her usual open and friendly self. Tim was quiet, which was standard for him.

Over that long weekend Sarah found the degree of compatibility between Tony and herself almost frightening. He seemed to be able to take the very thoughts out of her mind. She often felt that she knew what he was thinking before he told her. She was mistrustful of it – it was too much, too fast. But as soon as he left for the Coast she yearned helplessly for him. The softness of his moustache on her cheek, the silken rope of curly black hair that she had discovered growing on his back just below his waist, his good-morning kiss, always light and friendly and undemanding.

Now, three weeks later, Christmas lights adorned the trees in Rockefeller Plaza. The shop windows on Fifth Avenue sparkled.

Sitting at her desk Sarah thought of the upcoming holiday. She had better get started on her shopping. Very little time remained. There was a list to prepare for Robin too. And she'd have to make some decision about Tim.

John wanted him for the holiday. Tim and Peg both. Sarah had had the kids for Thanksgiving, he'd said matter of factly, as if that made a difference, so he was entitled to have them this time. She supposed . . . maybe . . . but just the same . . .

The phone rang. She picked it up, still thinking of her conversation with John, but expecting to hear Bonnie or Hy Berge, or any one of a dozen other business associates. It was Tim, saying, 'Mom? Is that you, Mom?'

Tim. Alarm swept her at the sound of his voice. It must be something terrible. He wouldn't call her at the office unless something was wrong. Something very wrong.

She could hardly choke out her question. 'Tim? What's the matter?'

She heard his deep breath before he answered, 'Nothing's the matter, Mom. I was just thinking . . .' The words faded. There was another deep breath. This time it was more of a sigh.

Whatever it was, it was bad. He was on the verge of stuttering, only controlling it by the greatest effort. She tried to keep her voice clam. 'Honey, what? What were you thinking about?'

'Well, see . . . I'd like to make a change.' She heard uncertainty. 'What it is, what I was wondering about . . . when are you coming down to Washington?'

'To Washington? I don't know. I hadn't planned. We had Thanksgiving together. And Christmas is coming up in a week.'

'Oh,' he said. 'Oh yes. Well, I can wait, I guess. I mean, I could talk to you then.'

'You're sure it's not an emergency?' Her alarm was fading now.

'Oh no. Not exactly. I mean, what I wanted to talk to you about is . . .'

Damn John, she thought. This is surely his doing. His doing, and Carla's. Plotting behind Sarah's back. Giving Tim ideas. Sarah asked, 'Is it about dropping out of school, Tim?'

'Oh. No.' His surprise was genuine. 'Not dropping out

94

of school. What I mean by making a change is . . . well, the truth is, I want a room to myself. That's what it really is. I know the expense would be awful. If I could only have a room to myself . . .'

Her alarm was completely gone now, replaced by quick anger. 'Tim! Tim, when are you going to grow up? You want a room to yourself so you call me here, at work, when you know I'm running myself ragged to keep things going for us.' She stopped herself, drew a deep breath. Then: 'Now, get together with Mark Downing and straighten it out. Whatever it is.' Mark was Tim's roommate. They had always got on well together.

'I'm sorry I bothered you, Mom. But I still want a room to myself.'

She watched the red light on the console blink to signal another call coming in. 'Okay. We'll talk about it. But not now.'

'When, Mom?'

'When you come home for the holidays.' She remembered John and Carla, and said, 'Your father asked that you and Peg go to stay with him for Christmas, but I think not. Not with this on your mind. You'll do it another time. All right?'

'I guess.'

The red light was still blinking. She said, 'I've got to run now. I have another call. I'll get back to you this Sunday. Sunday night. We'll discuss it more then. Okay?'

'Sure,' he said. 'That's fine, Mom. Don't forget. Sunday night.'

She assured him that she wouldn't forget and pushed the button. The connection crackled in her ear. She said, 'Sarah Morehouse.'

'Sarah? I'm glad I caught you.' It was the executive producer, Lyman Ogloe. He rarely gave his name on the phone, assuming, rightly, that he was important enough to be instantly recognized. He went on, 'We need to talk. I've been hearing some funny things. Is there anything that you'd like to tell me?'

He was thinking about the night before. Rita, her ivory

95

breasts and shoulders bare as she prowled the hotel room, wearing a silver half slip that clung to her thighs, and high-heeled silver sandals.

He had said, 'Come on now, baby. Come to Popsie,' and she'd stopped in her tracks, had swung around to glare at him. 'You promised you'd lay down the law to Sarah Morehouse. But the rumours are still flying. The guys are taking bets how soon I get written out. So what do you think? I've got a headache. How can I feel like loving when I'm so worried?'

'I *will* talk to her. When the time's right,' he'd said.

'I have a feeling I'm going to have a headache until I'm sure she's going to lay off of me.'

He had wanted Rita so much it hurt him. It hurt him between his legs. Even now, as he gripped the telephone, he could feel the pain coming on him again. Goddamn, why did things have to get so complicated? All he wanted was to get on top of Rita. And all she wanted was to work in *Oakview Valley*. But Sarah Morehouse . . .

And Sarah said, 'Something to tell you, Lyman? Not yet.' She could see his pale raised brows reaching for the rim of his shining bald head, his squinting ice-grey eyes. 'When it's settled . . . maybe another few days.'

'Thank God. They're making me crazy.' He meant Rita was making him crazy. She wanted him to make sure nothing was going to happen to her job. But he didn't feel ready to lean on Sarah. Not until he knew there was good reason to. Sarah was too important to the show. 'And,' he went on, 'I've got as much on my plate as I want.'

She laughed. 'Then I'll delay as long as possible. How will that do you?'

'It'll do me fine. But . . . listen, there's the problem of someone else. I've had a call . . .' He paused, thinking, feeling actually inspired. 'I guess I'd rather not say. Still . . .' He was implying that someone higher up was concerned that the rumours about Rita might be true. He was hoping she'd think it wasn't he, Lyman Ogloe, who was worried, only someone else. It might give her pause.

But Sarah said, 'I ought to have guessed.' She wondered if he thought he was fooling her with this little game. There might be someone else involved. It was certainly possible. But she didn't think so. She thought the someone was Lyman Ogloe himself, and he had the hots for Rita, and she'd complained to him, so now he was letting Sarah know that he was Rita's protector.

'And you still don't want to talk about it?' he asked now.

'Not unless you insist, Lyman.'

'I'd never do that. Keep in touch.' The line went dead.

She imagined him hunched over his desk, his cherub's face sagging, his bald head agleam with sweat. Poor guy. Was he worried about what Rita would do? Or what Sarah was going to do?

She went into the outer office. Robin looked up.

'Let me have a rundown on the fan mail tomorrow, will you, Rob?'

'Sure.' He sounded subdued. He didn't quite meet her eyes either.

Sometimes, he thought, he didn't dare look her straight in the face. He was afraid she'd guess what he was thinking. He'd tried so many girls, hoping to get over her. He'd believe for a while that he'd finally found the right one, the one who could make him stop wanting her. But then, he'd start comparing her to Sarah, and he'd lose interest in her. No matter how deep he buried himself in another woman, it was always Sarah he wanted, and he was always left empty and dissatisfied.

And now she said, smiling at him, 'We need a talk, Rob. How about a fast home-cooked dinner tonight?'

'Family only?' he asked.

'That's what I had in mind.'

'I'll be there.' Now there was laughter in his voice. A smile grew in his blue eyes.

That was better, she thought. She ought to remember that Rob needed to be specially noticed every once in a while.

*

Bonnie was half an hour early for her meeting with Sarah. That was a good sign. Another good sign was that she came in smiling.

They had met four times previously to discuss the changes in *Oakview Valley*. Bonnie had been pessimistic, mumbling that everything she thought of sounded as if it had been done before.

But with Sarah's encouragement and help they had developed a story line that soon began to have a life of its own. It would involve two new characters. Sarah was still not quite sure that what they had was right. Rita's Nella Rogoway had been a bitch. Soon the audience would learn that she had been a crooked bitch. One of the new characters was a girl whom Bonnie called Suellen. Sarah objected that that was too close to Nella, so they settled on Susan. Nella would be jealous of Susan, would somehow plant drugs on her, but she would be a woman cop . . .

When they had settled on the story line, they would need to break it down into scenes, with dialogue and sets. They would have to decide on the sequence of episodes that would move the plot.

Now Sarah went over the material one more time.

Bonnie fidgeted. She crossed her legs and uncrossed them. She stood up, walked around the desk.

Finally Sarah looked up. 'Good, I think.' Then: 'And not too many changes in the bible either.'

Bonnie let out her breath in a long sigh. 'I feel a lot better now.' But before leaving she asked, 'When are you going to tell Lyman Ogloe?'

She walked away while Sarah was still saying, 'Soon, I guess.'

Robin brought in the fan mail information Sarah had asked for.

She took her time looking over the total. Rita Porter had done well, but was falling now. The highest number had been almost three months ago. There had been a steady decline ever since. Hart Carow's mail was holding just about steady at high. More than three times Rita's at the moment. Everybody else was doing nicely. Sarah believed that fan mail reflected reaction to how well the writers were working as much as to the skill of the actors. But these numbers gave her the ammunition she would need for Lyman Ogloe, if he were to question her decision. She could tell him Rita was ruining the show, and that would weigh for a lot. But if she could tell him that, and prove by these letters that writing her out wouldn't mean a drop in the ratings, the meeting with him would take less time.

With a sigh she reached for the bleeping phone. Now who? She spent entirely too much time speaking into this receiver. There ought to be a better way. If only people would go back to writing the occasional letter . . . Then she said brightly, 'Sarah Morehouse speaking.'

Sunday night. Sarah lay curled against Tony. His body was warm, hard. It had solid substance against her. His eyes were closed, his lips faintly smiling under his dark moustache. He might be sleeping. She wasn't sure. She breathed softly, remembering the day before.

He called from LaGuardia Airport at ten-fifteen in the morning, only minutes after the red-eye flight had arrived.

Two hours later they had late breakfast together. Then, because it was a sunny day, though bitterly cold, they went for a walk. That night they'd gone to a show and had a sumptuous meal at the Ginger Man. Sunday morning they'd read the papers and lazed around until Hy Berge's cocktail party at five-thirty. They'd been there only an hour when Tony said, 'What do you think? Do we have to hang around? Or can we go?' They remained less than half an hour longer.

Soon they were in her apartment. 'I could hardly wait to get you away from there. I've been wanting to grab you since noon,' he said. Noon was when they'd finally got up.

She laughed. 'The same for me, but I'd better see what Peg's up to, and if Laylie has any messages.'

Peg was doing her homework, accompanied by the TV in her room. Laylie was talking on the phone, but she nodded and waved, acknowledging Sarah's questioning look.

When Sarah returned to Tony, he was lying in bed, thinking that his lucky star hadn't burned out after all. Always, since he'd been a kid in Detroit, he'd believed in his star. It was what he prayed to, and what gave him everything he wanted. Lately he'd thought it had faded, turned to ash, but now he knew better. Coming to New York was going to work. It would turn the whole thing around. He grinned at Sarah, opened his arms wide. 'Crawl in.'

She skinned quickly out of her clothes, skirt and blouse and panty hose flying, and soon he was holding her close, their breaths joining. It was as if, suddenly, her body had a strength and heat and will of its own, independent of her mind. It couldn't be denied. She rolled over him, their skin meeting like molten liquid, her hands fluttering at his loins, his shoulders, her lips sucking at his mouth, until with a swift smooth movement, he captured her between his thighs, his entry a slow strong surge that culminated in tiny flickering movements that sent sensation spinning through her . . .

Later, still holding her, he said, 'I missed you when I was away. I kept thinking about you. Where you were, what you were doing. Calling you. Or thinking about calling you. I'm on the phone so damn much for business. I don't want a love affair via long distance too.'

It was something she had thought herself. Too much life on the phone. What had he been saying? Something about a long-distance love affair? With a jolt she remembered that she had promised to phone Tim. Tim. I've got to call Tim, she thought. But she said to Tony, 'A long-distance love affair is much better than nothing. As I'm here to testify.'

'Nothing isn't the alternative.' He grinned at her. 'Suppose you were to be offered a job. One that you couldn't turn down. Would you consider moving to the Coast for that?'

She couldn't concentrate on what he was saying. Her mind could focus on nothing but her promise to call Tim. Move to the Coast? Why? What job? And what about Tony and her? She'd told Tim she was too busy to talk, and promised to call him. So that's what she'd better do.

She drew away from Tony, sat up. 'Tony, I'm sorry, but I've got to call my son. And it can't wait. Mark the place in our dialogue, will you? I'll be right back to pick it up.'

'I'll be here,' Tony said, 'but what's the matter?'

'Nothing, I hope.' She slipped on a robe and went into the kitchen to put through the call.

She was surprised at herself. She had very nearly forgotten her promise to Tim. Very nearly. There was a busy signal. It went on and on and on. She broke the connection, and immediately pushed the buttons again. Still busy. Damn! Damn! Why hadn't she called earlier? Sighing, she put down the phone. Kids. Tim, or maybe Mark Downing, could be on for hours.

Again Sarah tried Tim's number. Once more the line was busy. She drummed her fingers on the table. Tim had sounded so . . . uneasy. That was the only word she could put to it. Wanting to move to a single room. Why? She had a sudden frisson of fear, cold tickles between her shoulder blades where, only a little while before, Tony had pressed his lips, hair lifting at the back of her neck, where he had rubbed his moustache.

That time when she finally allowed herself to take up the phone, her hand trembled over the buttons. The line was still busy. There was nothing to do but wait and call again later.

Tony came into the kitchen wearing nothing but his blue jeans. 'What is it, Sarah?'

She told him about Tim's call during the week. About the constant busy signal she was getting now.

He listened. Then: 'Want me to drive you down there?'

She glanced at her watch. It was after ten. It would

take five hours. They'd arrive in the middle of the night. She said, 'We couldn't do anything when we got there.'

'Is there anyone else you can call in Washington?'

She thought of her brother, her mother. It didn't seem like a good idea. Not when she didn't know what was happening. She shook her head.

'We can probably charter a plane, Sarah.'

As he spoke, the phone rang. Sarah grabbed it.

It was Tim. 'Mom? Did you try to call me?'

'Yes. What's going on? The line's been busy. I couldn't figure out what to do.'

'Mark had the phone off the hook,' Tim said disgustedly. 'I didn't know until just now. I've been sitting here for hours, waiting to talk to you. See, that's what he does. Because his folks keep calling him. First his mother. Then his father. They keep calling him. And he stays up all night, walking around and muttering to himself, with all the lights on, and the stereo and the TV going. He's driving me nuts, Mom.'

Now she remembered her quick anger. She wished she hadn't blown up at him. What was bothering him wasn't trivial after all.

'Okay,' she said. 'Just calm down.'

'I'm all right. But you've got to understand. I'm not nuts, not yet. But I will be if this keeps on. I've got to get away from him.'

She made up her mind in an instant. 'I'll be there tomorrow. Around noon,' she said crisply. 'Go to sleep now, and go to your usual morning classes. I'll meet you inside the entrance of the main building at twelve sharp. We'll see your counsellor together, and get it all settled then.'

'You will be here, won't you?'

'I will, Tim.'

'And you don't mind about the extra money?'

'We'll handle it.'

He said goodnight in a shaky but relieved voice and she put down the phone.

Tony had been listening. 'What do you think?'

'I don't know. I can't figure it out. Tim's usually not a hysterical kid. It's very hard to understand.'

Tony said, 'Would you feel better if we left for Washington right now? We could stop at a motel near the school, and be there first thing in the morning.'

She stared at him. 'But Tony, you're leaving the first thing in the morning.'

'If you need me, Sarah, I can call and cancel. And I'll be glad to.'

'But you hardly know Tim . . .'

'I know you, don't I?'

She hesitated. It would be nice to have moral support. And it was a good idea to be there early. On the other hand, Tim's problem was most likely going to turn out to be a tempest in a teapot. Better not to be the hysterical mother of an hysterical child. She said finally, 'It's okay, Tony. I'll have them get my car ready and take off at six. That will get me there by noon, which ought to be early enough.'

She hoped her Honda was okay. It was kept in the garage under the building, and she paid in parking fees what some people paid in rent for their apartments.

'Are you sure?' Tony asked.

She nodded. 'But thanks.'

'Then let's go back to bed.'

They were up at five. While he was shaving, she made a list. Call Robin to explain. Call about the car. She dressed, made coffee.

They sat down with steaming mugs. Tony said, 'When Tim called last night, I was going to say I want you on the Coast with me, Sarah. But I know you won't leave NTN without having a better offer.'

'I couldn't. I've put too much into getting this far.' She supposed that that would be it. He'd be offended. He'd say she didn't care about him if she wasn't willing to jump at the chance to be with him.

Instead his smile flashed. 'I wouldn't quit Stell-Stat to

come to New York if I didn't have a better offer. Why should you? But what I want you to know is that I'll be working on that better offer for you. Would you like to be a producer at Stell-Stat? Doing night-time shows?'

'Would I?' she whooped. It was what she was working towards. Stell-Stat, or some other independent.

'Then start building a proposal. It'll take some time, of course. But knowing what your work is, and your reputation, I'm pretty sure we can swing it.'

They *would* swing it. They had to. To hell with his ex-wife Eve. Once, he had controlled Stell-Stat. Now he was manoeuvring to get himself back in control. He'd get Stell-Stat back one way or another. Beautiful, husky-voiced Sarah was a winner. He knew it. His instincts were always right. He saw them as a big-time team. He and Sarah . . . the two of them, together. She was the first woman he'd wanted, cared about, since Eve. And wait until Eve saw Sarah, saw her, her name in the credits, in the TV columns. Eve had said she'd outgrown him. Tony Statler wasn't good enough for her any more. Wait until she saw what Tony Statler had grown into. Beautiful, talented Sarah Morehouse . . .

She kissed Peg goodbye, told Laylie she'd call from Washington. She and Tony went down to the street together.

At the last minute, she changed her mind. She had the Honda returned to the garage. She rode out to LaGuardia with Tony. They parted at the gate to the Eastern Airlines shuttle. A quick hug. A kiss. Turning away from him, she hesitated. This was a man she hated saying goodbye to.

There were the usual delays. Air traffic kept the plane queueing for fifty minutes. When it finally took off, clouds blanketed the windows. Landing in Washington's National Airport was delayed by sudden fog. At last there was an opening. The plane slipped through, close to an hour late.

During the trip Sarah had told herself that everything was going to be all right. She would hear Tim out, and then, together, they would see the counsellor. If, between them, they weren't able to make Tim understand that moving wasn't the answer, then she'd insist that Tim have his own quarters. It would cost another two thousand a year, but she'd manage that somehow. Tim's happiness was worth it.

She felt, as she drove the rented car into the school parking lot, that the problem, whatever it was, was already resolved.

Beltraney Preparatory School for Boys was on a huge wooded lot a few blocks off Massachusetts Avenue, on a hill overlooking the west side of Rock Creek Park. Its main building had once been the home of a wealthy brewer. It was constructed of fieldstone, with huge arched windows and doors, and surrounded by formal gardens which had become the school campus.

As Sarah walked into that campus the confidence she had felt before suddenly drained away. A wave of foreboding swept over her. The big quadrangle seemed peculiarly silent. Several small groups of boys stood together, heads bent close in earnest conversation. There was none of the horseplay she was accustomed to seeing on her previous visits.

With a shiver she caught her breath, climbed the steps

into the main building. It was eleven forty-five. She was a few minutes early, even with all the delays.

Tim hadn't arrived yet, but she knew he'd be coming across the quadrangle soon, running as fast as he could. He never walked when he could run, bless him. She watched through the door's glass panes. The few boys remained where they were, stil talking. No one else appeared. There was an odd quietness in the building too.

There ought to be voices, the clicking of typewriters, the sound of phones ringing. There ought to be the noise of teenage boys clumping up and down the stairs. Her teeth tapped together in a funny little chatter of tension. The hair at the back of her neck prickled. Small quick flares of alarm built in her. She looked at her watch. Twelve noon. She pushed the door open to look, as if the glass panes interfered with her vision. Where was he? He'd been so anxious to talk to her. He wouldn't be late. Certainly not today. But he was nowhere to be seen. Again she looked at her watch. Now, she thought. Now, when I look up, he'll be running towards the steps. He'll lift his hand to wave, his lips already forming an apology. But when she raised her eyes, he wasn't there.

A door opened behind her. A man said, 'May I help you?'

She turned. It was the headmaster. Beyond him stood a tall policeman.

She cried, 'What's the matter? What's happened?'

The headmaster drew a deep breath. The policeman touched his peaked hat in a salute.

'I'm Sarah Morehouse,' she cried. 'Where's my son? Where's Tim Bradford?'

'Ms Morehouse.' The headmaster took her arm, drew her inside. He closed the door behind her. 'Sit down, please.'

She recognized the room. She'd been there when she first brought Tim down to school. It was dark-panelled, with dull red carpeting and dull red drapes. The furniture was upholstered and heavy. The chair into which she sank seemed to suck her in, to suffocate her.

The policeman remained on his feet. He asked, 'Mrs Bradford, Morehouse, whatever. Have you heard from your son?'

'Have I heard from him?' she repeated. She looked around wildly. 'What do you mean? Where is he?'

The headmaster cleared his throat. 'Tim was seen early this morning, at about six, leaving the campus.'

'Leaving the campus?' she echoed. 'But that doesn't make sense. I talked to him last night. I told him I'd be here at noon today. We arranged to meet in the lobby of this building.'

'What did you talk about?'

She rose. 'First you'd better tell me what's happened.'

'Tim hasn't been seen since he left the grounds.'

She stared at the headmaster. 'Why would he do that? What are you talking about?'

The headmaster said nothing, but his hands ground together in agitation. The policeman sighed.

'You called the police,' she said to the headmaster. 'You called *them*, but not me. I don't understand.'

'We've been trying to reach you since about ten o'clock this morning. Which was when we realized he was gone. According to your housekeeper, you had already left for Washington.'

'Yes, I had. But I don't understand what's going on. Tim knew I was coming. I told him we'd see about getting him a private room. He seemed uncomfortable with his roommate, Mark Downing. They'd been very friendly. But something . . . Tim said . . . the line had been busy for hours . . . I'd tried to call him . . .'

The policeman exchanged glances with the headmaster, then said in a deep quiet voice, 'As far as we know, your son is all right. There's no reason to think otherwise. We've put out an all points for him, and I believe he'll be found walking along a street somewhere not very far away. Perhaps he's in the park. We have people out looking. It oughtn't to take very much longer.'

'There's more,' she said with certainty. 'There's something you're not telling me. I know it.'

107

The headmaster cleared his throat again. But when he spoke, his voice was hoarse. 'Ms Morehouse, I'm very sorry this happened. We try to see trouble before it comes, but this time, apparently, we slipped up.' He paused. Then: 'Tim's roommate, Mark Downing, has been having family problems, we believe. A divorce is in the works . . .'

Sarah remembered what Tim had said. *His folks keep calling him. First his mother. Then his father. He stays up all night . . .* They must have been trying to get him to choose between them, to take sides. Oh God, how could they? How awful for Mark! She shuddered. At least she and John had never done that. And never would.

The headmaster was saying, 'Mark has reacted badly to the situation, it seems. He . . . this morning, he hanged himself. We fear that Tim may have found him, and . . . and run away.'

'Oh my God,' she breathed.

. . . her father, hanging, long ago . . . the handyman saying . . . 'I went into the storeroom, and he was there' . . . Sirens. An ambulance. Her mother screaming . . .

The policeman said, 'I know how you feel, but Ms Morehouse, there are things we have to know. Can you help us?'

'Yes,' she said tonelessly. Her knees suddenly collapsed beneath her. She fell into the chair, a wave of guilt overwhelming her. Once again she remembered her anger when Tim called her at the office. She'd bawled him out, too busy to listen to him. And now . . . now . . . Why hadn't she realized how important it was to him. Why? Why? But it was useless to wonder. The policeman was waiting. She had to help him. 'Yes,' she said. 'What can I tell you?'

'You spoke to Tim last night. And not since?' When she shook her head, remembering Tony's body against hers suddenly, the policeman went on, 'Who else could he have called?'

'I don't know.' She thought of her mother. Her brother.

But no, Tim wouldn't have turned to either of them. They just weren't close enough. They hardly knew each other. She had felt too little connection with her family to have passed on to Tim any deep feeling for them. But there was John. Unwillingly she said, 'He might have called his father.'

'Called him. Or maybe gone to him?'

'Perhaps. It's hard to know.' She hesitated. John would raise holy hell when he heard. She forced herself to say, 'I'd better find out.'

'Where is his father?' the policeman asked.

'Connecticut.'

The headmaster indicated the phone on his desk. She dialled the number, no push buttons here. John's secretary put her through as soon as she identified herself.

She had barely explained when John exploded, 'I told you, dammit! Why didn't you listen to me? No matter what happens, you always have to come first, Sarah. If anything's happened to Tim . . .'

She listened as long as she could, understanding how frightened he was, but finally she broke in, 'All right, John. I know. I know. But stop yelling and help us.'

'I don't know where he is. I haven't heard from him. And I'm coming down as fast as I can.'

'Maybe you'd better wait until we see . . .'

'If you think I'm going to let you handle this in your usual offhand fashion, you're out of your mind!'

The sound of the phone banging down echoed in the quiet office. Cheeks burning, she said to the two men, 'Tim's father's on the way.'

'Yes,' the policeman said dryly. And, 'I assume you spoke to him at his place of work. Could Tim have gone to his house?'

She said nothing.

'Will Mr Bradford think to call there to see if Tim's . . .'

She gave Carla's number, and name.

The line was busy on the first try. On the second, the policeman got through. John had already spoken to Carla.

109

Tim wasn't there, hadn't called. The policeman put down the phone, shaking his head. 'Now there's nothing to do but wait until I hear from downtown.'

'You've searched the grounds?' Sarah asked.

The policeman nodded.

The headmaster said, 'Ms Morehouse, I don't think this will take very long. But perhaps it would be wise if you took a room at a hotel. There are several only a few minutes away. I can get a cab for you . . .' He paused. ' . . . unless of course you want to return to your home. Now that Tim's father is coming . . .'

'Oh, no,' she said. 'I'm not going home.'

'Then a hotel room . . .'

'Tim's father . . .'

'I'll tell him where to find you when he gets here.'

'Thanks,' she said dryly. 'Just what I need.'

The headmaster gave her a pained look. He put a hand on her elbow, moved her slowly, but firmly, from his office into the hall and then down the too-quiet corridor to the wide glass-panelled door.

'You'll let me know the instant . . .'

'Of course.'

'I'll be at the Ritz Carlton. I have a car.'

'The Ritz Carlton. Yes.'

She drove down Massachusetts Avenue to the hotel. Within moments she was registered and in the small corner room that already looked like home and prison to her.

She closed the door behind her, put down her purse, took off her jacket. As she drew a deep tired breath, she suddenly saw before her an old scene, never actually observed but imagined a hundred times, before she was able to bury it deeply enough to have considered it forgotten.

It came back now in all its terrifying detail. Her father hung from a water pipe. An overturned stool lay close by. There was a darkness. And now there was a new picture. Tim was there, aghast and shivering. Frozen before a dangling body . . .

110

Deep shuddering sobs wrenched her. She fell on the bed and wept.

An hour later the phone rang. Composed by then, made up, her hair brushed, she raced to answer it. Tim! Had he come back? Had they found him?

It was Robin, offering sympathy, asking if he should come. He'd got her number from the headmaster and knew what had happened. Briefly she wondered how he had known to reach her through Tim's school. Then she remembered. She had telephoned Robin herself. God, she wished he were here, with her. But she thanked him, told him to stay put and watch over things for her there, asked him to speak to Annette Stone so that the associate producer would know how to reach her if necessary.

When Sarah put down the phone, it rang again. This time it was Annette. Robin had told her. She was sorry about Tim. Ought they to go ahead as scheduled? Sarah pictured the girl's eager face, imagined a poised knife in her hot little hand. Sarah said they should certainly go ahead. There was another call. Lyman Ogloe. He too had just talked to Robin. He wanted to know how he could help. Sarah said there was nothing to do but wait.

She told John the same thing when he banged on her door late in the afternoon.

'Jesus H. Christ! How can you sit there, calmly, with not a hair out of place, looking as if you're waiting for the cameraman to do a shot for you to yell at him about? Don't you care about Tim?'

Seeing her brought all the guilt back. He'd been the one to break up the marriage, although it had been *her* fault. It was *his* fault that he didn't see more of the kids. And he knew she was short-changing them as she'd always short-changed him. But what could he do? Except try to get her to be a better mother than she'd been wife to him? And now this . . . Tim. John had told her the boy should be at home with her or, if not that, then with him and Carla. But no . . . she wouldn't listen . . . she knew everything . . . it had to be her way . . .

111

'Don't be more of a bastard than you have to be,' she was saying.

'Okay,' he said. 'Okay.' He flung himself into a chair. 'Carla will be along later on. She had some things to do.'

Sarah didn't answer.

He said, 'Tell me what happened, Sarah.'

She went over it slowly. Tim's call. What he had said. What she had thought. Her arrival at the school. Her voice was calm, her words measured. As she spoke, she noticed that there was grey in John's thinning hair.

'Jesus!' he muttered.

She said, 'If you're going to stay here, you'd better get yourself a room. Otherwise just go home. You and Carla can have a great time tearing me to pieces.'

'Carla's on the way. As soon as she gets to the school . . .'

'I don't think it's necessary, John.'

'I know you'd rather I wasn't around. But I'm not going home.'

'All right. We won't argue about it. Go where you please. Just get out of here.'

He gave her a sour look, but got to his feet. 'Okay. I can take the hint. I'll be in the bar downstairs.'

'It figures.'

'You're in no position to criticize me, Sarah.' He waited, plainly hoping for an argument, but she ignored the bait.

When he was gone she called home. Laylie had to be told about Tim's disappearance. She had to know where to reach Sarah, just in case Sarah didn't get home that night. Or the next, or . . .

Peg answered the phone. She said, 'Oh, hi! I was just thinking about you, Mom.'

Sarah's heart gave a great jump. 'What's the matter, Peg?'

'Nothing. I was just thinking about you.'

Sarah asked to speak to Laylie. When the housekeeper came on, Sarah explained about Tim's disappearance.

'Oh my,' Laylie said, her voice suddenly shaky. 'Oh

112

my goodness.' And then: 'Don't you worry about us. We're going to be okay here. Just let us know, will you?'

And then, cutting through her words, Sarah heard Peg cry, 'Why Robin, hello. What's going on?'

'That's Rob just come in,' Laylie said, sounding relieved. 'You call when you can.'

Sarah felt relieved too. With Rob there to keep them company, Peg and Laylie would be okay.

The rest of the afternoon passed in a blur. Sarah tried to think about the bible changes Bonnie was working on. Her mind refused to do its job. She couldn't remember what plotting they had done, what she was planning, developing. She didn't care enough to struggle with it. She paced the floor. It was bad to be alone. She thought of her mother, of Jerry. But no. She couldn't call them. Katy would become upset, Jerry too. They'd start remembering . . . No. It was better, after all, to be alone. She looked out of the window at the darkening sky, at the long ranks of cars, headlights gleaming, that filled the street below. She stood over the phone, willing it to ring.

When, finally, it did, John said drunkenly, 'Well, what about it?'

'I haven't heard a thing.'

'What are you going to do?'

'Wait,' she said evenly.

'Cold-hearted bitch!' At least she could cry, pray. At least she could act as if she cared.

In the background Carla said something. 'I don't care!' he shouted.

Sarah hung up on him.

Soon after, Robin called to ask how she was, if there was news yet. Then, in rapid succession, Annette Stone, Lyman Ogloe and Bonnie each wanted to know what had happened. She spoke to them briefly, promised to keep in touch and put down the phone, hoping it would be silent . . . silent until the police called her.

She sat in the chair beside the table through the long hours of the night, sometimes dozing, rising only twice. Both times to say, 'Go away,' to John who came, progressively drunker, to pound on the door and shout useless questions at her.

At dawn she rose again, dishevelled and stiff. She took a shower, combed her hair, made up her face.

At a little past eight o'clock the headmaster appeared at her door. 'Good news, Ms Morehouse. Tim's been found.'

'Where?' she cried, swaying giddily. 'Why didn't you bring him . . .'

'The police took him straight to the hospital. It's only a few blocks from here. He was found in a garage behind an embassy only a mile or so from the school.' The headmaster's worn face glowed with a grin. 'I'll take you over right now. I have my car.'

She thought of John and Carla. 'I'd better tell Tim's father.'

'Surely,' the headmaster agreed.

Sarah got John's number from the desk clerk. She pounded on the door. Once. Twice. Three times. He'd gone to bed, at what time she didn't know, drunk. What had happened to Carla, Sarah didn't know. She pounded again. There was no response. Maybe she couldn't wake him up. Maybe she shouldn't even try. She was about to turn away when he jerked the door open. He stood there, swaying, unshaven and red-eyed. 'Sarah!'

'Tim's okay. He's been found. He's in the hospital. I'm going now.'

'George Washington,' the headmaster murmured.

'Oh, God!' John put clenched fists to his head. 'Wait for me.'

'I can't!' She ran down the corridor to the elevator.

Carla was just coming out of the coffee shop. Sarah acknowledged her cry, but hurried on.

It took only ten minutes to get to the hospital. It seemed like hours to her.

Finally she saw Tim lying against piled white pillows. She crossed the room to him, clenching her fists so that her hands couldn't shake. 'Timmy,' she said softly.

'Timmy, are you okay?' and bent over him with her arms opened wide.

He turned to her, white as the pillows behind his head, his face hollowed. Suddenly, in that single instant, his cheeks were wet with tears. 'Oh Mama,' he cried. 'Mama, it was awful!'

She held him tightly while he told her how he had awakened, the room dim with first light, and filled with an ominous silence. A silence so thick he could hear his heart beating. He had got up. Mark wasn't in the bunk across from his. Shivering, Tim went to get his robe from the cupboard. He pulled the door open. Mark seemed to jump out at him. He didn't remember much else. He had put on jeans, stepped into sneakers. He remembered slamming a door and running, running . . .

While Tim was speaking, John came in. He was combed, shaved, although his collar was unbuttoned and his tie hung loose around his neck. Carla was with him. Tim hardly seemed to notice their presence. He said, 'I'll never forget it. Never,' and shook in Sarah's arms.

'You will,' she told him. 'You will. I promise it. You will.'

Soon his weeping stopped. His breath slowed. He fell asleep.

In the corridor John said, 'What now?'

'We'll let him decide. It's too soon to try to make plans.'

'Yes,' Carla agreed. 'It *is* too soon.'

John turned on her, snarling, 'Oh, shut up. What do you know about it?'

Her face reddened. She bit her lip.

Sarah felt an instant's pity for her.

'I want Tim to come home with me,' John said. 'As soon as he can be moved. It'll do him good.'

'Be sure we'll do everything we can possibly do to . . .' That was the headmaster, anxiously twisting his hands.

John ignored him. 'Sarah, dammit!'

'I think we'd better let Tim decide what he wants to do. He can stay at Beltraney, if that's what he wants,' she told the headmaster. 'He can stay with you for a week or

115

two. If he wants to,' she told John and Carla. When John looked as if he were going to argue with her, she turned and walked away.

Later that same day Tim looked from Sarah to John. Go home. Stay with John? Change to a new school. Three choices. Too many to handle. Sarah saw in his face what he was going through. He didn't know what to do.

'You won't be burning any bridges behind you,' she said. 'If you want to change your mind tomorrow, or any other time, you can.'

Finally he said, 'I'd as soon stay at Beltraney, I guess. As long as I can have a new room. A place to myself.'

John was unhappy about it, and voluble on the subject. Sarah herself wasn't sure it was a good idea, but she admired Tim's courage. He wasn't willing to run away. He wanted to stand and face down his fears. She determined to help him as much as she could. But she would have to talk to him, to understand better what had actually happened.

She was relieved when John decided that he might as well leave, since neither Tim nor Sarah would listen to his advice. Carla gave them sympathetic looks and trailed after him.

When they were alone Sarah sat in the chair close to Tim's bed. 'Want to sleep for a little while?'

'No.'

'You keep thinking about it?'

'About before, Mom. If I could have done something . . .'

'What about the counsellor?'

'Duncie? Oh, he's okay.'

'Duncie?' she asked. 'Is that his name?'

'Dr Dunham really.'

'You told him about Mark?'

'Not exactly.'

Sarah waited.

'Well, see, I tried to.' Tim tugged at his blond hair.

116

'And?' It was like pulling teeth. But she had to know.

Tim sighed. 'He's a nice guy, Mom. But you go in, and you say a couple of things, and he, well then, he begins to tell you how he understands exactly. Because the same thing happened to him. And before you know it, your time's up. The secretary opens the door, and walks you out, and you're in the quad and you know all about his problems. But you don't know one thing about your own.'

'I see,' she said, determined to have a talk with Dr Dunham herself.

Soon after Tim went to sleep.

Sarah spent a restless night in the hotel. Early the next morning she went to the hospital. As soon as Tim was discharged, they returned to the school. She had a few words with the headmaster, and then helped Tim move his belongings to his new quarters.

At eleven o'clock she returned to the main building for her meeting with Dr Dunham who had, according to the headmaster, a PhD in psychology, with special emphasis on the problems of teenage boys.

Dr Dunham, it turned out, was a youngish man, perhaps thirty. He had curly black hair and wide-apart dark eyes and a fresh-faced rosy innocence that immediately made him suspect to her.

He got up to greet her. 'Mrs Bradmore? Uh, Mrs Moreford?'

Poor man. He had been reading Tim's school file, where under parents were listed John Bradford and Sarah Morehouse. That, she remembered, had been another thing that set John off into one of his long tirades about her inadequacies as wife and mother.

She corrected Dr Dunham, and while he apologized she seated herself.

'We regret the experience Tim has suffered,' the psychologist told her earnestly. 'We'll do everything we can to help him overcome it.'

'I understand.' She studied him for a moment. Then, 'I've spoken to the headmaster. He agrees with me that

Tim will need to be observed. Just that. I don't want you to talk to him. Not unless he specifically asks to see you.'

Dr Dunham leaned back in the swivel chair. 'That, it seems to me, would be tying my hands. Don't you think I should be allowed to decide how to deal with Tim?' He squirmed beneath her level green look. 'Yes, I realize. Mark Downing. Still, I know from my own experience, when I was a teenager, just your son's age . . .'

'You probably don't know that you're called Duncie, or Dr Duncie,' she said softly. 'Mostly because you talk when you should be listening.' She paused to allow her words to sink in, watching as a blush appeared at the edge of his collar and spread to his face. 'Now. Let me tell you what I want from you.'

'Mrs Morehouse,' he protested.

'Tim's asked to stay here, as you know. I'm not sure that's a good decision. But it's his. Okay. I need to be sure that he can handle it. I want you to observe him, check with the men who teach his classes. Make certain that he's not becoming depressed, changing his habits, withdrawing, falling behind in his school work. Do you follow me?'

'Well, yes, but . . .'

She rose. 'I'll call you once a week for your report.'

When she told Tim goodbye, she hugged him and said, 'Take care of yourself. If it doesn't feel right to you, just call me. And remember, now is when you start to forget.'

John said for the thousandth time since they returned home, 'I told Sarah. I knew he shouldn't be away at school. But she wouldn't listen to me.'

Carla stared hot-eyed into the darkness, wishing Sarah and her kids into distant oblivion. Carla was tired of hearing about them, thinking about them. She said coolly, 'Yes John. So you've said before. It's late. Why don't you go to sleep?'

'You're sore at me, aren't you?'

She hesitated. Then: 'Not exactly.' Now the coolness was even more pronounced.

'I'm sorry,' he said. 'It's just that she makes me so damn mad.' Sighing, he sat down on her bed.

'It's embarrassing,' Carla told him. 'The way you snap at me in front of her.'

'I didn't mean to. I'd had that extra drink, I guess. And Sarah's so absolutely infuriating.'

Carla said softly, 'Never mind. Let's just forget that for now.' She threw back the covers. 'Come on, get into bed with me.'

He climbed in beside her. 'The best thing is to let it go for a while. Then we'll see.'

'Exactly,' she agreed, snuggling into his arms.

Several nights later Sarah sat on the edge of her bed. The TV set was on. Ted Koppel doing *Nightline*. She neither listened nor watched. The fear, the bad memories, had been followed by the euphoria of relief. But now the letdown had set in. She was sunk in fatigue. She was glad that Peg had gone to bed early, that Laylie was out for the evening. It was better to be alone. When the doorbell chimed she swore softly to herself. Who could that be? Why hadn't the desk called to tell her someone was asking for her? She pulled a robe on, went to the door, and peered out through the viewer. Tony!

She opened the chain, unlocked the dead bolt. Tony! When the door opened he swept her into his arms.

Her fatigue fell away. She clung to him. 'Oh, what a wonderful surprise!'

'Just what I intended.'

He explained that the few words they'd exchanged on the phone hadn't been enough. He'd had to see her, to know she was really all right, to hear what had happened to Tim.

She made him a sandwich, brewed coffee, while she told him about the trip to Washington in more detail than she had before.

'I wish I'd been with you. I don't like to think of your having gone through that alone.'

'It was bad while it lasted. Very bad,' she said soberly. 'But it's over now.'

He held her within the circle of his arms, a hand curled at her breast. 'Over now,' he said. 'And I'm here.'

Wordlessly they went into her bedroom. They undressed, lay down together, bodies entwining. This time his lovemaking was gentle, soothing, and she was acquiescent, pressing small butterfly kisses on his eyes, his cheeks, into the hollow of his throat. He cradled her in his arms as they locked side by side to each other. And now his mouth pressed to hers, and still moving slowly, they climaxed at the same time . . .

At dawn they made love again, and then he had to get ready to catch his plane back to Los Angeles.

9

Sarah had prepared herself for an argument over where the children would spend Christmas, but John and Carla simplified everything by deciding that they would go to Pleasant Cove on St Thomas for the holidays.

So Tim came up from Washington. He was his usual quiet self. He didn't seem to want to talk about what had happened. Sarah didn't press him. She and Peg and Tim spent Christmas Eve at the Russian Tea Room. Christmas Day they'd unwrapped packages. Tony hadn't been able to come in from California, but his gifts had been sneaked under the tree by Laylie, and they'd all spoken to him on the phone.

Now, a few days after the holiday, Sarah sat at her desk, studying a stack of bills. She wondered how she had miscalculated by so much. At the other networks, programme budgets were dealt with in the Budget Office, but here at NTN the show's producer was responsible for calculating the cost of a show, and then sticking to it. *Oakview Valley*'s five episodes a week ran NTN about $500,000. But if the bills before her were a fair sampling, then she'd soon be running over. She kept checking the numbers. Finally she went through the costume file, comparing predicted costs with the bills themselves. She began an item-by-item study. Shoes. Jackets. Hats. Raincoats. Almost immediately she saw what was wrong. Four pairs of shoes. She had shown only one. Five raincoats. She had shown only two. One for Hart. One for Rita.

She put in a call for the costume designer.

An hour later he hurried in, breathlessly demanding to know what was wrong. She explained, showed him the figures.

'It couldn't be helped,' he said. 'Hart was complaining that his jacket was the wrong colour. Rita said hers made her look like a barrel. We had to do the changes, and you weren't here.'

'I understand,' she said. 'But how come you didn't go the usual route?'

By the usual route, she meant that only what was used was kept and paid for. The multiple choices and fits that weren't right went back to the stores from which they'd been bought, the cost being credited to NTN's account.

'Couldn't,' he said briefly. 'They were all too messed up for the bring-back-girls to handle.'

'Messed up?' she said.

'Tried on too many times, I guess.' He sighed. 'Actors. And Annette approved it, so . . .' He spread his hands.

Sarah nodded. 'Okay then.'

As soon as he was gone she sent for Annette Stone.

The associate producer was smiling when she came into the office. After a look at Sarah's face the smile became fixed. 'Something wrong?' she asked, nervously curling a lock of dark hair around her finger.

When Sarah asked her about the clothing bills Annette looked relieved. 'Oh, that,' she said. 'You see, it came up while you were away. When that awful thing happened to Tim.'

She made it sound as if it were months ago. It was actually only a little more than two weeks before.

She went on, 'We had to do something. And fast. We just couldn't wait.'

Sarah had been gone two and a half days.

'We just couldn't wait,' Annette repeated in the face of Sarah's stony silence. 'I knew you'd want us to go on. Remember? I asked you. You didn't want a delay. So I okayed the changes.'

'A rather large amount for a pair of shoes. A raincoat.'

'It took a number of tries before they made up their minds . . .'

'So I gather.'

'I knew you'd want them to look their very best. I was really thinking of you, and how you work.'

'Thank you,' Sarah said.

'I'd do anything for you,' Annette said fervently. 'You know that don't you, Sarah?'

'I appreciate it.' Sarah paused. 'And what about Lyman Ogloe? How did he happen to get into the act?'

'Since you weren't here, I had to get somebody's approval, you see. So . . .'

'Oh yes. I see.'

Lyman Ogloe had left a brief memo on her desk: *We do want to watch our costs, don't we?* She had the feeling that what he'd really wanted to write was *We do want to watch our step, don't we?*

Annette said, 'It's all right, isn't it?'

'Almost. But not quite. Next time don't let the cast run you around. When they try on, they've got to be careful. Whatever isn't used must be in good enough condition to go back. I don't want any more bills like these.'

'Oh sure,' Annette said. 'I'll remember.'

Alone, Sarah thoughfully leaned back in her chair. A helpful little soul. The girl would need careful watching. She had her eye on Sarah's job. Which was okay. In a way, that is. It would keep her hungry, which would keep her creative, useful and willing. But there was only so far she could go before she would need to expand her wings. As long as Sarah was producer, she would remain associate. Sarah smiled faintly. She remembered how it felt to be fighting her way to the top. She remembered the ruthless push. That same stony push was within her still. To get there was only the first step. To stay there was only the second. The third was to go on. Los Angeles, here I come, she thought. But not just yet. So, as she had told herself before, she'd better protect herself from Annette Stone's honed knife from now on.

Bonnie said, 'I thought the story line was going well. I was sure I'd be ready to start on the dialogue. You did too, didn't you, Sarah?'

'Yes. I told you so. I said keep going in that direction and we'd have just what we want.'

'I tried to, but . . .'

'But what?'

'Annette didn't like it at all.'

'Annette? What has she got to do with it?' Sarah demanded.

'You were away,' Bonnie said. 'I needed someone to kick it around with, so I talked it over with her.'

Sarah groaned.

'I know. It was dumb. It just seemed a good idea at the time. To see what her reaction was, I mean.'

'It was a lousy idea to discuss it with anyone except me. We aren't ready for that yet. Forget whatever she said. Just go on.'

But even as she spoke Sarah felt doubt rise in her. Maybe it wouldn't work. Maybe they'd have to start over. She decided to re-think the story line, but on her own, before she met with Bonnie again.

'You're sure it will fly?'

'It will with you doing it. And if it doesn't you'll find something else that works.'

'Okay . . .' Bonnie drew the word out happily. 'O-kay,' she repeated, smiling as she left.

Annette again, Sarah thought. She'd have to keep an eye on that one for sure. But meanwhile, Bonnie was back on an even keel again. For how long was anybody's guess. She was wonderfully talented, a skilled and fast writer, but she was a kite, easily unsettled by any breeze that came along. Sarah considered it her job to keep Bonnie steady. It wasn't simple, but it was worth the effort.

Some time soon, when Bonnie had got the changes in *Oakview Valley* under control, Sarah intended to talk to her about doing a story proposal for a night-time show. But she didn't want to bring that up yet. She smiled to herself. Tony would understand if it took a while.

Two mornings later, at seven, Sarah brushed snowflakes out of her hair and hurried into the NTN lobby. She was moments late so she went straight to the studio floor where the day's work would be done.

This area was two storeys high, its ceiling covered with stage lights, now dark. A wide centre aisle ran down the large warehouse-like room. It was edged on both sides with sets that had been hammered together by the crews during the night. There were twenty-two of them, one for each place in which a scene would occur during the day's taping.

Sarah took off her coat and sent Robin to her office for copies of the production facilities list. He returned within moments. From her briefcase she took the bible and a copy of that day's working script. The actors were gathering for the dry rehearsal. Many of them wore warm-up clothes. Several of the girls still had their hair in curlers.

Rita Porter looked as if she were already dressed for her first scene. She wore an extremely tight black sweater, black high-heeled ankle-strapped shoes and a flared red skirt. She was standing near a table.

Sarah could see the living room of Davey's home beyond her shoulder. Everything seemed to be in place, ready for when they started the actual taping. Chairs, sofa, vase of flowers. The same book stood open and very noticeable just over Rita's head. Sarah frowned slightly. *The Gun-Runners.* Still there. Was that all right? She went back. Checked the script set description. Yes. Not so much time had passed that it ought to have been read, put away, passed on to someone else. But . . . but a question remained in her mind. Something . . . something wasn't quite right about that book.

Hy Berge was speaking to the floor manager, who was nodding.

Sarah looked at her watch. The dry rehearsal, the preliminary reading of the script, had been done the day before in the rehearsal room, with the technical director, Robin and the production manager in attendance. Now, in another moment or two, Hy would lead them through the read-through. Sarah hoped that there'd be no complaints to slow them down. At ten they would do the blocking. Then there would be the walk-through. There would be a lunch break at noon, as required by the union contracts, in the fifth hour of work. After lunch there would be the run-through, then the camera rehearsal. The actors would go to wardrobe and hairdressers as scheduled, and then assemble for the dress rehearsal. As soon as that was finished, they would go to make-up, again as scheduled. When they were all finished they would gather for notes. That was when Hy would make suggestions to the actors. Sarah, if she had any comments, would probably make them to him for transmission to the actors. When all was digested, understood, probably by three o'clock, the red light would go on outside the studio door, Hy would say, 'Ready, Camera One,' into his mike, and the taping would begin.

But now Hart Carow walked down the aisle, saw Rita, and started for her, smiling broadly.

She drew herself up as he approached, her mouth a thin line.

'Hi,' he said. 'How're you doing?'

She put her hand over her mouth and nose. 'I'm okay.' And then: 'Just leave me alone.'

He winced first, then grinned. He leaned close to her. 'You're going about it all wrong, Rita. If you keep on being so rotten to me, I'm going to make a point of breathing right on you. And you don't know what'll happen if I do.' He was plainly teasing, half-laughing, trying to cover his hurt at how she treated him.

But she, instead of smiling, suddenly let out a horrified scream. She launched herself at Hart, kicking and scratching. He grabbed her by both shoulders and shoved her away. She took three quick dancing steps on her three-inch heels and tripped over a cable. She hit the floor with a loud thump, still screaming. Then, suddenly, she went limp, silent.

Instantly she was surrounded. Robin leaned over her, talking urgently. Hy patted her hand. The set designer patted her cheek. The floor manager raced for smelling

126

salts and returned with spirits of ammonia. Sarah stood by, tapping her foot, with one eye on her watch.

It was twenty minutes before the combined efforts of the whole group finally got Rita on her feet.

On the whole, Sarah thought critically, it hadn't been Rita's best performance. The scene had clearly been faked. Hart hadn't thrown Rita down. She had pulled away from him, and flung herself to the floor. Sarah looked at Hy and he looked back. They exchanged brief nods; that did it for Rita Porter. Sarah wouldn't have to make a decision over Bonnie's plan for getting rid of Rita. They would scratch it. There'd be only one script, a few minutes out of the forty-two minutes of the next episode they taped.

She took a deep breath. 'Hy, tell Rita that I want her in my office. And, if you don't mind, when you pass the shop steward's office, ask Sam Eich to call me.'

'It's not going to be easy,' Hy said, his voice a deep regretful rumble. 'Hart shares some of the responsibility for that little scene, Sarah.'

'Let me handle it,' she said crisply.

'I'll be glad to. She *has* been riding him. He did hold on as long as he could. A man's got a limit . . .'

Sarah said, 'I've been looking at fan mail figures, Hy. This isn't going to hurt us.'

'Oh.' He nodded bleakly. 'I see.' Then a grin warmed his face. 'That's why you produce, and I direct, isn't it?'

Rita had finally pulled herself together. Hart was his usual self. Hy Berge pretended nothing had happened. Crew and cast had continued with the day's work.

Now, at eight-thirty, after the final taping was done, Rita stood in the doorway of Sarah's office. 'Hy said you want to talk to me.' Her voice was cold, defensive. 'I don't know why they made such a fuss. *I* didn't do anything. It was Hart that knocked me down.'

Sarah said, 'I want to tell you that you're through. You've made your last scene here.'

'You can't fire me,' Rita said. Shrill. Combative. 'Just wait and see what happens if you do.'

Sarah answered, 'Okay. I'll see.'

'I'm telling you, you'll be sorry.'

'All right,' Sarah agreed. 'Maybe I will be.'

But the next day, early, she sat at her desk. Sam Eich, the shop steward, sat across from her. 'Listen,' he said, 'We've got a contract.'

She had dressed for their meeting, a soft pink shirt, silk, with a small lace-trimmed collar. Pearl earrings. A thin strand of pearls at her throat. Nothing hard, or angry, about her.

He had come in red-faced. Now he leaned forward, pulling a cigar from his shirt pocket. Another time she would have given him a forbidding look. This time she pushed a rarely used ashtray towards him.

Then gently, smiling a little, she said, 'Sam I know about the contract. I'm going to need your help on this.'

'These are my people, Sarah. Rita and Hart. What the hell's going on? How can you talk about me helping you do this?' He, along with Rita and Hart, and all the other actors on the show, belonged to AFTRA, the American Federation of Television and Radio Artists. It was Sam's job to represent the union and its members in any disagreement with management.

'Sam, you know perfectly well that Hart has been putting up with Rita's shenanigans for weeks.'

'It's a delicate situation.'

'Indeed it is. Rita's about to sink our show. You don't expect me to stand still for that, do you? Hy has talked to her. I've talked to her. All we want is for her to show a little civility, and for her to do her job, her best job. She's failed in both. And yesterday . . .'

'I know all about yesterday.' He blew a great gout of smoke in Sarah's face. She fought back a cough.

After a moment she went on, 'My back is against the wall, Sam. If I have to, I'll buy her contract out. But I don't think I do have to.'

'Well, there is that small-print clause about being cooperative . . . you know . . .'

She smiled at him. 'I knew you'd understand.'

'Only that's not so easy to pull off. It applies to morals, publicity, that crap.'

'It isn't limited to those things.'

'Maybe . . .'

She went on, 'There's a hard way and an easy way. If we have to, we can go to arbitration, of course.'

Sam groaned.

'I know,' she said sympathetically. 'It will be a mess. Because I'll have to explain, won't I?' She leaned forward, both slender hands on her desk. 'And I will, Sam. I mean business about this.'

'I guess I'd better talk to the kids again.'

'It would be a good idea.'

He struggled to his feet, cigar ash drifting off his waistcoat in a fine mist. 'I'll get back to you as soon as I can.'

She walked with him to the door. 'I'd like to think you understand. I'm not trying to be difficult. I've got to save *Oakview Valley*. I can't let one person wreck the show. Just think of what's involved. One hundred and ninety jobs, Sam.'

'I'm thinking,' he answered wryly.

She closed the door behind him, leaned against it. The office was very quiet. When the phone trilled it sounded like thunder to her. 'Oh, shut up,' she told it, and then lifted the receiver. 'Sarah Morehouse.'

'Sarah?' It was Lyman Ogloe. He drew a deep noisy breath. 'About this Rita thing . . .'

She slid behind her desk and into her chair. This would take a while. But she said, 'It's going to be okay. I've spoken to Sam Eich.'

There was an uncomfortable silence. She imagined him pulling his ear or scratching his round chin. He was wondering what the best thing was to do. Rita had just called him. Called him weeping, poor darling girl. *She's going to fire me. Fire me! After all we've been to each other . . . and oh, Popsie, how I'm going to miss your loving* . . . He wasn't going to give Rita up. No. No. Then how should he handle it? Finally he said, 'I wasn't talking about the union part of it actually. I know you can handle anybody there.'

'Then what's bothering you?' she asked brightly.

'I thought you understood.' He remembered that he'd said plainly that there was someone, very high up, who was interested in Rita's career with *Oakview Valley*.

'I'm afraid I don't. Is there something I should know about?' It was the only way to do it. Make him bring it out into the open. Fence until he did.

He said, sighing, 'I told you Rita's got a good friend, Sarah.'

'Oh, my! So you did!' Sarah cried in mock horror. 'And I suppose *he's* actually the producer of *my* show.'

Now was the time to say to her, *Never mind him. There's me to contend with. And I'm the executive producer of your show.* But he couldn't bring himself to do it. Not yet anyway. Maybe there was a way to avoid letting her know the truth.

He said, 'Now Sarah, you're the producer. But there are considerations . . .' The more worried he was the more pompous he sounded. He was very very worried now. He had to have Rita.

'I'm sorry if I'm stepping on someone's toes, but when toes get in the way, they get stepped on.'

'I think we should talk this over. After all, Rita was attacked on the set by Hart Carow.'

Sarah said, 'There are witnesses to what happened. Most of them feel Rita attacked him. That part of it is over. It's done, Lyman. Perhaps you'd better explain to Rita's friend. Whoever he is.' And she thought: If there is one.

Lyman Ogloe sighed. 'I wish I didn't have to.' He'd think of something. Some way or other, he'd see to it that Rita's career didn't end because she was disgusted by working with a fag.

'I also wish you didn't have to discuss this with anyone.

At NTN the show always comes first. But if you want me to, I'll do the talking for you.'

'You don't mean it!' He was shocked. How was he supposed to deal with that one?

'I do, and I will. If I have to. But I oughtn't to have to. It's really *your* job. Still, if you feel . . .'

'No,' he said hastily. 'I'll take it up with him, in my own way. But Sarah, I think you should know that I'm certain of his reaction. He's going to be very angry with you. He's going to feel that you're not a very cooperative person. And when your contract comes up . . .'

'Why Lyman, do you think he's going to threaten me? Do you think he'd risk the show's ratings for a girl like Rita?'

There was a long cold silence. At last Lyman said, 'I want you to understand your position, Sarah.'

And now it was clear to Sarah that Lyman was speaking for himself. Chubby cherubic Lyman, the executive producer of *Oakview Valley*, had proven himself to be as vulnerable as any man. Rita used men for what she could get out of them. Why not him? And she was accustomed to having them respond to her. As he so obviously had. It was that thought that made Sarah realize what must have happened between Rita and Hart. Rita expected every male to go for her. When Hart didn't, Rita felt challenged. Sarah could picture her throwing herself at him, being politely rebuffed with an honest explanation. That's how Hart was. Her pride hurt, Rita must have seized on the AIDS complication as an excuse through which to express her disgust with Hart, and with herself too.

No matter, Sarah told herself. The show couldn't be allowed to go down the drain. But a small ripple of worry stirred in her mind. Lyman Ogloe didn't make a good enemy. She brushed the thought aside and called Rob in to ask that he find Bonnie.

Soon the scriptwriter came in. She moved past Robin as if she were sleepwalking, eyes wide but unseeing, her face a frozen mask of misery.

131

He said, 'Hey, Bonnie . . .' and dodged around her, closing the door behind him as he went out.

She sank into the chair next to Sarah's desk.

Sarah looked at her for a moment, then asked, 'What's happened to you?'

'I figured you'd want me. After that stunt Rita pulled.'

'Yes. We have no time at all. I want one episode, and fast. She's out, and that's it.'

Bonnie said nothing.

'We'll scrap the jail bit. Everything we worked on. I'm sorry. I know you put a lot into it. But I want it much faster than that will allow. If I had my way I'd get her out of here today.'

Bonnie still didn't speak.

'What's wrong?' Sarah asked.

'Everything!' Bonnie said shakily. She took off her small glasses, rubbed them on her skirt and set them back on her nose. 'That's what's wrong.'

'Could you start at the beginning?'

'Can you turn me into a woman who can hold on to a man? Just for a couple of years? Okay, forget the years. Just for more than a month or two?' Her chubby cheeks sagged. Her big dark eyes looked drowned in unshed tears.

'Maybe if you tell me . . .' Sarah struggled to hold on to patience. There was so little time.

'You asked what's wrong and that's what it is. I'm fed up. I can't stand any more.'

Sarah had been through this with Bonnie before. She was accident prone when it came to men. Her choices were always bad. For her, at least. 'What happened?'

'Stan.' Bonnie's face crumpled. 'Oh damn! I just can't take any more.'

Sarah got wet paper towels from her washroom. She brought them to Bonnie. 'Look. We've got work to do. It'll all seem different to you tomorrow.'

'What do I care about work? My life's a mess, and it always will be. I can't do anything right. All he wanted was a loan. After all, I've been supporting him for three months. What more does he want from me? So I blew my stack, and said no as unpleasantly as I could.' Bonnie answered her own question. 'What he wants from me beyond bankrolling is nothing. I always knew he'd walk out on me. And he has. Oh God, he has, Sarah.'

'I'm very sorry,' Sarah said crisply. 'But you're much too good for him.' She knew that sympathy wouldn't work. Kindness wouldn't either. She said, 'Pull yourself together. We've got to do twenty minutes of new story line, and we also have to change the bible, and get some dialogue done, and do a good enough job so Robin can make the necessary copies for us p.d.q.'

'I can't think,' Bonnie wailed. 'My head . . .'

'I don't care about your head.' Sarah pulled a pile of paper towards her. 'Okay. Get in front of that typewriter. We're going to get started.'

Bonnie obeyed. She hit the on-switch. The machine hummed. She looked expectantly at Sarah.

Sarah said softly, 'There's always been a mystery in Nella Rogoway's past. She came to Oakview Valley alone, for no known purpose. For a while she seemed to be in hiding, remember? We can use that. She leaves Davey in the episode before. That's done. We won't change it. She starts driving. Suddenly she realizes that there's a car following her. There's a chase. She is forced to the side of the road. A man comes to her car. She cries, "Jordan! My God, how did you find me?" '

Bonnie's quick fingers danced over the keys, tapping out Sarah's words. Then in a monotone, she followed through on them. ' "Where did you come from?" And Jordan answers, "It's taken me a long time, hasn't it? I'll bet you thought you were home free. Home free, after what you did to me." And she cries, "But I couldn't help it. If only there'd been some other way . . . " He growls, "But there was only one way, wasn't there? Betray me, get the money. Run as far and as fast as you could." He laughs, "And you thought you'd be safe." He reaches for her. She screams, fights, but his hands settle around her throat. In a moment, she's dead.'

'Yes,' Sarah breathed. 'Yes. That's right. She's dead. Nella Rogoway is finished. And Rita Porter is out of the show.' She drew a deep breath. 'Okay. There's just a little cleaning up to do. Explain that Jordan is her husband. They pulled off a bank robbery together. She took the money and ran away. Okay?'

'Okay,' Bonnie said dully. 'I'll get on with it right away.'

Rita teetered on her high heels. Her voice shook with anger. 'I'm through, Popsie. Through. That's what Sarah Morehouse said, and Sam Eich said it too. I'm through! Just like that! After all you promised me.'

'If only you hadn't made that scene,' Lyman told her. 'I could have handled it, but you threw a fit, and . . .'

'Hart was threatening me! He knocked me down! What was I supposed to do? Let him?'

'Rita, please . . . we can't stand here on the corner. Come with me. We'll talk. I promise you . . .'

'Ho! I know your promises.'

'There'll be something. I'll find the part. You're going to be a star. Just come on now, and we'll . . .'

He wanted her so badly that it hurt again. He hurt all the time, even when he went home to his wife.

'I'll see you around the set. Until my last day. But don't expect anything. I've got a terrible headache. Permanently. As far as you're concerned.'

'Rita . . .'

She looked him up and down, then slowly shook her head from side to side. 'Poor Popsie,' she murmured, turning away.

10

The big apple dropped. There were whistles, horns, shrill cries. The cameras swung wildly from dancing couples to kissing couples.

Sarah turned off the television set. There was nothing more to watch, to wait for. It was January 1985.

Next year we'll be together, Tony had said on the phone a few hours ago.

Already that was last year. This was now.

There had been three invitations but none of them had interested her. She could have called several people to make some arrangement for the evening. But she had done nothing.

Peg was asleep. Probably Laylie was too.

She gathered a handful of reading matter and went into her bedroom, She stacked the pillows, took off her robe and settled down. She read a few pages of *Variety*, one article in *Advertising Age*, another in *Broadcasting*. Her attention wandered.

Tim had seemed all right at Christmas. Still, she was uneasy. She would talk to Dr Dunham within the next few days.

Peg was still working at her diet. Were her cheeks getting a little hollow? Sarah decided that she'd pay close attention to what Peg ate, and she'd ask Laylie to do the same. It was okay if Peg wanted to take off a little chubbiness. But anorexia nervosa was something else again. She didn't let herself go and look at Peg. That would be carrying panicked motherhood too far.

Instead she took up the New York *Times Book Review* from the previous Sunday. She flipped the pages. When she came to the list of hardcover bestsellers, she paused, remembering. A name jumped out at her. *The Gun-*

Runners, by Shields, was in the number two spot now. She frowned.

It had been at the bottom of the list when she first noticed it. First noticed it on the list. Also first noticed it standing on the mantel, appearing in every scene in *Oakview Valley* that was shot in Davey's living room.

The recognition hit her physically. A jerk in her muscles. A catch in her breath. The set dresser: Max Hollis! Damn him! Why hadn't she seen it before this? He'd been with her so long. And now a thing like this. She swore softly. What a way to start the new year.

It was the end of that week. Max Hollis sat before her. She waited for a long silent moment.

It was apparently too long for him. He said, 'Robin said it was urgent.'

'Yes.' She went on, 'You really do like that book, don't you?'

He coloured. Now he was the silent one.

'You *do* know the book I mean, Max.'

He shrugged.

'Week after week. Up there, on the mantel. Always right in the middle camera's range.'

'We needed something,' he said finally.

'Yes,' she agreed. 'And it could have been a bowl of fruit. Why wasn't it?'

He spread his hands.

'I'm disappointed,' she said softly. 'I thought I could trust you. I'd have sworn I'd never have to worry about what you'd do, your honesty, or your judgement.'

'It's not that important, Sarah.'

'But it is.' She leaned forward, her green eyes blazing now. 'You're using my show to huckster a book.'

'There are worse things to huckster than books.'

'What did you get for it?' she demanded.

He didn't answer. But his colour was fading. There was a white rim around his lips.

136

'I hope it was worth it to you. Because you're through here. I want you to pack up and get out.'

'Now wait a minute,' he cried. 'It's not that important. I know you're sore at me, but it won't happen again.'

'You bet it won't, Max.'

'Sarah, listen . . .'

'How much do you get per show?'

'You don't understand. It wasn't like that. Not for money. Not really for money anyhow. Shields is a friend of mine, see? A good friend. And we were talking about how anything that comes up on TV becomes a bestseller. And he said he wished it would happen to him. He's been trying to make the talk shows, but nobody's interested in fiction any more. That's what he said. I told him all you need is for a book to be seen on TV. Just seen. And one thing led to another, so I decided I'd prove it to him. And . . .' Max threw back his head and laughed. 'And the next thing I knew, he was on the bestseller list. So I decided to keep it going, see how far it would move. And now it's number two.'

'That's about what I figured had happened. Only I thought it was for pay.'

Max shook his head.

'I'm afraid your motive doesn't matter.' Her anger was gone now, replaced by regret. She had always liked Max, trusted him.

'I'll pull the book tomorrow. Nobody'll ever know. I'll set a plant there.'

'Yes,' she said. 'You do that. I'll be watching.'

'Sure. And you can bet I won't be that stupid again. Not even for Shields.'

'You didn't understand me. You'll finish this week. But I want you off the show. Speak to your shop steward about another place.'

'Sarah!'

'I'm sorry. That's how it is.' Her eyes met his. She wished it hadn't happened. But she had to trust the people on her crew. There wasn't any other way to handle this.

He got to his feet. 'After one mistake. Just one? And all these years I've worked for you?'

'I'm sorry,' she repeated, turning away.

Late in the afternoon, at the end of that same week, Sarah nodded at Hy, whispered, 'Yes. Okay.'

He grinned and spoke into his mike. 'Okay. Good. Go to black.' He looked back at Sarah, once again she nodded. He said into his mike, 'Thanks, kids. That's a wrap.'

Robin winked at her. Hy called to her as she rose. She ignored them both. Rita was coming towards her.

Sam Eich was suddenly at Sarah's elbow. 'Would you believe these kids? She actually thinks she's being mistreated, after how she worked Hart over.'

'But what about it, Sam? Does she go quietly, or do I have to push her?'

'She'll go quietly.' Sam cleared his throat. 'I want you to know that the union, i.e. me, advised her to.'

'Thanks, Sam,' Sarah said. Now she owed *him* one. She wondered when he would be around to collect it.

Rita had reached her by then, Sarah said her name softly. The girl was openly surprised. She had been prepared to walk past Sarah, small neat nose in the air, pretending that she didn't see the producer.

At the sound of her name she stopped, rocked back on her sandals. Brows peaked in her smooth forehead. 'Yes?' A chill drawl. 'Yes? You wanted something?'

'That was a fine performance,' Sarah said. 'You gave me chills and goosebumps. I always knew you were a good actress. I didn't realize how good until today.'

'Thank you,' Rita said in a go-to-hell voice.

'Some time you'll say "thanks" to me and mean it.'

'Sure. First you fire me, then you give me compliments.'

'You get what you deserve.'

Rita's face flamed. She spun away.

Sarah watched her go. Problem one, solved. *The Gun-*

Runners was now replaced by a potted plant, and Sarah would soon find a new set dresser. Problem two, taken care of.

From across the room she heard Annette Stone laugh. And there was problem three.

11

Problem three was resolved eventually with no effort on Sarah's part. Luck took care of that one for her. Sarah believed in luck. Her Aunt Ida paying her college tuition . . . the typing job at WTOP that first exposed her to television . . . What came after was hard work, sacrifice and direction. But there had been luck at the beginning.

And now once again it had worked for her.

The first story conference of March had just come to a close. Except that Lyman Ogloe had resolutely ignored her presence, Sarah was pleased with the way it had gone. She and Bonnie had tossed a few suggestions on the table. One of them concerned Davey, and the possibility of a new locale. A year before, Davey's younger sister, Lucilla, had disappeared. Bonnie wanted Davey to have news of her, to leave Oakview Valley in hopes of finding her. Someone had suggested Florida. Someone else spoke of Texas. Sarah said, 'I was thinking of a beach town, small, not too touristy.'

Bonnie looked unhappy. 'So many shows set in Florida these days. Same for Texas.'

'California?' Hy Berge asked. 'Small beach town . . . plenty of those. LA, Frisco . . . they're out. Already over-used. But maybe . . .'

A little more talk. Meantime Sarah was thinking that this would be a good chance for her to go to the Coast, see Tony. Normally it would be Robin's job to do the preliminary scouting. Then, when he'd narrowed the choices, she would check them out. *This* time she would do the preliminary scouting. Aloud, she said she would take care of it, and would have suggestions by the end of the month, in time for the next story conference.

She was smiling to herself, thinking about it, when she left the meeting. A whole weekend with Tony. He had been to New York twice, for a few days each visit, but they'd both been busy. They hadn't quite enough time together. Maybe that was good. Maybe it meant something.

Annette fell into step beside her. 'Sarah, I need to tell you . . . I want you to be the first to know anyway . . .'

'First to know? What's up, Annette?'

'I'm going back to Washington. After my thirty days' notice. It's a great opportunity . . . I couldn't pass it up. Just couldn't. Although working with you has been such a privilege. I've learned so much. And actually, if it hadn't been for that I doubt I could do the new show.' She paused, smiled, her eyes gleaming. 'Oh Sarah, it's so wonderful! I'm going to produce *Washington Women*. It'll be a twice-a-week show, on WETA. The women in politics, in Congress, the lobbies . . .'

'Fantastic,' Sarah said, thinking of Annette's uncle, the congressman. He would be very helpful. Maybe he had been already. 'I wish you all the luck,' she said. 'Let me know if there's anything I can do.'

So, by pure luck, the problem of Annette Stone was resolved.

She thought of calling Andrew Reynolds. He might be interested in mentioning a forthcoming Washington show. It never hurt to keep in touch with him. But already the next morning there was an item in his column. *Coming soon at DC's WETA*, Washington Women, *on pretty pols, before and behind the scenes, to be produced by Annette Stone, talented niece of Congressman E. L. Davis.* Sarah laughed when she read it. Like Sarah herself, very little got past Annette.

The next few weeks went by swiftly.

She spoke to Glory Ann, arranged to stay with her. Tony and Sarah would have all day Friday together, while she scouted locales he suggested. They'd have part of Saturday, a few hours on Sunday too. She'd leave late that night and be in the office on Monday morning.

141

She talked about the trip with Laylie and Peg, both of whom accepted the news without comment. They were accustomed to Sarah's comings and goings. The trips were part of the job, although this would be a longer one, in miles, than most.

But Wednesday night, while Sarah was packing for her morning plane, Peg came and stood in the doorway. She took several deep noisy breaths and waited.

Sarah heard, looked up. 'What Peg?'

Another noisy breath. Then: 'Do you *have* to go?'

'Have to?' Sarah repeated. 'No, I suppose not. But I ought to. And I'd like to.' She studied Peg. 'Do you want to explain?'

Peg shrugged. She shuffled her purple Addidas.

'Don't you feel well?'

Sarah saw that the girl's dieting was really beginning to show now. Where there had been plump cheeks there were now very definite hollows. Peg wasn't going to be a chubby teenager after all. That was to the good. But was it too much? Sarah wasn't sure. She knew that Peg's meals had been well balanced, because she'd been watching. And Peg didn't look sick. But still . . .

'I'm okay,' the girl was saying. But her voice was sullen. Her blue eyes evaded Sarah's.

'Something's bothering you. You've never minded my going away for a little while before.' Sarah resumed packing. But as she folded a half slip, she saw Peg's small hands clench and unclench.

She asked, 'Listen, Peg, would you want to spend the weekend with your father and Carla, instead of staying home?'

'Mom!' It was phony outrage.

'You would,' Sarah said lightly. 'And it's okay to admit it. I don't mind.'

'Are you sure?' Peg was red-faced, but smiling now.

'Go call and ask if they're available,' Sarah said, smiling too. But she did mind. It hurt to know Peg wanted to be any place but home. And this was home.

'It gets boring. I mean . . . when you're away, Mom.'

142

'I suppose it does. But it doesn't happen often, Peg.'

'Will you see Glory Ann?'

'Sure. I'll be staying with her most of the time. You know her private number. You can call me whenever you want to. If I'm not there, just leave a message. I'll get back to you.'

'You'll see Tony too, won't you?'

'Yes. That's one of the reasons I'm so anxious to go. To see him. But for a business reason too. I might be able to work out a deal.'

'So we could move out to LA, Mom?' Peg's eyes were sparkling now.

'If I got the right kind of job.'

'Near Glory Ann,' Peg said. 'Oh, I'll bet it would be wonderful, living there.'

'That's what I'm told. But don't count on it yet. It's a very iffy thing.'

'Well, I like the idea. I won't count on it, but I like it. A new place. A new house. A new school.' Peg paused. 'But what about Laylie?'

'I haven't thought that far ahead,' Sarah said. 'But when it happens, *if* it happens, then Laylie will have to decide what she wants to do.'

'I know she'd say yes.'

'That's one more thing you can't count on. Laylie's got her sister here. She mightn't want to leave her behind.'

'She will,' Peg said positively. 'I know I can count on that.'

'Ms Morehouse?' The stewardess bent over her. 'I have a message for you. From a Ms Stinkowitz. She says she'll meet you at the American Airlines baggage carousel.'

Sarah nodded her thanks.

The stewardess lingered. 'Anything I can get for you before we belt up for landing?'

'Nothing, thank you.'

'It's been a pleasure to have you aboard.'

Sarah smiled. Going first class was one of the perks of

being somebody, a producer with an on-screen credit. Another was her pink Ultra suede suit. She opened her briefcase, thrust a sheaf of papers into it, snapped the catches, and leaned forward to slide it under the seat in front of her.

The stewardess took it, knelt to stow it. 'Have a good time in LA,' she said as she walked away.

And that, Sarah thought, was the best perk of all. Wouldn't Aunt Ida be impressed?

Glory Ann was in one of her bag lady outfits. She wore a not very clean over-sized red shirt. Her blue denim jeans had holes in both knees. Her sneakers had holes at the toes. She flung her arms around Sarah, giggling. Her wig, black and teased like an Afro of the early 1970s was askew. Her make-up was grotesque. 'Oh Sarah, I'm so glad to see you!'

'How are you?'

'I'm great! All kinds of good things are happening.'

'What kind of things?' Sarah waved at a skycap, pointed to her small bag

'I'll tell you. But after. The limo's in a VIP slot. We'd better get out of it before he arrives.'

Moments later they were speeding away from the airport. There had been stares, murmured laughter when Glory Ann stepped grandly into the long sleek automobile, nodding at the blond chauffeur who held the door open for her and Sarah.

'That's Marko,' she said when they were seated in the back. 'Ralph got him for me, and a housekeeper because he thinks I can't get along alone. A lot Ralph knows.' She drew a quick breath. 'Anything you want, Marko will get for you. Any place you need to go, he'll take you.' She went on to the back of the blond head, 'This is my friend, Marko. She's the one I told you about. The one who gets the blame for every good thing that's ever happened to me.'

Sarah had insisted on casting Glory Ann in *Oakview*

144

Valley, giving her the exposure she needed. When her great chance came, Sarah had personally made certain she was released from the contract that had several more years to run. Sarah's confidence in her had given Glory Ann confidence in herself. 'If it hadn't been for Sarah . . .' Glory Ann said. 'If it hadn't been for her . . .'

Sarah asked, 'What about Ralph? How are things in that quarter?'

Glory Ann snorted. 'Non-existent. That's how they are.'

'You're not back together? You're not talking about it?'

'Nope. Don't you read the gossip columnists?'

'I don't believe everything they say, Glory Ann.'

'This time they've got it straight from the horse's mouth. And by that, I mean Ralph.' Glory Ann's voice thinned. 'We're finished.'

'I'm sorry. I thought it would blow over.'

'Me too.' The famous smile flashed. Sweet. Rueful. 'But . . . well, I guess it just wasn't meant to be.'

Sarah said nothing. Being philosophical wasn't Glory Ann's style. Something more was to come. But Sarah didn't ask. She knew that she'd find out in due time.

'Never mind. We've got lots to do. No time to worry about Ralph now.' Glory Ann grabbed Sarah's hand. 'Tell me, what about you and Tony Statler? Do you know that when he says your name, which is often, his whole face lights up?'

'I'm delighted to hear that.'

Glory Ann laughed. 'Now I finally know what's going on. Your face lights up too.'

Sarah grinned.

'Your taste is improving.'

'There was only one way to go,' Sarah said, thinking of Daniel Clermont. 'And that was up.'

'Sarah . . .' Now there was a tentative note in Glory Ann's voice. No joy. No exuberance. 'What do you think? Should I just give up on Ralph?'

'I don't know. Have you tried sitting down and talking with him?'

'Sure. He talks at me. One ultimatum after another.'

'That's all?'

'The thing is . . . he can't live in the limelight. I can't live without it. How do we compromise?'

'I don't know the answer to that one.'

'Give a little. That's what people say. But if you give a little, you end up by giving it all.' Glory Ann finished in a wail. 'Oh God, why do I get so mixed up?'

Later, when the phone rang, she spoke into it in a hushed whisper, lips closed, almost kissing it, crooning, 'Yes, oh, yes, of course I do.' And: 'Not now, no. But later on, maybe, I can. Sure. You know I won't forget. How could I? I mean, how could I?' And when she put down the phone, she raised a bland face to Sarah. 'An old friend . . . no one you'd know.'

Tony was tanned, smiling. His dark eyes narrowed appreciatively as he looked at Sarah over the table in Morton's. He liked being there, being seen with her, pointing out the television and movie personalities in the restaurant. He knew a lot of people, and a lot of people knew him, and Morton's was one of the places where he could be certain many paths would cross. He hoped she noticed how many people greeted him, and thought she did. Sarah was always aware of what was going on around her. He leaned towards her, said, 'It's good to see you, Sarah. I've been waiting a long time to get you here.'

'I'm glad I came,' she told him.

They had had a good day together. The weather had been wonderful, warm and sunny, once the morning fog had rolled away. They'd driven north, picking up Route 1 at San Luis Obispo, scouting locales. One at Harmony; the other at Cambria. Sarah was most interested in Cambria. It was a sun-silvered small town, with a permanent population of around three thousand, some of whom were artists who would never quite make it, and part-time artisans of various kinds, both, more often than not, supporting themselves by working at the nearby motels and restaurants, which catered to tourists visiting San

Simeon. Get away from those motels, Sarah thought, and she'd have a perfect spot in which Lucilla could hide.

The day had passed quickly. She had returned to Glory Ann's to change. Now they were having dinner before going on to friends of his for drinks.

'Have you thought any more about a proposal for Stell-Stat to consider?'

'I haven't *stopped* thinking about it, Tony. But I want something spectacular. A really outrageous idea. I'd like to make a movie that'll make everybody in TV sit up and take notice and start scrambling to do the same thing as fast as he can.' She grinned. 'I don't have it yet. But I'll get it.'

'I know you will,' he agreed. If anybody would, she would. He could always pick a winner. He'd already proved that.

'And how are things going with you?'

'Good. Better than I expected. I'm afraid to hope too much, so knock wood three times. But I may pull it off.'

He was referring to something he had told her about some time before; getting back into the driver's seat at Stell-Stat.

He reached across the table and took her hand. 'Keep at the proposal. Because if I make it . . .'

'Wait, Tony. Don't start making promises. You'll have to see what I do before you make me an offer.'

'I already know what you can do,' he said. 'One of the first things I did after I met you was to sit down and watch a week's worth of *Oakview Valley*.'

'You did?' She was startled, pleased.

'Sure. I was interested. Naturally I wanted to know what your work was like.'

When they had finished eating they went to his friends' home.

The drinks flowed. A butler passed trays of hors d'oeuvres. The talk was about television. The new technologies, the effect of VCR's, hand-held cameras. Stories, plot lines, properties, trends. Music, sets. Costs. Costs. Costs.

Tony introduced her to their hosts, then led her around

147

the room, pausing here and there to make sure she met certain people. One of these was a small pudgy man with a red face and glittering blue eyes. Sarah recognized him immediately. Jim Carstairs.

Tony began an introduction.

Sarah cut through his words. 'We've met. How are you, Jim?'

'Just fine, Sarah. And how are you?' Jim spoke as if he were barely able to get the words past his clenched teeth. He was plainly remembering their run-in years before. He, coming in late, drunk. Her angry denunciation . . .

She felt heat surge into her cheeks. It had been such a long time ago. But neither of them had been able to forget it.

Tony was saying, 'Jim's going to join us at Stell-Stat, Sarah.'

Her heart sank. There was no use in pretending to herself. If Jim was going to be at Stell-Stat, then she had an enemy there to balance Tony. Her chances had fallen to almost nil. The television community, although spread from coast to coast, was still a tiny community. Old friends remained old friends. It was the same with enemies. And Jim Carstairs obviously forgot nothing, forgave nothing.

She said brightly, 'That's good news for you, Tony. Congratulations, Jim.'

Jim smiled without warmth, then turned away.

Tony puckered his lips under his moustache for a silent whistle. 'So you're old friends, are you?'

'Not exactly. As you saw,' Sarah said. And: 'What's he going to do at Stell-Stat?'

'He's coming in as a line producer.'

'Keep your eye on him. It won't do you any good that he knows me. He hates my guts.'

That, Tony thought, was plain. And what the hell was wrong with the man that he could look at Sarah that way? But Tony laughed. 'So what? I'll be in charge, remember.'

Later, she was to recall him saying that, the brightness of his eyes, his teeth flashing. But that night she put aside her vague discomfort. Jim Carstairs was a nothing man.

Stell-Stat would find out. She reminded herself that she'd brushed him aside once and she could do it again.

Tony went to get her a glass of wine. An acquaintance from Sarah's Washington days stopped to talk. 'Are you planning a move, Sarah?'

'Not immediately. But if something attractive were to come along I'd be more than willing to listen.'

'I'd say something attractive already has come along,' the woman said. 'Tony Statler, for instance.'

Sarah laughed.

'But if you were referring to a contract, rather than to a male, I'd better warn you. Stell-Stat's not nearly as safe as it seems.'

'Really? How come?'

'Inside politics, Sarah. But you know plenty about that, don't you?'

Mystified, she shook her head. But the woman drifted on with a wave of her fingers.

Stell-Stat in trouble. It seemed unlikely. Tony had said nothing about that. Only about his own plans. She looked slowly around the room. Most of the guests were Stell-Stat people. Wouldn't they know if something was happening? Wouldn't they be talking about it? Not necessarily. It was possible for plots to build behind closed doors.

Tony brought her the wine. His fingers touched hers when he gave her the glass. He leaned down, smiling. 'Would it be rude if I said I can't take being here any more?'

Sudden warmth flooded her body. She hoped that she wasn't blushing. But when he began to laugh she knew that she was. She knew too that it was all right. She didn't have to pretend with him.

They spoke quick goodbyes to their hosts and left.

Tony linked arms with her, held her tightly until they were a few steps beyond the front door. Then, with a sigh, he pulled her into his arms. 'I've been waiting all evening for this.'

Their kiss was promising, deep and hot, but too brief,

interrupted as the front door opened, throwing a beam of pale light around them.

Jim Carstairs brushed by them with a wordless mutter. They were only a few steps behind him on the short walk to the parking area. He pulled out without acknowledging them.

Sarah knew that she ought to think about him. What he was planning. What he could do to hurt her, to damage Tony. She should discuss the Stell-Stat situation with Tony. But not now. She wanted nothing to distract her, him. They were together now. There wasn't much time.

She slid close to him, her head on his shoulder, his arm around her. The night seemed to slide by. The sky a deep blue, laced with occasional beams of silver light. The trees dark silhouettes. Small glinting cat's eyes winking from driveway markers.

They didn't speak, but the silence pulsed with feeling. She knew that neither of them wanted to spoil the moment with words.

When he pulled into the space in front of his rented bungalow, he pulled her into his arms, whispering, 'If Carstairs shows up now I'm going to punch him out.'

Laughing, they kissed. Laughing still, and breathless, they went inside.

'Want something to drink?' he asked.

She shook her head, consumed now by fierce desire.

'Music? Candle light? A fire in the hearth?'

She gasped, 'Tony, stop it.'

He opened his arms. 'Then come here.'

She lay against him, watching a ray of sunlight edge across the faded blue carpet. Sated now, she still wanted to take him into her arms, to hold him again as she had held him earlier. But he slept so sweetly, his face smoothed and young. Defenceless for the moment, different from the wakeful Tony, whose force burned in his eyes, and in his voice. Burned even in his love making so that there was

150

no part of her, from her head to toes that didn't tingle with his kisses.

A wave of longing swept her. Soon she would be leaving him. Thinking of him. Already wondering how quickly they could be together again. A momentary confusion shook her. What did she really want? What came first? Did she know? Had she ever known?

Tony stirred, turned to her. His fingers traced a warm triangle at the tops of her thighs. 'Sarah?'

She forgot her confusion. She wanted it all. She put her face against his bare chest, and kissed him.

Tony said he would pick her up in two hours for their luncheon appointment at the Beverly Hills Hotel Polo Lounge with Roy Carmack. It was Carmack to whom Tony looked for the money to help him regain his control of Stell-Stat. That was why Tony was behaving so nervously.

'Two hours from now,' he said. 'Is your watch okay? We don't want to be late. This guy is a nut for promptness.'

'I'll be ready. Don't worry about it,' she told him.

And then he wanted to know what she would wear. She told him she didn't know yet, hadn't thought about it. 'Well, think now. What?'

She shrugged. 'It doesn't matter. I'll figure it out.'

He was insistent. 'You've got to look special. He's one particular guy.'

She slipped from the car, laughing. 'I'll see you in two hours. And do you proud.'

She let herself into the house. There were quick footsteps.

Marko, the blond chauffeur, came towards her, hurrying, frowning. 'Ms Morehouse? Is Glory Ann with you?'

'With me?'

'Oh. She isn't.' He said it flatly. 'I was hoping . . . Did she say anything about going out last night?'

'I thought she planned to stay at home.'

'So did I.' Marko's tone was bitter. 'How she expects me to take care of her when she sneaks out, I don't know.'

'Take care of her?' Sarah repeated.

'Didn't she tell you? I'm her bodyguard as well as her driver.'

Sarah raised her brows. Bodyguard? Glory Ann?

The chauffeur understood. 'Kooks,' he said. 'A couple of them think they've been promised Glory Ann for their very own by God Himself.'

'You've checked the house and pool, haven't you?'

'Everywhere. Including her room, which is a mess. It looks as if she tried on every gown she has. And there must be a hundred of them.'

The two of them were looking anxiously at each other, not knowing what to do next, when the front door slammed open, then slammed shut.

Glory Ann yelled, 'Hey, where's everybody? I'm home. I'm home.'

Marko groaned softly.

Sarah hurried to meet Glory Ann. 'You scared us. Where did you go?'

'Out,' Glory Ann said happily. 'And I've had the most marvellous time.'

'If only you'd tell me . . .' Marko began.

She cut him off. 'Never mind. This was special. You didn't have to worry about this time.'

Marko shrugged and retreated to the back of the house.

Glory Ann flung her arms around Sarah. 'Oh, I feel so good. I hope you had a wonderful night with your man too! Now let's go gorge on rich and fattening foods and tell each other lots of lies!'

'You've got together with Ralph, haven't you?' Sarah said.

Glory Ann stepped back, her brows raised. 'With Ralph? Are you kidding?'

'Not Ralph then.'

'I can't tell you. But the most exciting . . . the most marvellous man . . . If only you knew . . . You'd never

152

believe it . . . Oh, Sarah, some times I can't believe I'm me!'

'I don't know what you're talking about, Glory Ann.'

'I know. I'll tell you some day. I promise. You'll be the first to know.'

Roy Carmack telephoned two messages to them at the Polo Lounge. The first one said that he was running late. He couldn't make it until one-thirty. At one-thirty there was a second message. He was sorry. He couldn't make it at all. Perhaps next week. Tony should call for a new appointment.

'That's that,' Tony said disgustedly, his heart sinking. Something must have happened. Why would Carmack suddenly be unavailable? 'Next week. When you won't be here.'

'Then you'll meet with him.'

'But you were to be my ace in the hole,' Tony said. 'That's why I specially wanted him to meet you now.' He made it sound as if he were halfway joking. But he wasn't. He'd been counting on Sarah. Her clover honey hair and level green eyes. Her husky voice, with its undercurrent of self-confidence. She was a successful woman, the kind of woman that only successful men have. That's what he'd wanted Roy Carmack to see. But when he explained it to Sarah, he put it differently. He said that Carmack was the chief executive officer of Tri-National Associates, a very large, extraordinarily rich conglomerate with assets in England, Canada and the United States. Carmack had millions at his disposal.

'Now I see,' Sarah said. 'And I'm glad the meeting is postponed. I'd want to have a concrete proposal to put before him when we meet.'

'He's somewhat eccentric. Goes by personalities more than by proposals, I think.'

'Just the same, I prefer to have something to offer other than my personality.'

'Then get a proposal together as fast as you can. I'll try

153

to set up a meeting in New York.' Tony grinned, feeling better. A small delay wouldn't hurt. And maybe she was right. Maybe having a story to talk about would be to the good. He said, 'And now, let's eat fast, and go and make love. I don't believe in wasting time.'

12

Monday morning. The sun just risen. Sarah was a little ahead of the first build up of traffic. TWA's flight 702 had been on time almost to the minute at Kennedy Airport, and she had been able to find a cab immediately.

She wished she could stop at the apartment, see Peg before she left for school. Peg had sounded glum when Sarah had called her from Los Angeles. No wonder. John had cancelled the weekend visit. Business, he'd said, Peg reported doubtfully. Sarah looked at her watch again. No, not today, it was impossible.

The cab finally stopped in front of the building. She paid the driver and stepped out. Running now, her purse swinging from her shoulder, her travel bag hitting her knees, she entered the still-empty lobby. The guard waved her past his desk.

The elevator doors hissed shut. Moments later she was in her office. Then a quick shower in one of the dressing rooms. A change of skirt and blouse. The quilted waistcoat, its red triangles matching the red triangles of her earrings. A quick brush at her hair. A fast make-up job.

She stood at her desk, checking her calendar. At this time yesterday she lay next to Tony, the warmth of his body enwrapping her. The window had been filled with an expanse of blue sky. Twenty-four hours ago. Three thousand miles away. She shook away sudden longing. That was then. This was now.

She sat down, hit the phone buttons with a pencil eraser. She had begun to frown at the fourth ring when Laylie said, 'Morehouse residence.'

Her voice was distant, blurred.

'Laylie. It's me. Is everything okay there?'

'Sure. You just get in?'

'A little while ago. I'm at the office. How's Peg?'

155

'Okay. She just left for school.'

'And you?'

'Okay, too.'

'Have Peg call me as soon as she gets home,' Sarah said.

'I will,' Laylie answered, as an outer door slammed and Sarah hung up. Several phones began ringing at the same time. Robin came in at a dead run, skidded to a stop, and said, grinning, 'Welcome home. Did you have a good time?'

He was glad she was back. He missed her when she was gone, even over the weekend, knowing he couldn't just pick up the phone, talk to her for a few minutes, if he wanted to.

'Yes,' she said. 'A very good time.'

'Good. Brace yourself. Sam Eich is outside. He says he *has* to see you.'

She sighed. She ought to have expected this visit. Even though Sam Eich represented AFTRA and Max Hollis belonged to NABET, they were old friends. Max would have talked to Sam. Ah well. Might as well get it over with as stall it until later.

'I'll see Sam now,' she said. As Robin started from the room, she asked him to get her the fan mail figures as soon as he could.

She didn't complain when Sam waved his cigar in her face by way of greeting. She smiled at him, leaned back in her chair.

'This is informal, Sarah. Off the record. Max came to me as an old friend. That's how I'm coming to you.'

'Sure,' she said encouragingly.

But he wasn't quite ready to get to it. He said, 'You're looking good. You always do.'

'Thank you, Sam.'

'A few days in LA agrees with you.'

Was there a hint in his voice? Had the grapevine mentioned Tony? She waited.

'Max Hollis came to see me the other night. He should have gone to his own shop steward of course, but since

156

we've been friends for years . . .' Sam let the words trail away. Then: 'He's very upset. About the mess he made.'

'He ought to be, Sam.'

'But you know, Sarah, this stuff isn't making any of us, any of the unions, look good.'

'I'm sorry. The unions are not responsible for this one. I know that. You know that. They know it upstairs too.'

'Still . . . these are union people. Rita. Max. What do they think they're doing?'

'I wish I knew.'

'This younger generation, Sarah . . .' He sighed. 'The thing is, did you have to take him off the show?'

'I'd have fired him if I could, Sam. But since I couldn't, because of the union agreements, I did the next best thing.' She paused. Then: 'It was partly his . . . well, his attitude.' Now she sounded rueful.

'You mean he was upset? That bothered you?'

'But he wasn't. Not really. At least not until I told him he was off the show. At first he was just mad at me. At me, Sam. I didn't do it. He did.'

'There wasn't any money exchanged. At least that's what he said.'

'I know. And it's probably true. This time. But who knows what he'll do next?'

Robin buzzed her from the outer office to say there was a phone call from Tony. He must have been near the phone when it rang, and answered because nobody else was nearby.

When he said Tony Statler, his voice put the name in italics. That was for Sarah's benefit. He himself had a bad taste in his mouth when he said the name. He'd never met the man, but that didn't matter. Robin hated the son of a bitch on general principles. He also hated Tony because Sarah so plainly didn't.

'Excuse me,' she said to Sam. 'A long-distance call. If that's all there was . . .'

'You wouldn't call him in? You know, give him hell, like I'm going to . . .'

'And give him one more chance on *Oakview Valley?*'

she asked. She understood the problem. The show to which Max had been transferred had folded. There was nothing else to put him on right now, as far as she knew. That would explain why he'd gone to Sam. Maybe the scare would have taught him the lesson he needed.

Sam purposefully smashed his cigar out in the ashtray on her desk. 'That's what I had in mind. One more chance.'

'Okay. I will. For you.' Win one, she thought. Lose one. Sam was a very important man. But suddenly she felt good, relieved. As if she'd dropped a load off her shoulders. She'd wanted to take Max back. She hoped she wouldn't be sorry.

Sam's grin warmed her. 'Take your call,' he said, ambling towards the door. 'When you want to talk to Max, give him a buzz.'

She picked up the phone. 'Tony?'

'I miss you.'

'Yes,' she said. 'Me too.'

'Good,' he laughed. 'I'm glad to hear it. When can you come back?'

'I don't know. When will you be in?'

'I don't know either. But things are happening,' Tony said. He'd been spending time with the guys at Stell-Stat. He knew he'd be able to turn them around. The trips to New York were doing him good. He'd told them he was working on something big to bring to Stell-Stat.

Sarah asked, 'Want to tell me what's going on?'

'Not yet. As soon as I can though.'

Inconsequentials, she thought. They weren't touching. She felt the lack of privacy. Faint voices on the line. A three-thousand-mile hum. Suddenly her breasts tingled.

She said goodbye, and rang off when Robin looked in, wagging his head urgently. Behind him was Lyman Ogloe. He elbowed the younger man aside, made shooting motions with his plump hands, and as Robin stepped back, slammed the door in his face.

'Sarah,' he said. 'I need to talk to you.' He stopped,

his fat cheeks sagging, his cupid's-bow mouth suddenly grim.

Now that he had brought himself this far, he didn't know how to go on. He wanted to say, *You goddamn bitch! You spoiled the best thing I ever had! Fix it, because I've tried to, and I can't!* But saying that would be saying more than he dared. There had to be another way.

He'd seen Rita. She let him take her to lunch. She accepted his presents. But she wouldn't go to the hotel room with him. She wouldn't let him touch her. And he ached. His balls hurt, and his heart hurt. He had to have her.

He said finally, 'It's about Rita. She's not doing anything much. A few commercials. But nothing that's going to go anywhere.'

For a moment Sarah's mind went blank. Rita? What about Rita? That was all taken care of. She wasn't Sarah's problem any more. But Lyman's grim face said she was.

He went on, 'You've got to do something for her.'

'There's nothing I can do,' Sarah said.

Lyman hadn't spoken to her until now since Rita's last day on the show. He had ignored Sarah at story conferences, and passed her in the hallway without a glance. Now this. What did he want? What did he expect?

He said heavily, 'Sarah, there's been a lot of trouble in your staff. Not just Rita. What about Max Hollis? Trouble we don't need, and shouldn't have. I want you to consider what that means. And whose responsibility it is. Good producers don't have such problems.' He got to his feet, went to the door. 'Think about that, Sarah.'

The door closed softly behind him.

She consciously forced herself to relax her clenched fists. She held her breath and felt her heart beating furiously against her ribs. Before his manner had been unfriendly, but now he'd come into the open. He'd been subtly threatening. And not so subtly, come to think of it. As executive producer he stood between her and management. If he wanted to, he could make big trouble

159

for her. What could she do about it? She would have to think of something. But what? What?

She rose, started out. Then, with a shake of her head, she went back to her desk and put in a call to Dr Dunham at Tim's school. He was in a meeting, couldn't be disturbed. He would return the call, she was told.

Once again she started out, planning to see Bonnie. But the girl wasn't in her cubbyhole, working over her word processor. She wasn't in the coffee shop, nor the library. Sarah left a note on her desk, then found her in the rest room.

Her round face white, her eyes red, she leaned against a sweaty tile wall. No, she muttered in answer to Sarah's question. No. She had no ideas. She'd been thinking, but not about anything worthwhile like a story. She doubted that she ever could. With a great wail, she fell into Sarah's somewhat unwilling arms. 'God, why can't anybody love me?'

'Anybody? Or Stan?'

Bonnie had been ecstatic when Stan had returned after their last fight. Sarah hadn't voiced her doubts. What was the use? And she didn't ask any questions now. It wasn't necessary. Obviously something had happened.

Bonnie said, 'I guess you won't be surprised to hear Stan's gone again.'

'Forgive me, Bonnie, but it's good riddance. There are plenty of other pebbles on the beach.'

'And they all end up the same,' Bonnie cried.

Half an hour later, powdered and rouged, she settled to work at her word processor. 'I'll just give a little polish to script three for this week before I turn it over to a dialoguer.'

'You won't forget this evening?'

'Of course not, Sarah. How could I? You're so good to me.'

'Really,' she said that evening as she curled up in a corner of the sofa, a glass of wine in her hand. 'You're so good to me, Sarah. If I were you, I'd run out of patience.'

'Never mind that. Let's think out loud together. We

160

probably don't have much time. We want something very new. Compelling. Contemporary. Touching a nerve. And for a mixed audience. We'll be thinking of night-time stuff on this one.'

'I know,' Bonnie said earnestly. She frowned, poked her lips out. 'For men and women. Between thirty and sixty. Hmm?'

The two of them batted some ideas back and forth. Then a sudden flush reddened Bonnie's cheeks. She said, 'The thing about Stan is, was . . . it all turned on money. I can see it now. Why didn't I see it before?'

Sarah said nothing. She was curious to know what subterranean connection in Bonnie's mind had brought Stan back into the conversation.

Bonnie went on, 'Right at the beginning, I paid for dinner, movies, whatever. Then he moved in. I paid the rent, for food. And then . . . then there was spending money. I guess so he could take out other girls. I was doing him a favour, see? I mean, I gave him money because I *wanted* to. But then, pretty soon, it was different. I mean. . . . when he asked me . . . sometimes I was almost . . . almost scared of him. Scared to tell him no. Not because he'd leave me. But because he acted as if I owed him. It was frightening . . . the way he acted . . .'

Sarah sat very still. She was remembering how her heart had pounded when Lyman Ogloe talked to her that day. The sound of his voice, his grim mouth. Threatening . . . She said softly, 'There's a lot of ways women can be frightened, frightened of men, or by them.'

'Or maybe they're frightened for nothing,' Bonnie said. 'Like Rita. I mean, Rita really didn't have to be scared she'd get AIDS from Hart. But she was.' Bonnie paused. 'And actually, although I realize she was completely unreasonable about it, I can't altogether blame her for worrying.'

'AIDS,' Sarah said softly. 'AIDS, Bonnie.'

Bonnie looked confused. 'What's wrong, Sarah?'

'It's a very contemporary subject, Bonnie. Very new

161

and compelling. And it interests everybody. It has to. Because everybody's involved.'

'A story about a girl who's afraid of getting AIDS . . .' Bonnie whispered. 'Oh, Sarah . . . it could be so exciting to do . . .' Bonnie seized a pad, began scribbling furiously. 'There's this girl . . .' She looked up at Sarah. 'I wish we could make her an actress . . .'

Sarah felt a quick surge of excitement. An actress! Rita! What if . . . She stopped her tumbling thoughts. No, no. It wouldn't do! The legal department . . . But she could deal with that as they wrote the script. She could be sure that she and Bonnie didn't get themselves out on a limb. And Rita! She'd be perfect for the part. She'd be perfect. And it would make her a star. If they got the script right . . . if they could persuade her . . .

'You see, if she were an actress, she could fall in love with her leading man.'

'Too close,' Sarah said. 'Let's have her fall in love with her director.'

'Directors aren't all that interesting,' Bonnie objected.

'There's no law. We can make him interesting.'

'Okay. She's in love with her director. But she's afraid of being in love. She's afraid of any man. She knows perfectly well that AIDS can be spread in a lot of different ways. Her fear turns her into a shrew . . . she's impossible to work with . . . her director . . .' Bonnie stopped. She looked sideways at Sarah. 'We're going to have to have a producer too, you know.'

Sarah didn't even blink. She agreed quickly. 'Yes. You're right. But Bonnie, bear in mind, this'll be a movie about doing a stage play. Not a television show. Okay?'

'Sure,' Bonnie grinned. 'Why not?' She bent her head over the pad again. When Sarah said nothing more, she looked up. 'What's wrong? Don't you like it? Won't it work?'

'It's going to work,' Sarah said fervently. 'I know it will. I know it!'

Laylie came in to say that dinner was ready. Bonnie went to the table, still working on the idea. While Peg picked at her food, and Sarah slowly ate, Bonnie stuffed herself with gusto, continuing to tear at the developing plot, working at it, changing and expanding it. She tossed out one development after another, seizing her pen to make a note when she began to feel overwhelmed by what was happening inside her head, and before her eyes. The scenes . . . one after another. The characters . . . the actress, the director, the producer.

Sarah listened, feeling almost drunk with elation. The story line was coming . . . If Rita would accept the part, Sarah need not worry what Lyman Ogloe was up to behind her back. If the proposal sold, she'd never have to worry about Lyman Ogloe again. Now, more than anything, she wanted to call Tony.

Bonnie was gone.

Peg was in bed.

Sarah called Tony. She let the phone ring ten times, then ten times more, but there was no answer. He wasn't at the bungalow. Just on an off-chance that he was still at the office, she called Stell-Stat. The answering service suggested that she call in the morning. She left her name and phone number, knowing that she'd try again the next day anyhow. She wanted him to know as quickly as possible that she and Bonnie had started working on the story line for the proposal.

Laylie came into the room. 'I've got to talk to you for a minute.' She looked glum, worried. Her shoulders sagged, and her usually well-disciplined braid seemed to be fraying.

'What's the matter, Laylie?'

The housekeeper sighed. 'It's my sister. She's had her fifth baby. It came along a couple of weeks ago. Sort of early, but okay. Only *she's* not okay.'

'Is she sick? What's wrong?'

'She's so down, she just sits and cries or lays in bed and cries. She won't feed the baby, nor change him, nor anything else. So the other kids are running wild, and they're just babies too. Her husband's already working two jobs. He can't do more than he is right now. And that's what I wanted to tell you. I've got to go see if I can get her back up on her feet.'

'Oh, Laylie . . .'

'I know. And I don't want to go either. But I've got to.'

'I know you do,' Sarah said. 'And we'll manage somehow.'

But in the morning, after Laylie had gone, Sarah wondered if they really could manage without Laylie.

Peg was still asleep, and time was ticking away.

At last Sarah went in to awaken the girl. She stood over her, hesitating. She hadn't realized how thin Peg had become. The dieting would have to stop. That was it. Enough was enough. When, finally, Sarah touched Peg's shoulder, Peg opened her eyes, sighing heavily.

'Time to get ready for school,' Sarah said.

'I ache all over.' Peg rolled over, buried her blonde head in the pillow. 'I don't want to get up, Mama.'

'What's wrong? Don't you feel well?'

'Oh, I'm okay. I just feel so tired though.'

'Better get moving,' Sarah said. 'You'll feel better after your shower.'

When Peg was dressed and sitting at the kitchen table, unenthusiastically stirring cold cereal with her spoon, Sarah told her about Laylie's sister, that Laylie would be gone for a few weeks.

'Oh, she can't do that!' Peg cried. Her eyes widened and filled with tears. 'I need her. She can't go away now!'

Peg cried so hard and for so long that Sarah finally said she had better not go to school. By then Sarah knew that something was wrong. Peg felt too warm to the touch. She had fallen asleep almost in the middle of a sentence, and now Sarah was remembering how often lately Peg had retired before her usual bedtime.

She made an appointment for noon with Peg's doctor, saying it was an emergency. She called in, told Rob that she'd be in later in the day. He knew she was upset by

164

the sound of her voice, but when he asked, she said, 'I'm all right. Something's come up.'

She didn't have to wake Peg up when it was time to leave for the doctor's office. The girl was ready, but she kept protesting that it was a waste of time. Sarah oughtn't to be taking time off work. Peg was just tired. But Sarah was convinced otherwise. *I need her*, Peg had cried, her eyes swollen with weeping. *She can't go away now!* Peg was talking about Laylie.

In the cab she retreated into silence. It was the same in the doctor's office. All she would say was, 'I'm fine. I just get tired sometimes. Everybody gets tired sometimes, don't they?'

The doctor spent a long time with her, both in asking questions, examining her, and taking blood samples.

Later he told Sarah that Peg's lymph glands, in her armpits and groin, appeared to be enlarged. She had a moderate fever. Those symptons were consistent with a number of different illnesses. He wouldn't speculate on what the problem was. He would wait for a laboratory report on the blood samples.

'And in the meantime?' Sarah asked.

'Let her rest at home,' the doctor said.

Sarah settled Peg in her room with stacks of magazines, the TV set on, a pitcher of orange juice at her elbow.

'I'm okay,' Peg kept saying. 'Stop fussing over me. You'd better get to work.'

Sarah knew that whatever was wrong with Peg had been wrong since the California trip. Peg had been losing weight, tired. Sarah winced, remembering. Why hadn't she realized what was going on? Swelling of the lymph glands, moderate fever, fatigue and weight loss. She wouldn't allow the word to form in her mind. If she didn't think it, then it couldn't happen. It couldn't be *that*. Leukaemia was the word she wouldn't permit herself to acknowledge.

Finally, to escape her thoughts, Sarah left Peg. As soon as she entered the NTN building she wished she were back at home. She kept thinking of Peg, wondering what the blood tests would show, and asking herself if she'd neglected Peg, hadn't given her the attention and care a twelve-year-old needed.

Preoccupied with her thoughts, she didn't notice that Daniel Clermont was among the others in the elevator with her. But when she stepped out on her floor he followed her, saying softly, 'Sarah, I wondered if I'd run into you.'

She looked up at him, her surprise evident on her face. 'Daniel! How are you?'

'Pretty good,' he answered. 'And you?'

'Okay. What are you doing here?'

He flushed. 'I'm job-hunting. I got fed up with Boston. So I'm making the rounds in New York.'

She remembered what had happened when she last saw him, but it no longer seemed important. She said, 'I hope you find what you're looking for.'

'If you have any leads . . .' His tone was diffident.

She said hastily, meaning it, 'I'll let you know of course.'

'You can leave a message for me with the Roysters.'

'Sure,' she told him. 'But now I'd better get going. I'm running late.' She smiled at him, hurried on to her office.

She made a note in her day book to herself. Daniel. A job in New York? Then she forgot him. Robin had some things for her to deal with. There was a pile of messages on her desk. Bonnie needed to see her. Lyman Ogloe asked for a meeting as soon as possible. They would be taping until five. And Sam Eich had a problem. Talking with him would take her at least until six. That meant she couldn't possibly get home before seven. And Peg would be alone. What a time for Laylie to be gone for a few weeks.

Sarah's heart suddenly dropped. Gooseflesh broke out on her arms. Peg! What was going to happen to her?

Sarah's hand shook as she checked the Rolodex for the number of the employment agency she'd used before. She put in a call, listing herself as needing a temporary housekeeper, one immediately available.

166

That done, she tried to reach Tony. She *had* to talk to him. His answering service took the call to his bungalow. Tony wasn't in. The service didn't know where he could be reached. The service didn't know when he would be back. The service agreed to take her name if she wanted to leave it. She tried Stell-Stat. He wasn't there either. She left word that he was to return the call.

13

There were three nightmarish days. Sarah could neither eat nor sleep. Her fear of what the doctor would say was wrong with Peg was so bad that she wasn't able to talk about it. Thus she told no one about Peg's illness. She hired a temporary housekeeper named Gilda Jones, and then concentrated on work, and on Peg.

When, finally, she learned that Peg had contracted mononucleosis, Sarah very nearly collapsed with relief. It was a temporarily debilitating disease, but not dangerous. The treatment consisted mainly of rest, nutritious foods and some medication. Peg, however, broke down, weeping, when Sarah explained it to her. 'Oh, Mama,' she cried. 'I tried so hard not to get sick. I know I'm so much trouble to you. And there's your job. What'll we do? Without Laylie . . .'

'We'll manage fine,' Sarah promised her.

'But your work . . . the show . . .' Peg wailed. '*Oakview Valley* . . .'

Sarah hugged Peg to her. 'You come first,' she said. 'Don't you know that? You come first.'

Somewhere, somehow, Peg had picked up the idea that Sarah's first concern in life was her work. Well, it was, Sarah acknowledged to herself. But not before the children, not before Peg and Tim. Briefly Sarah wondered about Carla, John. Had they put into Peg's head the idea that she was a burden to Sarah? She tried not to think about it. If it were true, there was nothing she could do about it but prove to Peg that they were wrong.

She devoted herself to reassuring Peg. She, Sarah, and the show, would go on. There was nothing to worry about. Peg and Sarah, together, could handle anything that came down the pike, and that meant this illness too.

Soon, calmed down, smiling, Peg promised to rest as

168

ordered every day after school. She agreed too to give up her dancing lessons for a while, and to remember to take her medicines as required.

Later Rob dropped by, saying he had been in the neighbourhood on an errand. 'How's Peg?' he asked anxiously.

'She's going to be okay,' Sarah said.

He didn't say anything, just drew her to him. Briefly she leaned against him. God, she was tired. Tired. It felt so good to let go for a minute. Then she pulled away.

After Rob had gone, Sarah called John to let him know what had happened. He said he'd drop in to see Peg as soon as he could. First, though, he informed Sarah that Peg wouldn't be ill if Sarah were a full-time mother.

To take the bad taste out of her mouth Sarah called Glory Ann, who listened, moaned sympathetically, and said, 'I'll be by on the weekend. I have to be in Washington, so I'll take a small detour.'

She swept in Friday night, bringing a family of teddy bears, which Peg immediately adopted, and a boxful of games to be sampled, one at a time, she insisted, over the next two weeks.

It was later the same evening. Andrew Reynolds was on the line. 'Sarah, do you know where I can reach Tony Statler?'

She answered, fencing, 'Why would I know that, Andrew?'

'He sublets the penthouse next to yours,' Andrew said. 'I thought you might have run into him in the elevator. He's got to be somewhere.'

'What do you mean?'

'I wouldn't tell just anybody,' Andrew purred. 'But since you're involved . . .'

'I am? What are you talking about?'

'Tony Statler,' Andrew said. 'And Stell-Stat. It used to be his firm, as you probably know. Then he lost it in a community property settlement when he and Eve Stellwagen, his wife, divorced. He stayed on as a paid employee, fighting to get it back. And it looked as if he was going to pull it off. Until a short time ago anyhow.'

Tony had lost Stell-Stat! She hadn't known that. She'd assumed he owned half the company, as he had for several years. She drew a deep shocked breath, remembering that Tony had never spoken of being the head of the company; she had simply assumed it. He'd been trying to recoup, Andrew said. And he hadn't made it.

So something *was* wrong. It was why she hadn't heard from him. She tried to sound casual, asking, 'What happened, Andrew?'

'Tony's out. Instead of being voted president by the board, he was fired. A new man is president. It was very undercover. They brought him in as a line producer, but the whole arrangement was a set-up.'

'Carstairs,' Sarah said slowly. 'That's who you're talking about.'

Andrew chuckled. 'You're nearly as good as I am, Sarah.'

She tried to pull together her scattered thoughts. This was why she hadn't heard from Tony in the past ten days . . . poor guy . . . With Carstairs president, her chance at Stell-Stat was gone . . .

Meanwhile, stalling for time, she said, 'My sources *are* pretty good, but I don't know where Tony is either.'

'I believe you,' Andrew said. 'So let me give you a tip. The best thing you can do for yourself and your career is forget Tony Statler.'

'What're you talking about, Andrew?'

'He's got the shove twice. It means he's bad news.'

'That's ridiculous.'

'You'll see.'

Sarah put down the phone. Andrew sounded so sure of himself. But then, he always did. Even when he was most wrong. Bad news. It sounded like a frightening epitaph. And like a warning. She understood what Andrew meant. She had seen it happen. It was one of the curses of the business. Somebody had a ratings drop. A show was badly received by the few critics who mattered. A job was lost

170

in some back-office political fight. That person became a
leper. Untouchable. It didn't matter how successful he
had been in the past. It was what was happening now that
counted. And this, Andrew was saying, was what had
happened to Tony. Why? Because he'd lost Stell-Stat in a
community property deal when he was divorced? Because
now, for one reason or another, the board of directors had
just voted him out? It just wasn't fair. Wherever he was,
he must be frantic.

She went into the living room. Glory Ann was saying,
'You just wait and see! I know you don't believe me now,
Peg. But one of these days you're going to see me in the
White House!'

'You're going to be our first woman president,' Peg
chortled.

'Nope!' Glory Ann danced around the room. 'But I'll
be there. And you'll know all about it. Just wait and see!'

She spent two hours on the phone that night. And the
next morning she left for Washington, saying, 'I have a
very important appointment there. And don't ask me with
who.'

The evening after Glory Ann had gone, Sarah stood on
the terrace. Faint sounds drifted up from the streets:
horns and sirens, and from somewhere closer, a few bars
of music. She wondered about Tony. Where was he? What
had happened to him? Why hadn't he called her?

A stocky silhouette stepped through the hedge that
enclosed her terrace. A voice spoke softly. 'Sarah?'

She stared, disbelieving. Had her own thoughts created
a ghost that looked and sounded like Tony? She found
herself laughing, saying his name. 'Tony! Tony! Where
did you come from?'

'Yes. It's me. I heard Peg's been sick. I hope she's okay
now.'

'She's getting there. I've been trying to reach you ever
since I last talked with you. I couldn't imagine . . .' Some
time she would ask him about Stell-Stat. But not now.

171

He said, 'I didn't know you'd called. I've been out of touch.' He was close, looking into her face. 'I didn't mean to worry you, Sarah. I just . . . I had some thinking to do. I borrowed a boat and went down to Mexico.' It was true as far as it went. He'd left some details out. He'd taken the boat trip with Eve, in hopes that he could finally persuade her to back him. It hadn't worked out. Now he knew that she'd just been proving to herself that he'd jump when she whistled. She'd had herself a stud, and crew, and in the end she'd said, 'Sorry, Tony, but business is business.' He told himself to forget it. His hands settled on Sarah's shoulders. He drew her close. His kind of woman. A winner. 'You don't know how much I've missed you.'

'You should have let me know, Tony.' Now she was thinking of Stell-Stat again.

'I couldn't. It all came down so fast. Right after you left for New York. But believe me, it was only the thought of you that kept me going. That's why I came back. It's why I'm here. Because of you.'

It was later. Sarah and Tony were in the kitchen having coffee. She didn't mention that she knew he'd allowed her to believe that he was president of Stell-Stat long past the time that he'd lost control of the company. She didn't tell him about Andrew Reynolds' call either, nor that she already knew Stell-Stat had dumped him. Tony, she was certain, wanted to tell her himself. So she allowed him to believe he was doing just that.

He said, 'Carstairs was friendly for a while. I thought we were getting along well.'

'He was sharpening the knife.'

Tony went on, 'Then there was the usual monthly meeting of the board.' Tony attended, as he always had in the past. He was expected to. But Jim was also there. That seemed odd. Line producers normally don't participate in board meetings. This proved not to be a normal board meeting however. The move against him was made

172

so quickly and unexpectedly that there was nothing Tony could do. He was out. Voted out of his own firm. Of what *had* been his firm, that is. Nobody would look him in the face, nor meet his eyes. Nobody said anything. He got up, stared at each of them in turn. In a dead silence. It was like being in a coffin. He left immediately. That night Eve called him. In the morning, they sailed. Afterwards he realized that she'd been in on the shafting. Maybe she'd even engineered it. Eve, using Jim Carstairs.

Sarah repeated the name quietly. 'Jim Carstairs . . .' He'd met Tony with her. He'd known Tony was her friend, if nothing more. Was it possible that Jim would carry his dislike of her so far? But no. She saw immediately that this move against Tony had originated in Stell-Stat long before. It was the reason for Jim's hiring in the first place. She'd even been warned when she was in LA by an acquaintance that things were unstable at Tony's company. She remembered how Tony had looked, dark eyes flashing confidence, when he spoke of regaining control. Nobody wins them all, she told herself. 'What's next?' she asked Tony.

'I don't know,' he said. 'I've been busy licking my wounds.' He grinned at her. 'That's over now. I feel better than I have since it happened. Which means I've done something right.'

'Coming to New York,' she said. 'That was right.'

'Yes.' He met her eyes. 'Because of you.'

She thought of the story line she and Bonnie had begun to develop. It had been for a proposal originally planned for Stell-Stat, to be submitted by Tony. That was out. But were there other possibilities?

And Tony asked, 'What about the proposal you were going to get ready for me?'

She'd seen before how often he was able to take a thought right out of her mind. Now he'd done it again. It pleased her to be prepared to say, 'We're working on it, Tony.' And to be ready to go on to describe it to him.

He listened intently, dark eyes narrowed.

She told him about the situation, the four main characters, explaining that Bonnie was working on the story line in her spare time.

'My God, Sarah!'

'What do you think?'

'It's good. Better than good. And I know just where to go with it!' He was on his feet now, pacing. It was the lifeline he needed. How right he was about Sarah! 'Roy Carmack,' he told her. 'You've got to get to him, talk to him right away.'

'We're not finished. There's a lot to do before we have the full proposal ready.'

'But you have the idea. You know what's going to happen. You can talk about it. You can sell him on it. The sooner we get started the better. I'll try to reach Carmack first thing in the morning.' Tony pulled her up, swung her around. 'It's going to work, I tell you! We're going to have a show!'

14

Early morning sun sparkled on glass and stone. There was warmth in the air. A hint of coming spring.

Sarah walked briskly across the lobby, returning the building guard's salute. She had a lot to do. But first, before anything else, she wanted to talk to Bonnie. Tony needed something on paper. A simple outline, if nothing else. Something to wave in Roy Carmack's face.

As soon as she got to her desk, she had Robin put in a call to Bonnie. The girl hadn't come in yet. Robin told Sarah, then asked, 'How's Peg this morning?'

'She looked pretty good.'

'Is it okay to stop in and see her the end of the week?'

'Sure. Whenever you want to,' Sarah said.

But Rob lingered. He wanted to tell her about Lyman Ogloe, but didn't know if he should. Before he decided, she asked him to get the fan mail figures.

When he brought them in he said, 'Lyman's been in and out the last few days. He was interested in your travel vouchers.'

'That so?' Sarah asked.

'And asking about your friends in California.'

'I see,' she said, knowing instantly what the executive producer was up to, and knowing what it meant. He was after her scalp, and looking for a way to get it. Even a hint of impropriety in the use of funds would damage her. She *had* scouted Cambria, but it would look bad if he could suggest she'd used NTN money to get herself to LA for personal reasons. She had to do something about Lyman right away.

She didn't like giving in, even appearing to. But she told herself not to care how it looked to Lyman. Let him think what he liked. She had to protect herself. If he thought he'd won, then good. She'd even the score another day.

She'd been waiting to talk to Rita about a part in the show until she had something to give the actress to read. But there was no time left. It was important to neutralize Lyman immediately.

She asked Robin to get Rita on the phone. While she waited she looked at the fan mail figures. A few letters still asked why Rita had to die. One writer promised not to watch the programme again, but a letter from the same person appeared in a stack dated several weeks later. Okay. The pattern of the fan mail supported her. She'd let Lyman know about that too.

When Rita was on the line, Sarah picked up the phone. 'Rita? How are you?' she asked.

The actress said she was doing fine, great, in fact. Her voice was filled with suspicion when she went on, 'What's on your mind, Sarah?'

'What about lunch today?'

'Today?'

'This won't wait, Rita.'

Still sounding suspicious, Rita agreed. They would meet at one.

When she hung up, Sarah glanced at her watch. Ten. Why hadn't Bonnie come by, or called? An hour passed, still no Bonnie. Sarah telephoned her apartment. There was no answer. Something about the long steady ring, repeated over and over, sounded ominous to Sarah.

Of course it could mean that Bonnie was on her way downtown right now. Maybe stepping into the elevator on the lobby floor. Maybe even rushing into her office.

But Sarah had the feeling that the phone wasn't being answered for another reason. She cut the connection. For a moment she sat still, staring off into space, a frown between her brows. Then she got up, took her bag, and made for the door.

Robin came surging up from behind his desk. 'Sarah! Wait! I have to talk to you.'

176

'No time now,' she said. 'I'll be back in a little while. Catch me then.'

'Sarah! It's important. A Mr Carmack called. You were on another line. He wouldn't wait.'

Carmack. He wouldn't wait. It sounded like the man. But she didn't stop. 'I'll take care of it later.'

The door closed between them. She hurried down the corridor, her mind already leaping ahead, full of terrible visions.

Bonnie . . . A scatter of clothing, overturned furniture, broken picture frames. A door half open . . . lamps burning, while daytime sun streamed through the windows . . . And someone crying, *Why didn't anybody care* . . .

A cab stopped at her signal. She gave him Bonnie's address, and at the same time she saw Bonnie moving slowly through the hurrying crowd on the sidewalk, dragging her feet, shoulders sagging.

Bonnie! Alive. Walking. Not crumpled in a heap at the bottom of a cupboard. Bonnie . . . on the way to the office.

She screamed at the cab driver to stop, threw a five-dollar bill at him and flung herself from the cab.

She yelled at the sleepwalking figure who drifted in the general direction of the building. 'Bonnie!'

The girl turned. Her plump face was pale. Her dark eyes were sunken in pads of red and swollen tissue.

Sarah caught the girl by the shoulder. 'Bonnie, what's wrong with you? Are you sick? Have you taken something?'

'It's Stan,' Bonnie said.

'I ought to have guessed. Pull yourself together.'

'I have to go to the office.'

'Of course you do. You've got a lot of work.'

'Stan might call me. If he changes his mind. And he might. He did last time. Maybe he'll think it over . . .'

'If he changes his mind? Again? Are you crazy? Would you let him come back?'

177

They stood on the sidewalk, Sarah clutching Bonnie's arm, buffeted by tides of hurrying people.

Sarah said, 'What do you need him for? So he can scrounge off you for another six months?'

'I love him.'

'You love him,' Sarah said disgustedly. Then: 'Come on. Let's go inside. I'll buy you a cup of the worst coffee in town. And I'll give you half an hour so you can tell me how you can't get along without Stan. And then you're going to go to work. And this evening, when you can put *Oakview Valley* aside for a while, I'll tell you what you have to do for me. Because we don't have any more time left. I'm going to need my own proposal fast. We've got to get a story line together. Something down on paper. A few great scenes. Some stuff that's good enough to show.'

'I can't,' Bonnie said. 'My heart's broken. I can't think.'

'Never mind your broken heart. You think with your head anyhow.'

In the elevator Bonnie said, 'It's no use. I don't have what it takes. I don't want to be a scriptwriter any more. I just want to be a girl in love.'

'Then you'll have to find another man. Stan is in love with himself. And maybe with your money. He's certainly not in love with you.'

'Easy for you to say,' Bonnie told her. 'You never have man trouble.'

'There's not a woman alive who hasn't had man trouble,' Sarah retorted. But she said nothing more. It wouldn't help Bonnie to know that Sarah too had spent her share of hours staring at the ceiling, wondering. Asking herself why the phone didn't ring. Why Tony didn't knock at the door. Now, suddenly, it was hard to believe it had happened.

She got Bonnie coffee, seated her at her desk. 'Okay.'

Bonnie didn't answer.

'Don't forget. I want you at my place at six. I've got a lot riding on this, Bonnie.'

A lot riding on this, she thought. It was the understatement of the century. This proposal's going to get me to

LA. It's going to keep Tony in the industry. And indirectly it's going to get Lyman Ogloe off my neck.

'What's it about?' Rita demanded the instant she settled in her seat.

'It's something I'm working on. On my own. It'll be a while before we get started. But I want to know if you'll be available. If I can list you as my star.'

'Star?' Rita repeated. 'Me? But you fired me, Sarah. Why would you want me to come back and work for you?'

'I told you how good you were,' Sarah said. 'Remember your last day?'

'You really meant it, didn't you?' Rita looked as if she almost believed it. She went on, 'What's this thing about?'

'I'm doing the proposal now. For an independent. A night-time TV show. It's about fear. The fear of AIDS, in a way. But mostly, really, about how fear can change a woman's life.'

When Sarah had said the word AIDS, Rita's eyes narrowed. She made a small hissing sound. Finally she said, 'Like me. And Hart Carow.'

'Just a little.'

'A little?' Rita laughed.

'You'll see.' Sarah hurried on, 'It'll be a wonderful part. Great emotional scenes. There's this actress in love with her director. They're doing a show for Broadway. She's been told that he's gay, although he isn't. She loves him, but she's afraid at the same time. And then he gets hepatitis.' Sarah paused. Rita was no longer listening.

Her face showed that she saw herself in conflict. Fighting her love. Fighting her fear. She saw herself taking care of the man she adored, even though it endangered her own life. She saw a death scene, she on her knees, weeping hopelessly . . .

'And what happens?' she asked finally.

Sarah didn't know what was to happen next. But she said, 'We're working on it. A terrific finale . . .'

'You really want me?' Rita asked.

179

Sarah nodded. 'You're the first, and the only, person I've thought of.'

'I'll do it,' Rita said positively.

So that was settled before they had even started on lunch. They ordered. When their salads came, they ate, talking about the story. About AIDS. How it was changing the lives of women as well as men, either gay or straight. Nobody was really sure how the disease was transmitted. Through certain kinds of sexual contact maybe. Through contaminated blood.

Possibly by contact with a prostitute. And there could be other ways, as yet undiscovered.

'I'll call you as soon as I have the story fully developed,' Sarah said, certain that in a little while Rita would be telling Lyman Ogloe about her lunch with Sarah.

'I hope I hear from you soon,' Rita told her. 'I'm excited. I think you've got a great idea.'

Now it was as if she had forgotten that there was anything about the story that could seem familiar to her. It had a good part. For her. That was what mattered.

And, Sarah supposed, once they'd begun production, Lyman would have a rude awakening. When Rita didn't need him any more, she'd drop him.

But that was none of *her* business, Sarah thought on the way back to the office.

'The call from Mr Carmack is on your desk,' Robin said. 'And there's the *Oakview Valley* story conference. You're having a big day.'

'Yes,' she said.

He put a hand on her shoulder, said as lightly as he could, 'You're pushing yourself, Sarah.'

'All in a day's work,' she answered, thinking about Carmack.

Robin let his hand drop away, but he could still feel the warmth of her skin against his fingers. His mouth was suddenly dry. He was glad she had gone into her office.

He knew that he had come very close in the past few months to pulling her into his arms.

Sarah checked Carmack's number, then called it. Within moments she had him on the line.

His deep booming voice said, 'Ms Morehouse? Sarah? You don't mind that, do you?' And before she could answer, 'I'm sorry I missed you in Los Angeles. It couldn't be helped, I assure you.'

She said she understood.

But he went on, 'Tony Statler has been in touch with me. He told me how to reach you. We must talk. As soon as possible. When are you free?'

That night wouldn't do. Bonnie was coming. And the proposal wasn't ready. Or was there actually enough to talk about? At lunch with Rita, it had seemed that there was. But Rita wasn't Roy Carmack. Sarah wished she had free time during the afternoon so she could see him then. But there was the *Oakview Valley* story conference. She couldn't miss that. She had to see what the reaction was to the new Lucilla and Davey episodes in Cambria.

She said, 'How about tomorrow evening?'

'I'm at the Pierre. We'll have dinner.'

High-handed, she thought. She'd gathered that from the way he'd kept Tony and her waiting, and then cancelled their meeting. He had the money, but now she could be high-handed too.

She said, 'I suggest you come to my apartment. We can have something to eat. Very informal of course. And we can talk.' She waited for him to mention Tony. But he didn't.

He said, 'Let me have the address.'

She gave it to him.

He repeated it, added, 'Seven then,' and rang off.

Not only high-handed, but decisive. Brusque. He wouldn't be the easiest man in the world to work for. But that was all right. People who knew what they wanted were never easy to work for. She was one of them.

She dialled Tony's number. He'd be anxious to know what had happened. If Roy Carmack had called her, what

181

had been arranged. He had an answering service in New York as well as Los Angeles. And it was the service that answered now. She left her name. She'd have to tell Tony later.

It was time for the story conference. She grabbed the script and hurried out.

'Here? You're having him to dinner here?' Tony asked incredulously. He looked around the luxurious room as if the deep beige carpet were in tatters, the upholstered furniture in shreds. 'My God, Sarah, the man's a millionaire. Why do you want to give him a home-cooked meal?'

'Why not? We can talk here as well as in a restaurant.'

'Over the dirty dishes,' Tony said disgustedly. 'What kind of image is that going to project?'

'I'm not worried about the image. If he likes the idea, then he'll like it. He won't care where, or how, it's presented.'

'You're making a big mistake,' Tony said. 'Carmack is accustomed to Hollywood types. Glamour. Pizzazz. You're going to make him think of you as a housewife manqué, for God's sake.' Agitation pushed him out of his chair, set him to pacing back and forth. His eyes flashed at her. 'I can't figure you out, Sarah. Where did that dumb idea come from?'

She watched him, her gaze speculative. This was an odd reaction. He was too concerned. What was really bothering him?

She said aloud, 'Peg's improved a lot in the last couple of weeks. But I don't like leaving her alone too much. And since it's not absolutely necessary . . .'

'I'm afraid you've thrown it away, Sarah.'

'If I have, then I have. But I don't think so.'

'You don't realize how hard I had to work to get him to see you,' Tony answered. 'The man's besieged by people trying to sell him something.'

'I don't doubt it. And that's what I'm hoping to do too. Why should I pretend otherwise?'

182

'You could put your best foot forward.'

'My best foot is my work, Tony. If I'm wrong about this, then I'm wrong. But I don't think it matters.'

'It matters. You'll see.'

When Bonnie arrived, Tony excused himself, although he'd been asked to stay and have dinner with them.

Gilda Jones served the meal. Peg joined the two women. After they'd eaten she went back into her room to read.

Sarah said, 'Okay, Bonnie, what about it?'

'Stan didn't come back.'

'That's not what I meant. Have you got any further along with the story?'

Bonnie got her purse, took out three sheets of paper. 'I've got this much down.' She pushed her small glasses to the end of her nose. 'A synopsis of sorts. I don't know how I did it. But here it is.'

Sarah beamed. 'Good girl.' She read the pages quickly. The producer, a minor character in their previous discussions, had emerged into an interesting woman. Sarah saw elements of herself in the role, but she made no comment about that. 'Very good girl,' she said when she was finished reading. 'You have it all here.'

'I do?' Bonnie asked doubtfully.

'Let's see how it breaks down into scenes.'

They discussed that for the next few hours. Bonnie became more enthusiastic as they talked, made notes, added bits and pieces along the way. By the time she left, she was spinning out dialogue and planning a move to LA.

Later Sarah told Tony, 'We have enough to go on now. I didn't think we could be ready by tomorrow night. But there's plenty to talk about.'

'Good,' he said. But he didn't ask what they had. When Sarah began to tell him about the proposal he told her to save it for her meeting with Carmack.

'But don't you want to be prepared?' she asked.

'Nope. You're going to do all the talking.'

'You know him, Tony.'

'That's why you're going to do all the talking. There's

183

nothing Carmack likes more than a good-looking woman. He'll be so busy watching your legs, he'll agree with everything you say.'

She laughed. 'Nobody invests the kind of money we're talking about on the basis of a pretty pair of legs.'

'You don't believe that, Sarah.'

A faint unpleasant echo . . . the whisper of rumour . . . every woman in the business had heard it . . . she slept her way up . . . with men, with women . . . it didn't matter if it was true or false . . . it was said.

She said slowly, 'You're not joking, are you?'

He didn't answer.

'We give the man my proposal. If he wants to pay for it,' she said firmly. 'That's how I do business.'

There were times to argue. Times to give in. Tony knew this was give-in time. He said, 'Of course. What are we arguing about?' He drew her into his arms. 'How about we stop talking shop for a little while? And pretend, instead, that we're real people.'

'We are real people,' she said, her mouth against his lips. 'That's why we feel the way we do.'

But she was thinking about the proposal now. She would need to do a lot of work before Carmack arrived the following night. Pricing. Dollar signs danced in her head. Support staff. Cast. Sets. Music. Names floated through her mind.

Tony's tongue moved on her lips, slowly pressed into her mouth. Her arms went around him. Later.

The phone rang. Tony swore sleepily.

She raised up on an elbow, staring into the darkness. The illuminated dial of the clock said two-fifteen. The middle of the night. Oh God, Sarah thought, something's happened.

'Don't answer it,' Tony yawned.

But she was already fumbling the receiver to her ear. Tim? Who? What? Oh, God, it had to be bad news. There

184

was nothing but bad news when a call came through at that hour.

'Sarah Morehouse,' she said, her voice shaking, dry, full of terror.

'Sarah? It's me. It's Glory Ann. Can you come?'

'Glory Ann? What's the matter? Where are you?' Fear pricked through her body. She tried to think, to listen at the same time.

'It's awful,' Glory Ann said, sobbing now. 'A terrible mess. You'll hear pretty soon. But that's only the half of it. Can you come?'

'Where are you?' Sarah asked again.

'Washington, Sarah. I told you. That's where I was going. Remember, I was so happy?'

'But where?'

'The Fairview. I can't go out. I'm all alone. I don't know what's going to happen. Can you? Would you?'

'As fast as I can get there, Glory Ann. Hang on. I'll be on the way in fifteen minutes. I'll drive down. It'll take me about five hours. Okay? Can you hold on that long? Or shall I charter a plane?'

'I'll be waiting,' Glory Ann whispered.

'Sit tight. I'll be there soon.'

'Hey, Sarah,' Tony was saying in the background. 'Hey! Wait a minute! Where the hell are you going? Plane? Drive? Carmack's going to be coming here in about twelve hours.'

She ignored Tony. Glory Ann was saying, 'You'll come?'

'As fast as I can.' Sarah put down the phone, threw back the covers.

'Sarah, wait, What's going on?'

'Glory Ann's in Washington. Something's happened. I don't know what. But she's in bad trouble, it sounds like.' As she spoke Sarah went to the wardrobe. She pulled out a skirt, a blouse.

'And you're going? Just like that?' he demanded, his mouth thinning beneath his moustache.

'When I've been in trouble she's always come to me, and I haven't had to ask.'

'You must be kidding. What do you think Carmack's going to do if you stand him up?'

'He'll understand when you explain it to him. You can even show him the synopsis. Tell him I'll price it for him later.'

'Sarah, we've got too much to do. We've got to plan the meal, and what you'll wear. You've got to get yourself ready. Most of all, you've got to talk to him. I'm not kidding. I can't sell your proposal for you. Not to him. I know the man. I know what he wants. And it isn't listening to me.'

What the hell was Tony selling? But there was no time to consider that. She said crisply, 'Do the best you can.' She was putting on her blouse, stepping into her skirt. She gave her hair a quick brush. As she started to make up her face she paused. 'Peg! I almost forgot. I can't leave her alone, and it's going to be Gilda's day off tomorrow.'

Tony said nothing. He was up, dressing.

Sarah gave him a quick glance. His face was set, lips white. He wasn't thinking about Peg.

He caught her glance. 'I can't believe you'd throw a chance like this away. You don't know what Carmack's like. One rebuff and he's off you for life.'

'Too bad.'

'And you *do* know Glory Ann. She's hysterical. She screams when she gets a paper cut on her finger. By the time you get there she won't remember why she called you.'

'Maybe. But if she needs me, then she gets me.'

'You're crazy.'

'Okay, I'm crazy.' He wasn't going to offer to stay with Peg, and she wasn't going to ask. She took up the phone. There was one person she could always depend on. In a moment she heard Robin's sleepy voice. She explained. When she put the phone down, Tony was gone.

She would think of that later, she told herself. Not now. Not now. She had things to do now.

186

She took her purse, a suede coat, and went into Peg's room.

The girl was sound asleep. Sarah hated to waken her, but she couldn't go out without telling her. She touched her shoulder. Peg said sleepily, 'Laylie?'

'It's Mama, honey. Laylie'll be back in a few days. Can you wake up? I need to talk to you.'

'What's the matter?' Peg cried, suddenly awake and alarmed.

'It's all right. Don't be scared,' Sarah said soothingly. 'It's okay. I wanted to tell you that I'm going down to Washington now. Robin's on his way over to stay with you. Remember, this is Gilda's day off. He'll be here in a little while.'

Peg gasped. 'Washington? Tim! What's wrong?'

'It's not Tim,' Sarah said quickly. 'It's Glory Ann. I've just talked to her. She's upset, and she asked me to come down. But she's okay, Peg. She truly is. I talked to her myself.'

'Then what's wrong? Can I come too?'

'You're not ready for a trip yet. You'd better stay here with Robin.'

'Is Glory Ann going to be okay?'

'Sure. And I'll call you before you leave for school. But don't go if you feel too tired.'

'Don't worry about me. Give Glory Ann a big kiss.' Peg was yawning now.

Sarah tucked the quilt around her, and left her.

Within moments Robin was at the door. His dark hair was tousled. A shirt tail hung below his windbreaker.

Sarah let him in, grabbed her bag.

He said, 'Be careful driving. Play the radio so you don't fall asleep. Okay?' Their eyes met. Before he could stop himself he gave her a quick hard hug.

'Thanks, Rob,' she said. And: 'I'll call you as soon as I can.'

As she stepped into the elevator she gave a single glance at Tony's apartment. Then, with a shrug, she pressed the button and was on her way.

15

The seven o'clock sun was smog grey, Connecticut Avenue traffic already heavy. Street vendors were busily setting up buckets of daffodils on their pushcarts, and bags and berets and filmy head scarves on their wooden stands.

Sarah pulled her car into the hotel driveway and got out. There was a stack of newspapers at the side of the canopied door. She gave it a quick glance as she went by. Glory Ann stared up at her from the front page of the Washington *Post*. Above her grimacing face an inch-high headline announced, *Hollywood Beauty Injured in Georgetown Brawl*.

Sarah grabbed a paper, flung a dollar bill at the doorman, and hurried inside. In the photograph Glory Ann's golden hair was dishevelled. Her eyes looked wide and terrified, and there was a dark streak of blood on her right temple.

'Ms Champion,' Sarah told the receptionist, who shook her head. 'Not registered.'

'She must be. She's expecting me. Tell her Sarah Morehouse is here.'

'We don't have a Ms Champion,' the small grey-haired woman said irritably. 'I told you. She's not staying here.'

'Glory Ann. The actress.' Sarah thrust the newspaper at the woman. 'This one. Call her. Now.'

'Why didn't you say so?' the woman complained. She spoke into the phone in a whisper, then gave Sarah the room number even more softly.

Sarah spun away, a bellhop hurrying beside her. Still clutching the newspaper, she darted into the elevator. The bellhop hit the express button, then the floor number. He smiled at Sarah.

Within moments the elevator doors slid back.

The entrance to the suite was a few steps to the left. Its door stood ajar. Sarah pushed it open, calling, 'Glory Ann! It's me!'

As she turned to close the door, shutting out the gaping bellhop, she saw Glory Ann, who had been hiding behind it.

A small patch of white covered the actress's temple, but there was a livid bruise on her jaw, another under her left eye. The left side of her face was so swollen it looked as if she had an orange in her mouth. She was unmade-up, hair flying like a witch's web in all directions.

'Sarah! You came! Oh, thank you!' Her voice was shrill and strong at first, and then broke, and finally she burst into tears. Sarah led her into the living room, where she fell into a blue velvet sofa, sobbing.

Sarah held her. 'Tell me. What happened to you, Glory Ann? What's going on?'

'He never said he was married!' Glory Ann wailed.

'Who? What are you talking about?'

'Don't you remember? I told you and Peg that pretty soon you'd see me in the White House. Oh, it was so exciting!'

Sarah sighed. It was impossible to make sense of what Glory Ann was telling her. But she said, 'Don't you think the President is a little old for you?'

'Not him, Sarah! Not now. But soon. I mean after he gets elected.' Glory Ann sat up. 'Oh, damn! Why can't I stop crying? Why am I so upset? It's just so awful.' A new flood of tears ravaged her smooth cheeks. 'And the limousine . . .'

'You have a limo yourself, Glory Ann.'

'But his is a stretch limo. And silver. And it makes you feel like a princess in a tower.'

'Who is the man the limo belongs to?'

'Kenneth Burton. You know. The senator.'

Sarah knew the name. Kenneth Burton wasn't just a senator. He was the leading contender for his party's nomination to the presidency. He was also the contender most likely to win the next election. Sarah had known that he was married. But Sarah read the newspapers, watched the news on television. Glory Ann did neither.

Now Glory Ann said, 'That's why we had to keep it a secret. Because he's going to be the next president. Afterwards it wouldn't matter if he went around with an actress. But first he had to get elected.'

'I see,' Sarah said.

'So I suggested that I register as Ms Stinkowitz, but he didn't like the idea. I got dressed in my bag lady outfit, and he refused to recognize me. So we never did anything. The other time I was here, we just stayed in the hotel. And drank champagne. And a few times we drove around, looking at the sights, from the limo windows. That *was* exciting.'

'And . . . ?'

'But this time I wasn't having any more of that, thanks.' Glory Ann straightened up. Her wide eyes, bloodshot and still glistening with tears, fixed on Sarah's face. 'After all, I have my own standards. My own feelings. If I wasn't good enough for the people who were going to vote for Ken, then . . . well, then . . . So anyway, I insisted we go out. Just for dinner. And I wasn't trying to look like an actress. I was just being me.' She added hastily, 'Not Ms Stinkowitz. Just me, I mean.'

'And the rest is history,' Sarah said. But she sensed that there was more. There had to be.

'The rest is in the Washington *Post*. Or some of it is. Not all. Because they don't know all. But some.' Glory Ann took a deep breath. 'I just couldn't believe it was happening. I was eating a tuna roll, dripping soy sauce on my blouse, and then, all of a sudden, this woman was there, leaning over the sushi. Shouting. Yes, she was shouting so loud it sounded like thunder to me.

' "You Hollywood hussy! You stay away from my husband! Maybe you can get away with that stuff in California where you belong. But you can't get away with it here. Not in Washington" '

Glory Ann's eyes once again filled with tears. 'Imagine

it, Sarah! Me, and Ken sitting next to me. And that woman . . .'

Sarah did imagine it as Glory Ann continued. The woman was small, with light sandy hair cut short and close to her head. A small straight fringe hung over her pale blue lashless eyes and pale unshaped brows. Her face was narrow, dead white except for a red slash of a mouth that made her look like a vampire caught in mid-meal. She picked up Ken's drink and threw it at Glory Ann. Scotch and blood dripped down Glory Ann's cheeks. The man with her was a detective. He kept saying, 'Mrs Burton, you promised me . . .' And, 'Mrs Burton, please . . .' His deep slow Southern voice was like a Greek chorus to the wife's continuing shrieks.

'And I couldn't believe it!' Glory Ann wailed. 'I mean, in the corn belt they wear blue jeans with high heels. I ought to know. I've played the type often enough. High heels and blue jeans, and T-shirts so tight that the legend stretches across the breasts and almost meets in the back. And usually they say things like "Hug me hard". And there she was, his corn-belt wife, wearing a black jersey top, with a rose in her cleft. And calling me names!'

'It must have been awful,' Sarah said. But she waited. Something else had happened. She was certain of it.

'It *was* awful. It was probably almost the worst thing that's ever happened to me in my life.' Glory Ann gulped. 'Except for what came afterwards.'

'Yes?' Sarah said. 'And what was that?'

But Glory Ann shivered, gingerly touched her swollen face. After a moment's silence, she said, 'And you know what Ken did?' She paused dramatically, then whispered, 'Nothing.'

'Nothing?'

'It was her, and the White House, I guess. Or me . . . and . . . and just me.'

'I see,' Sarah said. 'The man's a damn fool of course.'

'They've cooked up some story. How I was with some-body else. And she made a terrible mistake. They got it all worked out. I told them, "Sure. Go ahead. I don't care

191

what you say." So they'll make it look good.' She sighed deeply. 'But I've lost Ken.'

Sarah looked at her, then took her hand. 'I understand,' she said gently. 'But that's not what's upset you so much, is it, Glory Ann?'

'No,' Glory Ann wailed. 'It's what I did after. And what happened. Oh, how could I be so dumb? How could I do it? I'm so ashamed of myself. And I know I deserved it. But just the same . . . just the same . . .'

'What happened, Glory Ann?'

The actress gingerly touched her face again. 'You see? You see? Ken's wife didn't do it. Just this little cut here, where the tape is. That's hers. But the rest . . . Oh Sarah, I thought he was going to kill me. And maybe he would have. Maybe . . . if I hadn't had all that money in my purse, and kept talking and talking . . .'

'Glory Ann! Who? What are you talking about?' Sarah cried.

'It was after they all left. Ken. And his wife. And the detective. They left. And I was just sitting there. Finally I got up and left too. And I walked down M Street, feeling just awful. Awful, Sarah. You know what I mean. So I stopped in some place to have a drink. Just one. Maybe two. To make me feel better. And there was this guy . . . We got to talking. It was more than one or two drinks. It was a lot of them. And laughing and talking . . . So I began to feel better. Skunk drunk actually. He suggested we have a couple more. Only some place else. Which we did. And somehow we ended up in a hotel room . . . And he went crazy. Calling me names, hitting me. I really thought he'd kill me. Finally I blacked out. When I came to, he was gone. So was my purse. I sneaked out, walked here, sneaked in. And now look at me! Just look at me! What am I going to do?'

'Glory Ann! You're a very lucky girl.'

'I know. But what am I going to do?'

'You take a long hot bath. I'll go buy some stage make-up. After that I think we should begin to think about getting out of here.'

The phone rang.

Glory Ann whispered, 'What if it's Ken? Or her? What if it's *him?*'

Sarah answered it. Ralph Champion was asking for Glory Ann. Sarah identified herself, went through the 'hi, the how are you, the what the hell is happening to Glory Ann this time?'

After the appropriate responses Sarah passed the phone to Glory Ann, who said, 'Yes?' in a small frightened voice, and then, 'Ralph! Oh my God, Ralph! How wonderful to hear your voice! I never thought, I never dreamed . . . Oh Ralph, yes, yes, yes! I'll be there. Oh, yes, I'll be there all right. And as fast as I can!'

She had breakfast with Glory Ann, and did her best with the make-up she'd found at a nearby shop, and to keep the actress's mind occupied, told her about the new proposal she was working on for Roy Carmack and Tri-National. Glory Ann was enthusiastic, demanding to know who she was considering for the various parts. Sarah explained she hadn't decided about the other roles, but had asked Rita to do the actress. Glory Ann made a face, but agreed that Rita would do a good job, and added that she'd also be so happy with the part that she'd forget to be her usual troublemaking self.

When they had finished eating, Sarah paid Glory Ann's hotel bill, gave her plane fare and travel money, and put her into a cab for the airport.

Sarah then took a room at the hotel and had a two-hour nap. Refreshed, she spoke to Tim on the phone, and then, on an impulse, she stopped by to see her mother.

Katy looked well. She had a new hairstyle, a small neat cap of silver waves. She had a trim figure, too. She admired Sarah's suede coat. She admired it and admired it some more. Then she tried it on, and admired it again. The coat remained behind when Sarah left, having met the 'someone' Katy had mentioned months before.

His name was Bennett Ames. He was a neighbour, a

small dapper man with brilliant blue eyes. 'I'm happy to meet you,' he told Sarah earnestly. 'I've heard a lot about you. All good.'

Sarah liked him, and told Katy so before she started back to New York.

The first thing Robin said when she got home was, 'Are you okay?' The second was, 'What about Glory Ann?'

They were sitting down to eat the meal that he and Peg had prepared when Laylie walked in.

Peg screamed, 'Oh Laylie, I thought I'd never see you again.'

'I haven't been gone that long,' Laylie told her. And to Sarah, 'I heard on the radio about Glory Ann. Is she okay?'

Sarah gave the three a somewhat edited version of what had happened. She left out the part about the man Glory Ann picked up after the incident with the senator's wife. She finished by saying that by now Glory Ann ought to be stepping off the plane and into Ralph's arms.

Then she sent Robin and Peg into the living room, so she could speak to Laylie privately about Laylie's sister, and about Peg.

Her sister, Laylie said, was up on her feet and trying. Which was all Laylie, or anybody else, could ask. Maybe, if only she didn't have any more babies, she'd make it. Laylie had had a long, pretty embarrassing talk with her brother-in-law, and was hoping that would help.

Sarah told Laylie about taking Peg to the doctor, and what had happened since.

'Just when she needed me,' Laylie said. 'That's when I wasn't here. I'll make it up to her somehow.' She reached for her apron. 'Get rid of the temporary, whoever she is. There's not room enough for both of us here.'

Sarah made that call, then went into the living room.

She let herself drop wearily into the sofa. She had spent most of the drive back thinking about Tony. There was a side to him that she didn't know. The same as it had been with Daniel. More, she suspected, than she wanted to admit to herself.

194

Now, something in Robin's face made her say, 'I feel so mixed up. I'm always telling Bonnie that she picks the wrong men. I'm beginning to think I'm the same.'

He leaned towards her, saying gently, 'I know what you mean.' And he was thinking, That's good, Sarah. Doubt Tony Statler. Wonder about him. And maybe you'll begin to notice me.

'There's something . . . I'm not quite sure . . .'

'Intuition?' Robin asked.

'That. And clues too. But . . .' She smiled suddenly. 'You're so easy to talk to, Rob.'

'You can say whatever you want. You know that.'

She nodded, rose. The moment was over. She had things to do.

Almost immediately after Robin left, Tony was at the door.

He was smiling, his teeth gleaming white under his moustache. His dark curly hair was freshly brushed. He looked well-cared for and confident. A man who knew who he was, and where he was going. The first thing he said to her was, 'I set your meeting with Carmack at the Russian Tea Room. Just the right atmosphere. Much better than dinner at home, with the kid in the background.'

Not a word about Glory Ann . . . Not a question about Sarah herself . . . what had happened . . . the long drive down and back alone.

All business, she thought. Concentrated. Direct. As if there had been no frantic call. That was a game she could play too.

'When is the meeting?' she asked.

'Tomorrow, Sarah. At one o'clock sharp.' Tony chuckled. 'I think you did yourself some good, actually. He was impressed that you'd drop everything for Glory Ann.'

'You told him that?'

Tony looked surprised. 'Certainly I told him. What else could I do? The man was entitled to an explanation.'

195

'He'll be more impressed when he finds out that Glory Ann likes the idea for the show.'

Tony's white teeth flashed. 'Be sure and tell him.'

Sarah said nothing. There was unfinished business between Tony and her. It had to be talked about. The air had to be cleared. She kept remembering that there was a Tony she didn't know. That maybe she didn't want to know.

She settled into the sofa. 'I thought you were angry when I left for Washington.'

'I was sure you were making a bad mistake,' he said cheerfully. 'It turns out that I was wrong. Going off to rescue Glory Ann was the best thing you could do.'

'Some things come before other things.'

'Sure. And I didn't agree with you. But never mind. Let's talk about tomorrow. What are you going to wear?'

'Clothes,' she answered. 'I haven't considered which ones yet.'

'You'd better. You know how first impressions are.'

'I'm more interested in the proposal. I'll want to have figures for him.'

'Certainly. But even if you haven't got the numbers together, you can fake it,' he said confidently.

She didn't have to fake it. She was ready, having worked at her desk until midnight, glad of the excuse to send Tony back to his own apartment early.

There had been only one brief interruption, and that had been immediately after Tony left. John had phoned to ask how Peg was doing, then to talk to her. Since she'd been ill, he'd sent two cards, called twice, visited once. Sarah reported her progress, then turned him over to Peg and concentrated on the proposal.

Her figures were rough, but close enough, and based on taping the show, rather than doing it on film first, then transferring it to video tape as was most frequently done with Los Angeles-made shows for television. She preferred video tape, being a TV person, and considering it to be

196

the wave of the future because it had an extraordinary quality of immediacy that nobody could get on film. She would explain all that to Roy Carmack, if he questioned her on it. Meanwhile she factored in studio rates, which covered the production facilities' three cameramen and cameras, six technicians and a technical director, audio and tapes. That came to about $7500 per day, including estimated overtime. Then there was the production staff: the producer and associate, production assistant, writers, all on weekly fees. She included travel and related expenses, tape stock, the post production costs, and finally administration, which covered legal fees, accounting, insurance. Without the principal cast, perhaps to include as many as ten, her estimate for the show was $850,000, and that was cutting it very close.

She and Tony were at the Russian Tea Room at five minutes to one. Roy Carmack hadn't arrived yet.

She ordered a pot of tea. Tony had a martini, muttering, 'I hope he doesn't pull the same no-show as last time.' He'd had two more drinks by the time Carmack arrived.

He turned out to be a big man, heavy in the shoulders and arms, with a round red face. He moved slowly on spindly legs, leaning on ebony crutches that braced him at the elbows.

Tony rose to make the introductions and help him into his chair.

Carmack acknowledged neither the help nor the introduction. Seated, he leaned his chin on a ham-sized fist and sat staring at Sarah, breathing hard. When the waiter appeared he spoke for the first time, ordering two bottles of Perrier. Then he said to Sarah, 'Tell me about yourself.'

Tony said, 'Sarah is the producer of *Oakview Valley* on National Television Network. It's known for being the most innovative soap in the business, and has been consistently receiving the highest or second-highest Nielsen for all daytime series. Her reputation in the industry speaks for itself. As I explained to you . . .'

'I want her to talk,' Carmack said without turning to look at Tony.

She said, smiling, 'Let me tell you about my idea.' She drew the synopsis, expanded now to six pages, from her briefcase.

He accepted it, then dropped it on the table. 'We can discuss that later. First tell me about you. Are you married? Divorced? Do you have a family? Where did you go to school?' Carmack smiled slightly, 'In short, let me have an oral résumé. But of your personal life. We'll get to your professional life eventually.'

The rich eccentric, she thought. A spoiled brat. She said, still smiling, 'My personal life isn't relevant, Mr Carmack.'

Under his dark moustache, Tony's mouth compressed. He nudged her ankle beneath the table.

Carmack said coldly, 'Obviously I must think it is relevant. Otherwise I wouldn't be asking.'

'We can discuss our pasts another time,' she told him evenly.

'The past,' he said, ' is what comes before the present. It's the foundation. What do you have to hide?'

'We seem to be talking at cross purposes, Mr Carmack.'

'I don't know what you mean by that. I'm asking you a question, and you're stalling instead of answering it.' Now he smiled faintly. 'I have about ten million dollars at my disposal. Doesn't that entitle me to ask whatever I want to? As long as I think I have good reasons for wanting to know what I want to know?'

'Of course,' Tony said soothingly. 'What Sarah means . . .'

Carmack waved a big hand. 'Please. Let her talk for herself. She doesn't need a translator, I hope. If she does, then she's not going to be any use to me.'

Tony sank back. Elbows braced on the table. His eyes were shining. Maybe from the martinis, she thought. Maybe from all those millions.

She said to Carmack, 'Your money entitles you to ask me about my credentials. And I'll be happy to give them to you.' Quickly, concisely, she gave him a list of her jobs, with whom and when, and what she had done. She

198

described her responsibilities at the network, mentioned the various productions with which she had been associated.

Carmack listened, nodding slowly. Occasionally he sipped the Perrier.

She ended, 'I guess that's about it.' She felt talked out, tired, dispirited even. Put into words, organized, all the effort of the nearly twenty years before didn't sound like very much. No résumé could convey the power and passion that had kept her going.

He seemed to be considering what she had told him. Considering it, but not reacting. Finally he asked, 'Where were you born?'

'Washington, DC.'

'Is that a fact? I never met anybody actually born in Washington before. Was your father in government?'

'No. He wasn't.' She went on, dry now, 'There are quite a few people in Washington who aren't.'

'What did your father do?'

She smiled tightly. 'We're back to irrelevancies, Mr Carmack.' Her father had worked his guts out, and never had anything to show for it. But that was none of Carmack's business.

He said tonelessly, 'You shouldn't be ashamed of your family. My father was a tailor. A not very good tailor at that. In Toronto. We lived upstairs. Over the shop. You could always smell fabric. Dust. Machine oil. Steam. I hated it. I got out. That's what I want. People who want to get out.'

She said nothing.

He sighed. 'Never mind then. We'll get back to that another time. Suppose you tell me what you want from me.'

'It's not a question of what I want from you. It's what I can do for you. Do for you, Mr Carmack.'

He laughed. 'Okay. I'll settle for that. I like it. What you can do for me. So tell me. And tell me, also, what it's going to cost.'

She leaned forward. 'Statler Productions will do one

199

show for you, or four, or as many as you like. I'll budget each one separately, and you'll be free to pick any of the proposals you like, or turn down those that don't seem right for you. As underwriter, you can decide how you want to handle the use of Tri-National's name. I can do commercials for you. Or I can flash the name as a credit.'

He cut in. 'Statler Productions?'

'Tony's company. I'll be working for him.'

Carmack turned in his chair. He looked long and hard at Tony. Then: 'What do you do?'

'I run the business end,' Tony said. 'You should understand about that.'

Carmack grunted. He swung back to Sarah. 'Okay. What's this show about that you've got written up here?'

Once again she handed him the six-page synopsis. 'This will give you the idea. The story line. My writer is working on the scenes now.'

'I don't want to read it,' he said. 'Describe it to me in your own words.'

She went through the story quickly. The actress who loves a director she thinks is gay. Her fear of AIDS, and how it dominates and finally changes her life.

In words, sketches, bits of improvised dialogue, Sarah showed him what she planned to do. All the time she spoke, she watched his face for clues to what he was feeling. But it was impossible to read his expression. The dimpled chins didn't move. The pale brown brows remained fixed. His eyes remained on her.

Finally she stopped, said, 'That's about it.'

'And the cost?' he asked.

'It breaks down this way.' She began to show him the figures, the estimates from the night before.

He said, 'It's all there, isn't it? Then I can go over that later. What's your total?'

'About $850,000. Plus additional actors' fees. That depends on whom we cast. Probably something like another $600,000. It's a bargain. This would be quality advertising, coming off a quality show.'

'Yes,' he said.

She went on to tell him that these numbers were based on video taping, and why she preferred it over filming.

He shrugged that away. 'It's your decision. All such matters would be in your hands,' he said. 'Now let's order. I hate to talk business when I have a meal in front of me.'

The waiter came. Carmack chose dishes for the three of them, ignoring Tony's, 'What did I tell you? Isn't she great?'

Beet borscht, with sour cream and boiled potatoes, garnished with spring onions. Cold salmon with sliced tomatoes. More Perrier all around.

He ate silently, his eyes fixed on his plate. When he was finished he got the bill from the waiter. As soon as he had signed it, he pushed himself to his feet. 'I'll let you know. Meanwhile, come to my hotel for dinner tonight.'

He was looking at Sarah, speaking only to her.

She answered, 'I'm sorry, Mr Carmack. I can't.'

Once again Tony kicked her.

She went on, 'I'm busy this evening.' She thought she heard Tony mutter something about a damned kid.

Carmack jerked a thumb at him. 'With him?'

'That doesn't concern you,' she said pleasantly.

'You have an overdeveloped sense of privacy, young lady. What about tomorrow night?'

She shook her head.

'You don't want to be alone with me, do you?' He grinned. 'All right. I'll accept that for the moment. As soon as I decide I'll let you know where we stand.'

'Yes. Thank you.' But now she was being only minimally polite. She scarcely cared where they stood. The possibility of being funded by Roy Carmack, by Tri-National, was much less appealing than it had been before she met him. He would be a hard man to work with, to work for. She wondered what he thought he was buying. And then she wondered what Tony thought he was selling.

They separated on the sidewalk. Carmack climbed into

one cab, she and Tony into another, for the ride to the NTN building.

As soon as they were alone he said, 'That wasn't the performance I expected of you.'

'It wasn't, was it?'

'Don't you like the man? What is it? What happened?'

'I didn't know anything had happened,' she answered, looking at her watch. It was two-thirty. She had a meeting at three. Hy Berge. Lyman Ogloe. Hy had problems to discuss. Lyman, who had lately reverted to his usual smiling self, probably because he knew of Sarah's lunch with Rita, wanted to help. She wanted to think about that meeting, to forget Roy Carmack.

But Tony was insistent. 'You did just about everything you could do to turn the man off. And why, for God's sake, would you refuse to have dinner with him?'

'Did you notice that the invitation did not include you?' she asked, slanting a green glance at him. Of course he had noticed. It wouldn't have been possible not to.

Tony was saying, 'I don't give a damn if he includes me or not! What's that got to do with anything? As long as you get the funding we need.' Jesus! he thought. What was wrong with her? Was she going to turn out to be another Eve? Another woman who couldn't keep her eye on the main thing?

'I don't intend to find myself racing around the hotel while he chases after me on his ebony sticks.'

Tony laughed. 'Why not? You can handle him.'

She knew that she could. Carmack or any other man. It was a matter of her own conviction. How sure she was of herself. The woman who traded sex for favours assumed that she had nothing but sex to offer.

'You're really anxious for this, aren't you, Tony?'

'Of course. Aren't you?'

'I'm not so sure.' But she didn't go on to voice the reason for her doubts. She was not that certain of the reasons for them herself. And she was in a hurry. Hy and Lyman would be waiting. The cab pulled up in front of the NTN building. She reached for the door.

But Tony held her arm. 'We talked it through. What goes?'

'Later,' she said. 'I've got to run.' And jumped out.

Only moments after she arrived home Tony was at the door.

She let him in. He wanted her to forget about having dinner at home, to go out with him. To talk. Alone. Just the two of them. There was a lot to consider, he said. They had to make plans. He kept saying that Roy Carmack always made up his mind quickly. It wouldn't be long. She'd be surprised at how soon they'd know what his decision was.

But she wanted to stay home. Laylie had prepared dinner. Peg was up and about. Everything was getting back to normal.

She switched on the TV set.

Tony paced the floor. 'You'll hear in a day or two. I'll fly back to LA. Set up an office first thing, of course. You can move later, stay at the bungalow. We'll need to get a crew together. But that'll be easy. There's a lot of people out there already.'

Sarah found herself thinking about Peg at the bungalow. And what about Tim? And was there going to be an argument with John when he heard that she'd be taking the children away from New York?

She stopped herself. Why was she thinking of that when the deal hadn't been closed? She was as bad as Tony.

She said aloud, 'Let's not make plans yet. We don't know what Carmack's going to do.'

'But he'll want to get started right away. He's the kind who wants to see results yesterday.'

'I'm sure of it. But let's wait until we've signed with him.'

'It's going to work, Sarah. I know it. I feel it. *We're* going to work.' He hugged her, pulled her to her feet, danced her around. Over his shoulder she saw Tom Brokaw's face on the TV screen. He said, 'This is the beginning. There's no end to what we'll do. We're going to be the best team the industry's ever seen. Nobody can stop us. You and me. Statler Productions.'

He remained on that high of excitement and expectation for the following week.

That was when Roy Carmack called. He said, 'Miss Morehouse, I want you to be in my suite at the Pierre at five o'clock. It's urgent. What I have to say I want to say face to face. Will you be there?'

'How long will the meeting take?' she asked.

'Less than an hour, I'd suppose.'

She hesitated. He hadn't mentioned Tony. How come? What did that mean? She said, 'I'll be there.' And added, 'I'll have Tony meet me.'

Silence. A faraway bell rang. The wires hummed. Carmack said, 'You force me to say it now. No. I don't want Tony Statler to attend our meeting.' Then, after a moment, 'But if you don't want to be alone with me, bring your secretary.'

'I'll see you at five,' she said coolly.

Roy Carmack didn't rise when a servant ushered her into his suite. 'Excuse me,' he said. 'I'm having a bad day.' He pointed at his two ebony crutches.

Sarah took a chair near the sofa on which he half lay, half sat.

The servant went out.

Carmack sat looking at her in silence for a few moments. Then, wiping his face with a white handkerchief, he said, 'Let's make this short and sweet. You're wondering why I said I want to see you alone. That's because I want to give my business to you. I like your way of handling yourself, and I like your proposal. It's going to be timely, dramatic and informative.'

'Good,' she said crisply. 'I'm glad you're satisfied. But what's this about Tony? We work together.'

'And that's your mistake, young lady.'

204

She squared her shoulders, tipped her head back. 'I am able to choose my own partners.'

'And so am I. I chose not to do business with him. The man's finished. He lost Stell-Stat once, and then he lost it again. He hasn't done a damn thing in years. Maybe he never has. Maybe it was Eve Stellwagen who built up Stell-Stat, and he hung on to her coat tails. Anyhow, he has about two thousand dollars in the bank. He owes money on his car. He owes back rent for the New York sublet, and the bungalow in Los Angeles. He even owes for the clothes on his back. Just what can Statler Productions do for you that you can't do for yourself?'

She said nothing. She had never asked Tony about his resources. Of course she knew that he'd been hard hit when Stell-Stat let him go. But she'd assumed that he must have something. On the other hand, he'd never lied to her. He'd made it clear that he was anxious for the Carmack deal to go through. Still it shocked her to hear how bad things were for him. How had he planned to open an office for Statler Productions? How could he have hired a crew? Had he planned to rely on what Carmack agreed to as an advance?

Now Carmack was leafing through the pages of her proposal. 'Look,' he said. 'You've got yourself down here for a fee of seventy-five thousand for the show. Right?' At her nod, he went on. 'And you show twenty per cent of the show's cost for overheads. Right?' Again she nodded. 'That would be Statler's cut. We could add it to your fee.' He grinned at her, his pink round cheeks dimpling. 'I'll set you up. You do the shows. You. Alone. Morehouse Productions.'

It was tempting. She could very nearly taste how sweet an opportunity it was. But it was sour at the same time, and she could certainly taste the sourness. She could accept Carmack's offer, and forget Tony. Why not? He hadn't been completely honest with her. He'd been too anxious for the deal to let her know everything. She wondered briefly if, were the situation reversed, he would have hesitated for a moment. Still, telling herself that she was being foolish, she said, 'I'm sorry, Mr Carmack. I thought you understood. The deal includes Tony Statler.'

It was hard to explain it to Tony without telling him straight out that Roy Carmack had decided he didn't need Statler Productions.

She said, 'We couldn't come to an agreement. I told you before. He's a very difficult man. It's just one of those things.'

Tony was white-faced, sweating. He'd worked so hard. He'd been so sure. What had happened? What had Sarah done to spoil it? He said, 'You must have thrown it away.'

'Maybe I did. In a way. But I couldn't help it.'

'You couldn't help it,' he mocked her.

'Tony, you don't understand. The man's impossible.'

He slammed his glass on the table. 'What aren't you telling me?'

She hadn't told him what Carmack had said about him. She did now, reporting everything that Carmack had told her.

Tony listened, his face expressionless. Finally, when she had finished, he said, 'If you'd handled it right we would have been okay. He wanted you, didn't he? That's all that counted.'

'You mean I should have accepted those terms?'

'Of course. And this isn't set in concrete either. We can still save it. All you have to do is call him. Tell him you've changed your mind.'

She wondered if Tony really meant it. Or was it just a gesture? Even if I'm out of the deal, you take it. It's what you've always wanted. Was that what he was saying? Something inside of her couldn't accept that.

'No, Tony. I won't call him. I haven't changed my mind.'

'But you've got to.'

'I don't want his money.'

'But I do, damn it! I have to have it. Just do this for me. Take his terms. What difference does it make? Take

206

his terms. Then you can hire me. Independently. Call it a part of administration. You can take me on as an employee.'

'Statler Productions is your firm,' she said. What he was saying was feasible. There was nothing Roy Carmack could do to stop her from hiring Tony once she and Tri-National had signed an agreement. But she didn't like the idea. In the end it would taint her relationship with Tony, as well as her business connection with Carmack.

Tony was saying, 'Without his money there is no Statler Productions, Sarah.'

'We'll find another sponsor,' she told him.

Tony got up, stalked out of the apartment.

The next day Harry Stowe told her that Mr Statler had packed up unexpectedly and taken off for the Coast.

It happened that she had a very busy schedule. She had no time to think about anything but work until after six o'clock. Then, suddenly, with the phones silent, the offices empty, it hit her.

Tony was gone. It was over. She didn't want to think about him, to wonder why, once again, she had chosen the wrong man. She called home, told Laylie she wouldn't be there for dinner, and would probably be home late.

Then, taking her bag and briefcase, she left the NTN building. She walked for hours through the April evening. Dusk fell. Darkness came. She found herself before a small café. She was tired now. It was time to rest. She went inside, sat at the bar.

It was a place she had been before, but she didn't realize that then. When the bartender asked her what she wanted, she looked at him blankly. White wine? Scotch? No. Neither of those. She wanted something that would work, and quickly. Something that would stop her circling thoughts. She asked for a martini, a double, on the rocks.

The glass was set before her. She raised it, took a small sip. The drink was bitter. She felt it burn as she swallowed it. No matter. After the third sip, she decided it was the medicine she needed.

A man sat next to her, offered her a cigarette. She shook

her head, looked away from him when he tried to engage her in conversation.

She finished her drink, asked for another. Now she felt nothing. The bitter medicine had done its job. She took a big swallow. Soon she'd go home. But not yet. Not quite yet.

Suddenly Robin said, 'Sarah, what are you doing here?'

She turned, smiling. 'Rob? How did you find me?'

'Find you?' He took in her shining eyes, faintly dishevelled look. 'I didn't find you. I often come here for a drink. Don't you remember? My apartment is in the middle of the block.'

'It is?' she said, laughing delightedly. 'Isn't that funny? I was out walking, and ended up almost right next door to you, and I didn't even realize it.'

'I'm glad you did,' he told her. And: 'How many of those things have you had?'

She looked at her empty glass. 'This is the second, I think.'

'That should do you, Sarah.'

'Oh no,' she said earnestly. 'I would like another.'

'Okay. One more.'

When the bartender brought her drink, she sipped it slowly. She kept looking at Rob, smiling. 'It's such a coincidence. I can hardly believe it.'

'You know what?' Rob said. 'You are loaded.'

'No, I'm not. I'm just fine.' She nodded solemnly. 'I have to admit that I don't much care for the taste of martinis. But they work. They do what they're supposed to do.'

'And what's that?' He steadied her as she wavered on the stool.

'They make you feel better.'

'Why do you need to feel better? What's wrong?'

She looked into her half-empty glass. What's wrong? It was a good question. But she wasn't going to answer it. She wouldn't know where to begin, or how. Suddenly her lips felt numb. There was a tightness in her cheeks. She

208

whispered, 'Something's wrong with me, Rob. I feel very peculiar. I think I'd better go home.'

'I think so too.' He paid for the drinks she had had, helped her down from the stool.

She shivered in the cool air of the street, looking vaguely around for a cab.

'We'll get you some coffee first,' Rob said. He put his arm around her.

It felt good to lean against him as he led her down the block, then into his apartment house. She hardly noticed the short elevator ride to the third floor.

Inside, he settled her in a corner of the sofa. 'I'll only be a minute.'

She murmured, 'Sorry to be so much trouble,' and leaned back, closing her eyes.

It seemed only seconds before he was back. But by then she had stretched out. When he offered her the steaming coffee, she shook her head, 'No, no. I need to rest,' she said drowsily.

He slid a pillow under her head, loosened her skirt, and gently undid her blouse buttons, trying to make her comfortable. She made soft murmurings as she snuggled into the cushions. He sat on the floor beside her. Suddenly there were tears on her cheeks.

'Sarah! What's the matter?' When she shook her head, he moved to the sofa. He took her into his arms and held her. Gently he kissed the tears from her cheeks. For a long while he held her, not knowing if she were awake or asleep. Then her hands came up to cup his face, and her fingertips stroked his lips, and their two bodies fitted together on the narrow space of the sofa. They lay that way, entwined, for a long while, and then she raised her mouth to his and he kissed her until they were both without breath. Some time in the moments of that kiss, their bodies shifted, and gently, slowly, lingering over each caress, Rob leading her, Sarah leading Rob, they began to make love, not as if it were their first time together, but as if they had always known and loved each other . . .

At moments after midnight, Sarah suddenly awakened in Rob's arms. He still slept, his lashes dark against his cheeks, his arms tightly enfolding her.

The evening, their meeting in the bar, the walk here, her collapse on the sofa, all came back to her in a quick overwhelming rush. Oh God! What had she done?

But she knew. She remembered. Rob's mouth on hers. His body on hers. It had been so good. They had been so right together.

But no, no. She mustn't remember it. If only she hadn't stopped in that particular bar, had those martinis. If only . . .

Cautiously she slid away from Rob, got up. It hadn't meant anything. He was too young for her. Too many martinis, a bad mood, and Rob's kindness . . .

As she smoothed her hair, hesitating, he slowly opened his eyes. 'Sarah?'

'Rob, dear,' she said. 'I feel such a fool. What luck that you rescued me and brought me here before I blacked out.'

He swung his feet to the floor, rose. 'Blacked out?'

'Weren't you saying something about coffee when I passed out on you?'

He took a deep careful breath, his face expressionless. He remembered every curve of her, every kiss, the way she rose up to him in passion, the way her eyes gleamed in the dark. And it meant nothing to her. He said, 'Coffee coming right up, Sarah.'

'Oh, Rob, you're so good to me,' she said. 'I do appreciate it.'

'Sure.' He brought her a cup of hot coffee.

She drank it as quickly as she could, and then he got a cab and took her home.

She thanked him again, gave him a quick goodnight peck on the cheek, and hurried inside.

Okay, he thought wearily as he took the elevator down. If that's how she wanted to play it, then that was how it would be. She would pretend that nothing had happened. Then so would he.

16

May was quiet. Peg had been given a clean bill of health from the doctor and had gone back to her usual active life. Laylie had got the apartment under control, so that it seemed she had never been away.

At NTN the Nielsens were holding. *Oakview Valley* maintained its number three position for three weeks in a row. Then moved to number two. The scripts fell together smoothly. The rehearsals went without more than the accustomed number of glitches. Some time soon, Sarah told herself, all hell had to break loose. It was in the nature of the business for a crisis to brew when it was least expected. So Sarah expected trouble. It didn't come. Even her personal life was calm.

She visited Tim in Washington once, spoke to Dr Dunham weekly. All went well in that quarter too, although John continued to insist that Tim leave Beltraney at the end of the term in June.

Sarah had heard nothing from Tony Statler. In the beginning she had imagined long conversations with him in which he explained why he had gone away without a word. She pictured accidental meetings when, suddenly, he would walk across a room towards her, his dark eyes sparkling. But soon she allowed herself to face the truth. They had had something good for a while. But it was a Daniel Clermont situation all over again. Perhaps she should have seen that from the start.

Carmack had disappeared from the world she moved in. Andrew Reynolds had had a brief mention of him. *Tri-National's CEO, disappointed by his NYC failure, is sulking in Toronto and considering new moves*. It sounded as if the item had come directly from Carmack, but she couldn't imagine him bothering.

Now, in the middle of a meeting, she looked around.

Bonnie was radiant. Obviously she had found a new man. Sarah wondered where. It seemed to her harder and harder to meet men she considered suitable, although she met plenty that she didn't.

She was relieved to be in that situation at the moment. She had Peg and Tim. And the crew. Hy was his usual self. Hart Carow had continued in his good spirits and performances since Rita's departure, and Rita continued doing commercials at Halloran, Fox and Deerling, impatiently awaiting a call from Sarah about the night-time movie script. Ursula, the new girl brought in, was a joy to work with so far. The cameramen were, as always, preoccupied with technology, caring for nothing beyond the knobs and dials they handled. Max Hollis, back again as set dresser, was always polite, but no longer as friendly as he'd once been.

And Robin . . . as she looked at him, their eyes met. A sudden blush spread to his dark wavy hair. She looked away quickly, remembering how their bodies had fitted together on the narrow sofa in his apartment, remembering the warmth of his lips.

He lingered after the meeting had broken up. 'Sarah?'

'Yes.' Now she was crisp, in a hurry to get back to her office.

'We haven't had a chance to talk for a while. How about having dinner with me tonight?'

'Not tonight, Rob. I can't.' She didn't give an excuse because she couldn't think of one. 'But I'll tell you,' she added quickly, seeing his crestfallen expression, 'let's make it tomorrow. Come over for pizza.'

Later, at her desk, she checked her calendar. She couldn't see Robin the next night after all. She was going to the opera then. She found Robin, told him, suggesting Friday instead.

'Have dinner out with me,' he said. It would be more like a date that way, he thought. It might lead her to think of *him* as a date. A man she was out with.

'I'd rather stay home. If you don't mind. I've had so many nights out.'

It had all been business one way or another. That's what her social life had become. To the opera on Thursday. But with Mac Johnson, public relations man for the City Ballet. Monday it had been dinner with a Georgiana executive and his wife. Tonight she wanted to stay at home with Peg.

Robin was looking at her quizzically, waiting.

'What, Rob?'

'I'm just wondering if you ever see me, that's all.'

'See you? Of course I do. What are you talking about?'

Give her time. That's what he'd always told himself. Don't push her. Let it be natural. But now he couldn't stop himself. 'I'm talking about seeing me,' he said evenly. 'I mean, realizing that I'm a person. Not just your production manager. A person. A man.'

'Robin! What's the matter?'

'Nothing.' He grinned suddenly. 'The trouble is, if we stay at home, as you call it, then it's like family.'

' "As I call it." What do you mean by that?' she demanded. 'What else should I call it?'

'When you say stay at home, you mean stay at *your* home. Not mine. I'm not staying home. You are.'

'Okay,' she said. 'And . . . ?'

'And all the connotations of comfort and satisfaction refer only to you.'

'Oh, I see,' she said slowly. 'Okay then, I'll come to your place, and we'll stay at home there. So you won't think I'm a selfish bitch.'

'I don't care if you are a selfish bitch. I'd just like to take you out to dinner.'

'Fine.' She smiled at him. 'You pick the restaurant.'

'I will.'

She went into her office, settled down. But in a moment she raised her head from the papers she was studying. She looked at the door, almost expecting to see Robin standing there.

It had been a peculiar conversation. She tried to remember how it had gone, but couldn't quite bring it back. There had been nuances, she was certain, that she

213

hadn't caught. Something in his smile, in the tilt of his head, in the way his blue eyes had met hers. Perhaps he too had been remembering how they had seemed to belong together . . . the sweetness of their lovemaking. Perhaps he knew that she hadn't blacked out, and only allowed her to pretend that because he understood that she had no other way to handle it.

She moved restlessly in her chair, recalling now that she'd particularly noticed that there were hardly any lines in his throat. Laugh lines near his eyes, yes. But none, nothing marking his throat. She recalled too noticing that his voice was unusually deep. A nice boy, Robin; and talented too. As well as attractive. Oh yes, he was very attractive indeed. Blue eyes, steady and serious. A trim build. Wide shoulders. Narrow hips. A flat behind. And very nice hands, muscular but long fingered.

Hey, Sarah . . . come on. Remember the guy's only twenty-five or so. She wasn't sure. But no, that couldn't be right. He'd been around twenty-five when she first hired him out of WZBT in Boston. He'd been one of three production assistants there, and hungry to get to New York to work for NTN. Daniel had introduced them. Robin had come to the station fresh out of the communications division at Syracuse. Three years ago. Then he would be twenty-eight or twenty-nine. Still a child. No, that was ridiculous. Not a child. But too young for Sarah. Not that such combinations were all that rare any more. She knew several women in the industry who had young lovers, even young husbands. But she didn't see herself as one of them. No. It wasn't for her.

She tried to work. She took several phone calls. She wrote a few letters. But it kept bothering her. How old was Rob? Finally she pulled his personnel file. Twenty-eight.

When she arrived home she wished that she'd taken Robin up on his offer.

Peg sat expectantly on the sofa. Carla and John were there. They exchanged greetings and then Peg said, 'If it's okay with you, I'm going to have dinner with Dad and Carla tonight.'

Carla said, 'We were in town. I ought to have phoned first, but it was a spur of the moment thing.'

John said, 'I was sure you wouldn't mind.'

Sarah wanted very much to say she did mind. She wanted to say she was entitled to some notice before they made plans for Peg. It was convenient enough, Sarah supposed, tonight. But it mightn't be some other time. Instead, she smiled. 'Of course it's all right. If that's what Peg wants. But I hope you won't keep her out too late. She still needs a lot of rest.'

Carla promised to keep an eye on the time. They rose to go.

But then John said, 'I spoke to Tim yesterday. He sounded fine.'

'I know,' Sarah told him. 'I've also spoken to him.'

When she'd talked with him the day before, Tim had been excited about the soccer game the school had won. 'I got hit on the head. Twice.'

'Oh, Tim . . .'

'It's *all right*, Mom. I didn't get hurt. And I got two goals. And . . .' He went on, as if he'd almost forgotten, 'Dad called this evening.' Tim was always careful to tell her whenever he'd talked to John. He had to be sure she knew he never hid a contact with his father from her. She had to be sure that Tim knew it was okay. He remained his father's son. No matter what his father was to her now.

'It's worked out well,' Carla said. 'Apparently.'

'I think so.'

And John, feeling the usual heat rise in him, remembering the thousand times he'd seen just that same expression on Sarah's face, had to say, 'Of course, there are hidden scars . . .'

'I doubt it,' Sarah said coldly.

Peg, galvanized to action by the increasing chill, hurried to kiss Sarah goodbye and then rushed John and Carla out.

Sarah turned on the TV set. MacNeil/Lehrer. She watched until the programme ended. A good one, as always. Then she wandered into the kitchen. A pot simmered on the stove. The table near the window was set for one.

Laylie opened her door, looked into the room. 'Ms Morehouse, when do you want to eat?'

'Later. Maybe in an hour or so.'

'Fine.' The door closed.

Sarah went back to the living room. There was plenty of work to do. The proposal . . . the story line should be completed. Bonnie ought to be getting on to the scenes soon. There was casting to think about. But what for? Stell-Stat was out as long as Jim Carstairs was there. She knew how he'd manage anything that came in about her. 'Oh, yes, I know her. But there's something . . . I don't know what it is. She doesn't have the right touch with crew. We worked together once. But she turns people off. Very difficult.' And then, with a shrug, he'd cast her proposal, and her, aside.

As for Carmack . . . well, he wasn't the kind of man who looked back. Or changed his mind. If he'd wanted her badly enough he'd have taken Tony with her. As it was . . . as it was she'd probably been foolish. Tony had been right. She should have gone ahead with Carmack, Tony or no. Why hadn't she? Why had she thrown away the best chance she had?

She couldn't remember now. It had been stupid. The job with NTN was making her lazy and blind and self-satisfied. Was she going to do soaps all her life? The answer to that was no. If she hadn't got to where she wanted to go in the next couple of years, then she'd be stuck nowhere, with nothing to look forward to. After forty, you didn't go up. You went down. Everybody in the business knew that. After forty, you were as good as dead.

But there were other independents. What about Lorimar? Or Tandem? What about the others? She shouldn't give up on the proposal. It was too good. It would make a great television movie.

She went into the bedroom, but instead of settling at her desk she turned on the TV set on the dresser. *Hill Street Blues*. She watched for a moment. Good production values as always. She went to the mirror, leaned close. Intent green eyes. A few lines, but not many, not deep. Yet. A faint fullness under the chin? No. No way. Again, not yet. But she didn't look twenty-five any more.

Immediately she thought of Robin. A child.

She wandered into the living room. Sherlock Holmes expounding. She reached for the channel changer. But the phone rang. Laylie would answer it. She waited.

Laylie came to the door. 'It's for you. Somebody named Radnor.'

Radnor? She didn't recognize the name. 'Say I'm out. Take the message if there is one.'

Laylie nodded, disappeared.

Soon after the phone rang again. Laylie returned. 'It's Mr Berge.'

'I'll call him first thing in the morning.'

Once again Laylie disappeared.

If Glory Ann were in New York that was who Sarah would want to be with. Glory Ann would cure whatever it was that ailed her.

Sarah went back to her bedroom, sat at her desk. The proposal was centred on it, its blue folder barely marked by handling. It was so good. So good that whenever she thought about the story she got gooseflesh on her arms and down her back. She knew what that meant. Damn Roy Carmack. And damn Tony Statler.

Gone without a goodbye, a thank you, an apology. Just gone. And somehow, although she'd tried to fool herself, she had expected nothing different . . .

Oh, it was good, Glory Ann thought. Good to lie in the poolside chair and watch Ralph from beneath her lowered lashes. Good to look at him, and listen to his voice. She enjoyed it so much she forgot to pay attention.

Ralph stopped, put the script down. 'What do you think?'

'I don't know,' she said. 'What do *you* think?'

An accumulation of scripts had been forwarded to her by her agent. Ralph was slowly going through them.

'Lousy. Like the rest.' He smiled at her. 'And, if not lousy, then not good enough for you.'

His wiry body was brown, hard-looking. His red hair glistened. It seemed impossible that months ago he'd stamped out, saying he was through, couldn't and wouldn't live in a fish bowl any more. It seemed just as impossible that she'd thought she'd like going to the White House with what's his name. She and Ralph belonged together. She was going to make sure they stayed that way. Maybe, if they worked together, and he was as involved just as much as she was . . . maybe then . . .

She rose, spread her arms wide and did a quick cart-wheel. Her breasts sprang from her bikini bra. When she was on her feet again, she re-positioned the bra, saying, 'There's that story Sarah was working on . . . I told you about it, didn't I? I wish I could do that.' She took three quick steps, and suddenly she was Sarah . . . the tilt of her head, the fast confident walk. 'See? And it could be a wonderful show.'

'Then why don't you?' Ralph asked. 'You can do whatever you want, Glory Ann.'

'She's having money trouble. What she needs is funding . . . some company willing to take the chance on a pretty important subject.'

'Funding,' Ralph said thoughtfully. Then: 'Do you really want that part?'

'Oh I do, Ralph. And what I wish is . . . I wish you could get Universal . . .'

'No,' he said. 'Not Universal. Then I wouldn't have control.'

'Control?' she asked innocently. She fixed her eyes on

218

his face and held her breath, waiting. And now . . . now if only he'd take it one step further.

'Call Sarah,' he said. 'Find out if the story is still available. Maybe I can get the backing we need. It would be great working with you. The same project. We'd be together all the time.'

She let her breath out in a jubilant, 'Wow!' and wrapped herself around him. 'Oh Ralph! What a great idea!'

Moments later the telephone rang in Sarah's apartment. There was a longish pause. Then Laylie came towards the bedroom, calling ahead, 'It's Glory Ann.'

Sarah grabbed the receiver. 'Ms Stinkowitz, I presume?'

'Sarah! Hi! I'm sitting here next to the pool. Thinking of you. And suddenly I thought . . . well, why not? Why not? I'll just call and tell you what I'm thinking about.'

'I was thinking of you a little while ago too, believe it or not.'

'You were! Really? You're not just saying it? Because that means something. It really does, Sarah. You just wait and hear what I was wondering.'

'And what's that?'

'That story you were working on. Remember? The one you told me about in Washington?'

'I remember all right. About the actress who's afraid to love . . .' Now there was grimness in Sarah's voice. Tony Statler. Roy Carmack. Her own mistake. It was never far from her mind these days.

'Because of AIDS,' Glory Ann said. 'That's what I was wondering about.'

It was no use trying to hurry Glory Ann. In her own way, in her own good time, she would get to what she was talking about.

'What happened to it anyway?' Glory Ann went on.

'Nothing. That's the trouble.'

'Good,' Glory Ann said. 'Because Ralph . . . the two of us . . . We've been sitting here next to the pool . . .' She

219

paused. 'Come to think of it, Sarah, did I ever tell you that Ralph and I got together again?'

'You didn't. But Andrew Reynolds did.'

'You've seen him? How is he? What's happening in his life?'

'His column, Glory Ann.'

'Oh. I thought maybe you'd been to lunch with him and had gobs of gorgeous New York gossip to tell me.'

'LA gossip is probably much more interesting. But tell me what you were wondering about.'

'Wondering about?' There was a dead silence. Sarah thought, I should have kept her to the point. Now she's forgotten all about it. Whatever it was.

Glory Ann giggled, 'Got it!' Sarah began to suspect that the actress was pulling her leg. Was it possible that Glory Ann's scatterbrain act when she wasn't acting was an act too? Hmm. Like peeling an onion maybe. 'Yup. That's it. We were wondering about a couple of things. Like, have you committed the story to anybody?'

'Not yet.' Sarah didn't explain further. It would only distract Glory Ann to hear about Tony, about Stell-Stat, and then about Roy Carmack.

'And what about casting?'

'Nothing, except Rita Porter as the actress. I told you about that. When the proposal didn't go, I dropped it for a while. I'm going to pick it up now . . .'

Glory Ann didn't let her finish. 'Listen, Sarah, wait. How about the producer? Is that free? Because if it is, I'd love to do it. I keep thinking about that role. Boy, imagine! Me, playing you! I'd be brisk, cool, bossy as hell! Always in control, yes. But volcanic inside! What do you say, Sarah? Will you let me do it?'

'Glory Ann! What do you think? Of course! But I couldn't afford you.'

'Oh, just talk to my agent,' Glory Ann said airily. 'I'm not rigid about price when there's something I really want to do. And I really want to do that producer.'

Sarah said, 'You know how much more saleable the proposal gets if I can offer you in it. Are you sure you . . .'

'That's the thing,' Glory Ann said. 'It's what Ralph and I were talking about. You'd better consider the proposal committed, sold, off the market, whatever you want to call it, as of now.'

'Glory Ann! What are you talking about?'

'Oh Sarah, really! It's not that complicated. Ralph's been reading scripts to me for weeks, and he hates everything he's seen as much as I do, and what I want is, to do your story. And Ralph says, if that's what I want, then he can find somebody to do it. What do you say to that?'

'I say hooray!'

Glory Ann went on, 'Or we might even establish our own production company. Ralph's going to figure out the business part.'

'Okay,' Sarah said.

'So don't do anything until you hear from us.'

'Okay,' Sarah repeated, laughing.

As she put down the phone she thought about Ralph Champion. She knew his work. He'd been with NTN before he went to Universal in LA. Sarah knew she could rely on him just as she could rely on Glory Ann. And Glory Ann . . . she might sound goofy sometimes, and she might have some goofy ideas. But you could trust her. Always. For ever. A promise was a promise to Glory Ann.

If Glory Ann said so, then it was going to happen! Suddenly, unexpectedly, Sarah began to feel wonderful. *It was going to happen*. The AIDS story was going to be her first night-time television show!

Her green eyes glowed. Her mouth spread in a joyful smile. She would send the proposal out by express mail first thing in the morning. That would give Ralph something to work with. And she would get on to Bonnie. They needed the scenes now. Casting: Rita Porter, the actress. Glory Ann Champion, the producer. And for the director . . . never mind. There was time for that. And the crew . . .

Laylie said from the doorway, 'How about your dinner?'

'Not right now, Laylie.'

'I was going to watch *The Colbys*.'

'Go ahead. I'll worry about dinner later.'

'You sure?'

'I'm sure, Laylie.'

As soon as the housekeeper had gone, Sarah reached for the phone. She had to tell someone. Before she knew what she was doing, she tapped out Robin's number. She heard his voice almost immediately. It was as if he had been right at the phone, waiting for it to ring.

But why was she calling him? She'd said she couldn't see him that night. She put down the phone.

It would be embarrassing to explain. And it didn't make sense anyway. He was a child. Twenty-eight years old. Not quite young enough to be her son, it was true. But ten years . . . ten . . . That really wasn't very much of an age difference. Good God, what was the matter with her?

She tried to reach Bonnie, the logical person, after all, to talk to about the story. Bonnie was doing the script. She had a real interest in what happened.

But it was Bonnie's new man who answered. He sounded angry when he said that Bonnie was out, he didn't know where, and didn't know when she was coming back.

Sarah told herself to be braced for trouble soon. Bonnie and the new man weren't getting along well. Bonnie would be a mess, unable to concentrate on dialogue, on suspense, on pacing, on production values. She'd only want to think about the new man and wonder what was wrong with her.

Sarah got up, walked around the room. She went into the kitchen and poured herself a small glass of white wine.

Was it possible that Glory Ann could really pull it off?

Suddenly Sarah found herself at the phone again. That time, when Robin answered, she said, 'Rob, it's Sarah. I'm having second thoughts. I need to talk to you. Can you come over?'

Robin hadn't taken the time to change. He wore blue jeans and a white cotton shirt with the sleeves rolled to the elbow. He listened, frowning, while Sarah recounted her conversation with Glory Ann.

'Of course,' Sarah said, trying to sound dispassionate, although there was elation in her voice, and in her eyes, 'nothing's really definite. I don't know if it's going to happen. Maybe I've jinxed it for ever by talking about it.'

'I don't believe in jinxes,' he said. 'It'll work out.' He didn't seem impressed, nor enthusiastic.

'But you're wondering, aren't you?' Now her own excitement began to ebb. There hadn't been a real commitment. Why had she begun to count on a few ephemeral words? Still . . . Glory Ann . . .

Robin said, 'It might take some time. But I think you'll end up with exactly what you want. And when you do, you'll pack yourself and the kids up, and fly out to the Coast, and that will be the end of that.' There was a heaviness in his voice that reflected the heaviness he felt. His eyes didn't quite meet hers.

'The end of what?' she asked.

'You know, Sarah.'

'Rob, you're not making sense. I know what?'

'I'm making sense. You're just not following me,' he said.

'It would be exactly what I've wanted for years, Rob.'

'Sure. But it also means that you'll be leaving *Oakview Valley*. And me.'

'Rob! You know me better than that! If I go to the Coast, you'll go with me. You're ready to move up to associate producer. I'm sure I could work that out.'

'I don't care about that, Sarah.'

'Of course you do. Are you crazy? You've worked your head off, just for a chance at it.'

She couldn't believe what she was hearing. Robin had the same kind of ambition she did. She couldn't imagine him willing to go on for much longer doing a job which was no more than a stepping stone to something better.

'You know a lot about television, Sarah. But not a lot about me.'

'I've known you for nearly four years now. And pretty well too, if I do say so myself.'

'Which isn't saying very much,' he told her.

She stared at him. 'Rob, we're good friends. I know something's been bothering you for a while. Don't you want to tell me about it?'

'I do want to. I've tried to. You just don't hear me.' If he said 'I love you, Sarah. I want you,' what would happen? Suppose she laughed at him. It would spoil what he did have. Her trust in him. Seeing her every day. Being a part of her life. He hesitated, waiting.

She saw his indecision, but instead of encouraging him, she busied herself giving them both more wine. She decided that she didn't want to push him any further. She had the feeling they were moving into dangerous territory. It was better left alone. Whatever was bothering him, and she supposed it was girl trouble, was his problem. Maybe she'd better not involve herself in it. She wouldn't know what to say, how to deal with it.

He was looking at her, plainly waiting.

She put aside her glass, and rose. 'Let's go have dinner. It's getting late. You must be starving by now.'

'To tell you the truth, I'm not hungry.'

But when she had served him he wolfed the salad, the veal casserole. He gulped his wine. He kept looking at her, his blue eyes dark now, but he concentrated on eating.

She nibbled the food, her excitement rising again. 'It'll make a wonderful show.' And then: 'Could it really happen just because Glory Ann's my friend?'

'Television's network,' he said. 'Everybody knows everybody. You know that.'

'Yes, but this . . . this . . . it's so . . . it's almost too easy.'

'Easy?' He laughed. 'You put in . . . how many years anyway? working up to this moment. How can you say it's too easy?'

'Years,' she said. 'Yes.' She remembered Washington. Still in school. Taking the bus home in the middle of the night. Walking two miles through frightening darkness

224

because suburban Maryland had no transport that late in those days. Doing the scut work, picking up shirts for her boss, buying his anniversary presents for his wife, dodging the friendly pat on the ass that he liked to bestow. Years.

'You've paid your dues,' Rob said.

'I guess I have.'

He suddenly pushed back his chair. 'I'm glad you told me. And don't worry. If this chance doesn't pan out, then something else will.'

She nodded.

He cleared his dishes from the table, drained his glass. 'If you don't mind, Sarah, I'll be going now.'

'If you have to.' She didn't relish the thought of the rest of the evening. Empty. Quiet. Peg would soon be coming home, but she would go to bed. Sarah would be alone again. But she wouldn't ask him to stay.

He was saying, 'Yes, I think so. It's time to go.' He had to get away before he made a fool of himself. He needed to kiss her, hold her, to pretend, at least for a little while, that she was his. The only thing to do was leave.

After he had gone she wandered restlessly around the apartment. There was the emptiness, the quiet, she had anticipated. Her excitement at the possibilities that lay before her was gone now. She felt let down. Champagne gone flat.

Peg came in, yawning. She'd had a good time with John and Carla, but now she was tired. She went to bed.

When Sarah finally went to sleep she found herself clutching her pillow to her and thinking of Robin, of the curve of his cheek, and the line of his mouth just before it broke into a smile.

17

That weekend, although neither of them knew of each other's plans, both Robin and Sarah decided to visit Tim in Washington.

Rob caught an early Eastern shuttle and took a cab to the Beltraney campus. He and Tim had a late breakfast together and went for a walk in Rock Creek Park.

They talked about soccer, and what Tim wanted to do the next year. 'Dad wants me out of here,' Tim said. 'Although he hasn't mentioned it lately. But I don't know. I only have one more year.'

'Don't worry about it now,' Rob suggested, thinking of the possibilities that lay before Sarah. 'Just wait and see what happens.'

Tim grinned companionably. 'That's what I plan on doing.'

They headed back to the campus, Tim thinking that it was nice to have a grown-up friend, Robin feeling close to Sarah in his pleasure with Tim's company.

Later the same morning, Sarah took Peg and flew to Washington. She rented a car and drove up Massachusetts Avenue on the way to the school.

Peg said, 'I'm dying of thirst, Mom.'

Sarah glanced at her watch. 'Let's get Tim and go and pig out on something huge and sinful. Okay?'

Peg said, 'Sure.' There was a brief silence. Then: 'Listen, Mom. I hope it's okay. I feel kind of funny about it, but when I was with Carla and John, she got to asking me about Tony. And I said he wasn't around any more.'

'It's true. Why not say so?'

'I don't like talking about your business. Only he is my father. Somehow, when he asks me . . .'

'When *he* asks . . .'

'She's the one who brought it up. Only I could tell he wanted to know, was listening, waiting for an answer.'

'No matter. Either way. We don't have anything to hide from them.'

John, no doubt, had said to Carla afterwards, 'See, I told you. No man lasts with her.' And that would only have been the beginning. Never mind.

Sarah was not going to explain the facts. The facts, as she saw them. John and Carla were very interested in Sarah's life, marital plans, comings and goings, expenses and whatever. For a very good reason. John was shelling out a pile every year for Tim's schooling. They'd like very much to slide out from under that responsibility. A change in Sarah's status could give them the excuse they needed. That was one reason why Carla had offered to take Tim. If he went to them, enrolled in a local school, they'd save those big bucks. If Sarah remarried, they'd save the half that John contributed to the children's support. John did very well, Sarah was certain. No need to worry on that score. But for Carla, very well wasn't enough, it seemed. Sarah smiled faintly. She wouldn't adjust her plans to their needs. No way, and no how, would she ever do that. On the other hand, she wouldn't cut off her nose to spite her face, or theirs either.

Peg and Sarah checked in at the school reception desk and were told that Tim had signed out with Robin Denver only a few minutes before.

Peg said, 'What's Robin doing here?'

'I don't know.' Sarah was suddenly apprehensive. Could Tim have called Rob? Was something wrong? And how could she find them?

The finding was easy. When she and Peg went out they saw Rob and Tim walking across the quadrangle. Tim almost as tall as Rob, gangling, his blond hair shining in the sun. The two of them were relaxed, smiling.

Sarah studied them as they came closer. It was okay. Nothing was wrong. Then why had Robin turned up here?

They approached, colour flooding Rob's face. He said hastily, 'I was in town. I decided to stop in and see Tim.'

'In Washington? How come? I didn't know you had friends here.'

He didn't answer.

They drove into Georgetown together. Tim led them to an ice cream parlour on Wisconsin Avenue.

Peg sat next to Robin, announced, 'This is where we do our huge and sinful thing.'

They ordered combo fudge sodas at Tim's suggestion.

The waitress brought them. Sarah took a single taste of hers, then pushed it aside. She listened to Tim and Robin talk soccer. Soon they were all four off on new movies. The time went quickly.

Robin pushed back his chair, rose. 'I've got to get going.'

'Wait a minute,' Tim protested. 'I've still got lots of time.'

Robin shook his head. His goodbyes were brief.

When he'd gone Sarah said, 'I didn't know he was going to visit you today.'

'Neither did I. He just turned up. But I'm glad he did. He's easy to be around, isn't he?'

Sarah thought, there was only fourteen years, a little less even, between Tim and Robin. Hardly enough for a father and son relationship. Then what did Rob have in mind? She wished she understood. But she was sure she wouldn't ask him. He'd known Tim long enough, she supposed, for him to have uncle privileges. Maybe that was it.

Peg and Tim had dinner with her. The teasing was as usual. It was reassuring to watch them. Tim was himself. Peg was too. There was no reason now to think that either of them had been permanently hurt by their separate experiences. Tim with Mark Downing. Peg with her illness. Still, how did anybody know?

Sarah shivered inside. She wouldn't think about it. She wanted her kids to be okay. More than okay. She wanted them to be safe. But how did you accomplish that? Even if you were a full-time mother, married, with a home in the suburbs, you couldn't guarantee your children's security any more than you could guarantee your own.

Rob's visit to Tim was still in the back of her mind when she went to the office on Monday morning.

She didn't intend to mention it, but suddenly she heard herself saying, 'It was nice of you to go to see Tim. He enjoyed the time with you.'

'I enjoyed the time with him,' Rob said flatly. 'He's a good kid.'

She wondered how to suggest that she and Rob get together for dinner at the end of the week. And even as she thought it, she realized that this was the first time she'd felt uncomfortable with him. Before, always, he'd been Robin, her right arm, her production assistant, even her friend. Now, he was . . . well, what was he? It was ridiculous that she should become too shy to offer a straightforward invitation.

But he gave her no time to figure it out. He said, 'I'd better get started on this stuff you've lined up for me. And Bonnie left word that if you had time to see her, she'd get up here as soon as you call.'

'It might as well be now, I guess. Want to tell her?'

Rob nodded, left the office.

Bonnie came in a few minutes later. She was wearing a white linen shirt, a blue skirt, both so wrinkled that they looked slept in. Her glasses had slipped to the end of her nose. She sank into a chair, said in a whisper, 'Sarah, you're not going to believe this.'

More man trouble, Sarah thought. Save me, save me, from young women. Also middle-aged and older women.

Bonnie waited expectantly, shivering.

Sarah obliged. 'I won't believe what?'

'That's why I didn't call you over the weekend. Because I don't believe it either.' Again Bonnie stopped. This time as if she'd run out of breath and words.

'But you wanted to call me,' Sarah prodded gently. 'About what?'

'This could be so big. For both of us, Sarah.'

229

Sarah said, 'You know you're making me crazy. What could be so big? What are you talking about?'

Bonnie said earnestly, 'It's my agent. He called me late Friday.' She gulped, took a breath. 'Do you remember my novel, Sarah? *Shining Star*.'

'Of course I do.' Sarah had read *Shining Star* when it came out, the first novel by an unknown writer, Bonnie Walker. It had seemed a perfect property for television. Sarah had contacted Bonnie through her agent, and had been delighted to learn that the girl was supporting herself by writing TV scripts. They'd never been able to work a deal on the book, but when Sarah was looking for a new writer for *Oakview Valley* she remembered Bonnie. Now she said, 'Of course I remember your book. What did your agent have to say?'

'There's this syndicate. California Television Company. Have you heard of them?'

'It sounds familiar. What about it?'

'It's expressed interest in *Shining Star*.'

'Yes?' Sarah asked, knowing there was more. There had to be. Bonnie now had the look of a cat who'd swallowed a canary.

'They want me to do the script.'

'I should hope so. They surely know your work with *Oakview Valley*.'

'Yes. And they asked me who I most like to work with. As producer.'

'Oh?' Sarah said.

'I told them you.'

'Me?' Sarah laughed. 'Since when would they let a scriptwriter pick a producer?'

'This is special,' Bonnie told her. 'Would you be interested?'

'It depends on the deal. I'd certainly be interested in knowing the details.' She paused. She hadn't intended to say anything to Bonnie until she heard from Glory Ann. That might be weeks, months. She hadn't even told Rita Porter about the possibility for that reason. Still, Bonnie had to have an idea of what might happen before she

230

made a commitment to California Television. She made a note to check on the company as soon as she could. Then she said, 'There's something else, Bonnie. I want you to get going as fast as you can on the script for the AIDS proposal.' She went on to explain about Glory Ann's interest in doing the show, and her attempt to find money for it.

Bonnie listened, wide-eyed and breathless, awed that Glory Ann would want to be involved. With Glory Ann's name in the cast, it would surely be made, and would become a success. When Bonnie reached to adjust her glasses, she knocked them off, and then went scrambling to retrieve them.

Finally back in her chair, she said, 'It's hard to believe . . .' Her voice trailed away. 'I don't know . . .'

She was scared, Sarah knew. She said, 'Let's not tell anybody, Bonnie. Not yet.'

'You feel the same as I do.'

Sarah crossed her fingers. 'You bet.'

At the door Bonnie turned back. 'Sarah, thanks.'

'You'll get to work on the script?'

'You bet!'

It would have been pleasant, Sarah thought, if she could sit at her desk, contemplating the two beautiful possibilities that had opened before her. But there was no time for that. *Oakview Valley* presented its own demands.

First she went to see Lyman Ogloe. He was a happy man now, his affair with Rita going smoothly. He greeted Sarah with warmth. But he *was* nervous about some budget problems. He wanted reassurance from Sarah.

She said, 'I'll do the best I can, as always. But the important thing is to bring in good shows, and to hang on to our Arbitrons and Nielsens. Do you think I'm going to risk the ratings to save a few bucks?'

'Sarah!' He acted shocked. 'Would I ask you to do that?'

After repeating her promise to do her best, her very best, not to overspend, Sarah returned to her office.

There was a message that Handy Sawyer, the IATSE

man, wanted to see her right away. IATSE was the union to which some movie cameramen, as well as stagehands, belonged. But *Oakview Valley*, like most other shows now, was done on video tape, and the people who handled that belonged to NABET, the National Association of Broadcast Employees and Technicians. So whatever the problem was would be with the stagehands.

Sarah and Handy Sawyer were buddies. He was not only the shop steward but was also a past president of the union. She had worked with him for four years. She called to let him know she was available immediately.

When he came in he was frowning. He said, 'Sarah, you know I hate making waves for you. Only I think I'd better talk to you before we have a real incident. You know how quick on the trigger some of my boys are.'

'I'm always glad to see you, Handy,' she said, smiling. She was glad that she'd remembered to send a wedding gift when Handy's son married a few months ago. He had the look of a man bringing her a platter of trouble.

'You've got some people, they don't know their places. Anybody else, I'd have had to call a walkout. I don't want to do that to you.'

It was taking him so long to get to the point that she became seriously concerned. What could have been happening that she didn't know about?

He said, 'Do me a favour, and you a favour too. Tell your set designers to keep the hands off the furniture. They want something moved, they go get somebody of mine to move it for them. Okay?'

'They know, Handy. But they forget. They're in a hurry, and they don't stop to think sometimes. Between you and me, it's not the greatest sin in the world.'

'I agree,' he said. 'But what can we do?'

'We can stop it from happening again. And we will.'

He grinned at her. 'The thing about you is, you're so easy to work with. And you're pretty too.'

'Thanks,' she said. 'Let me know if there's anything else I can do.'

'Oh I will, Sarah. I'll have to. Besides, it's always a pleasure to come and talk to you.'

When she was alone she made a note to herself. Find out what the set people have been doing to bug Handy.

Rob brought in the morning paper. He had it folded to Andrew Reynolds' column. He asked, 'See this, Sarah?'

Andrew had written, *Glory Ann Champion's Ralph is scouting production money. A mole tells us Sarah Morehouse is in on the deal that should be a deal soon. What'll happen to Oakview Valley if that comes off?*

'I wonder how he got that,' she said.

'There's nothing new?'

She shook her head.

'You must be getting antsy.'

She shrugged, feeling his eyes on her but not looking up. After a moment he went out and she heard him talking to someone. Soon the costume designer came in. He seated himself, twitched his trousers, examined his nails.

'How goes it?' Sarah asked.

He raised his brows, wagged a hand at her. 'Comme çi, comme ça.'

'Lyman has been on my back about the budget.'

The costume designer gave her an aggrieved look. 'I can't help it. Things are so expensive, Sarah. What do you want me to do? Shop at Sears?'

'If you could manage by shopping at Sears, I'd say yes. But I guess you can't.'

'It's our image. We've got too much at stake to wreck it. Half the audience turns on just to see what creations we come up with next.'

'Yes. But we've got to deal with it. You know what's coming up. A 1985 audience is too mobile to be satisfied with staying in Oakview Valley. They want to get around. So do our characters. So Davey will be going to Cambria on the California coast to look for his long-lost sister. It's going to cost plenty.'

The costume designer pouted at her. 'That's your problem, Sarah. You pick the places. I only do the clothes.'

233

She smiled. 'You're right. I was thinking out loud. But do us both a favour and try hard to cut costs. Beg and borrow. Steal. Whatever.'

'That's a very limiting suggestion,' he said reproachfully.

'I'm sorry. Try.'

Sighing loudly, he went out.

Moments later the phone trilled. Rob put a call through.

It was Daniel Clermont. His voice was slow, careful. 'Sarah. How are you?'

Daniel. She hadn't heard of anything that would do for him, though she had been paying attention. Why was he calling?

'Daniel,' she said. 'It's good to hear from you. What are you doing these days?'

'I'm working. A temporary job. Not very much.' Then: 'I read about you in Reynolds' column this morning, and wanted to wish you luck.'

'It's good of you to call. There's nothing certain yet.' And then, even as she thought it out, she went on, 'If the project *does* go through, would you be interested? I'd need a business affairs manager. Of course I can't make any promises right now. But if you were available . . .' It wouldn't hurt to do him a good turn. They'd had some pleasant times together. And he was a good man on the job. She certainly didn't need any more Jim Carstairs in her life.

'Would you really . . . after what happened . . .'

'Why, Daniel,' she said. 'This is strictly business. I know you'd do a terrific business affairs manager for me.' And suddenly she saw another advantage. Rita liked men. Here would be a new one for her to concentrate on. And Daniel liked success. He'd be drawn to Rita as soon as he laid eyes on her.

He was saying, 'If you want me, I'll make myself available whenever you need me.'

'Then I'll be in touch as soon as things are definite,' she promised.

*

234

She was at the door. Everyone was waiting. She walked in, crossed the room. Rob was looking at her. As she became aware of his gaze, her heart seemed to give a quick hard thump against her ribs. He was looking at her the way a man looks at a woman he wants. It was like being enfolded in a wonderful warmth. It was like a caress.

She sank into a chair, busied herself with notepad and ballpoint pen. Hy Berge nodded at her, then spoke into his mike. The floor manager signalled.

The scene was between Hart Carow, playing Davey, and Ursula Rein, who had joined the cast after Rita was written out, playing the new role of Karen.

Hart said, 'Karen, are you sure there isn't something you want to tell me?'

'Nothing,' Karen answered, looking into his eyes. 'Nothing, Davey. I've never hidden anything from you. Not ever.'

'Those phone calls, Karen?'

'Some kook, Davey.' Karen shrugged, turned away from him. But she didn't turn quite far enough. She was upstaging Hart. Deliberate? Accidental? Sarah wasn't sure. She didn't move nor speak, waiting to see what would happen.

For an instant Hart stopped being Davey. A look of anger flashed across his handsome face. Then he became Davey again. He and Ursula played out the scene.

Later Sarah told Hy, 'Did you see Ursula? That doll's beginning to feel her oats.'

'I saw.'

Sarah grinned. 'They always try it on, don't they?'

'The smart ones do.'

And then Hart came up, saying heatedly, 'I'm not going to put up with it. I had enough trouble with Rita. I don't want any more. Not with Ursula.'

Hy soothed him. Sarah soothed him. He promised to leave it to them to handle.

Hy told Sarah he'd talk to Ursula. Sarah was delighted to allow him that joy.

She went back to her office, hungry, with the beginnings of a headache. When would she hear from Glory Ann? How long before Bonnie knew if there was a deal with *Shining Star?* And what about Rob?

She wished now that she hadn't called a cast and crew meeting. But there were noises in the outer office. The group was gathering. The unit manager, set dressers and costume designer, the script typists, Bonnie. Robin stuck his head in. 'Everybody's ready.'

'Except me,' she said. 'How about some Tylenol?'

He brought her the pills, water. 'Anything special?'

'Just this day.'

The cast and crew filed in, took chairs. The office was crowded, airless. She waited until everyone was settled, then she told them about Cambria, remembering when she and Tony had gone scouting locations together. What a beautiful day it had been. It seemed a long time ago now. She went on, explaining that Lucilla had been hiding in the small beach town, and now Davey would go there for several episodes.

There was a general chorus of enthusiasm before the second thoughts poured in. The shits and fucks flew. Mainly from the younger women. Sarah remembered when she too had spoken that way, believing that it gave her an aura of toughness, proved she was her own person. Now the strong language seemed dull, or even worse, empty.

Finally she cut in, 'We'll all have to make personal adjustments when we go on location. Notice that I said when, not if. It's in the cards. I just want you to know about the situation as it develops. And I also want you to know that I'll help in every way I can with any problems that arise.'

When they'd all gone, Robin said, 'Well done, Sarah.'

'All in a day's work.' Then, without stopping to think about it, she asked, 'Are you available for dinner tonight by any chance?'

'Sorry. I'm not.' He didn't look at her now.

She wanted him to. She wanted him to look at her the

236

way he had when she entered the rehearsal. She wanted
to feel enwrapped, caressed. She wanted to feel loved.

But she asked teasingly, 'Heavy date?' playing the older
sister to hide her hurt. He was her right arm after all.
Which meant he was supposed to be always available.

He didn't respond to that. He nodded at her, said
goodnight, and left her.

What was wrong with him?

She flipped the Rolodex. Meet somebody for a drink?
But who? She got her purse, remembering the small café
near Rob's apartment, the evening she had ended up
there, drinking martinis, and later, Rob's arms around
her. No. She didn't want a drink. She'd go home, spend
the evening with Peg as originally planned.

Only without Rob.

Good God, she thought. What's wrong with me?

18

Peg said, 'Mom, what's wrong with you? You've been pacing back and forth and jumping every time the phone rings. And generally acting as if you've got a burr in your butt.'

Sarah winced. 'We can do without the burr in butts bit, Peg.'

'Okay,' Peg grinned. 'But what's wrong?'

'I don't know. I'm a little restless, I guess.'

'Wondering when you're going to hear from Glory Ann?' Peg said, her sympathy so adult that Sarah's throat tightened.

Peg looked well, not as thin as she had been, but slender. Her cheeks were no longer hollowed. There were no shadows under her eyes. She was her old energetic self.

'I do wonder. I can't help it,' Sarah told her. 'But I know I shouldn't count on anything happening very soon. These things take time.'

'Carla doesn't expect you to go to LA,' Peg observed. 'I heard her tell Dad, when he was grumbling about our maybe moving out there. My moving, that is.'

'Is that right?'

'Carla says doing soaps isn't all that much anyway. And that it's a big jump from an *Oakview Valley* to prime-time TV movies.'

'Really?' Sarah rose, prowled to the window and peered out. The lights thirty-five floors below seemed to belong to another world. She and Peg, in the penthouse, were in a separate universe.

She didn't want to know what Carla thought, but she didn't want to make too much of it by telling Peg to shut up. It was good that Peg felt comfortable enough with the

238

divorce to talk about Carla and John. Sarah wished that Tim was as casual about it. But he couldn't be.

And of course, Carla was partly right. The chance of Ralph's being able to put together a deal for a TV movie was iffy. The chance that Bonnie's book would be bought by California Television Company was even more iffy. Sarah had checked the firm out. It had been set up by three young people, none of whom had any money of their own.

That's what Sarah told herself. On the other hand, she hadn't been able to get the two possibilities out of her mind. She hadn't been able to resist putting out small feelers for information either. She'd collected the names of several private schools, in case that was what Tim wanted. She knew of two good schools for Peg too. She'd boned up on the neighbourhoods that would be suitable. It was all written down in her day book. Just in case.

Peg said thoughtfully, 'You know, Mom, I think Carla's very jealous of you.'

Sarah laughed and hugged Peg, and suggested they try a quick game of Chinese checkers.

Carla sat so that her face was shaded from the spring sunlight. It dried the skin, made for wrinkles. She didn't need any, thank you. Her complexion was good. She intended to keep it that way. She wished John would make up his mind. When he did, she would know how to plan. But she waited, said nothing. She had learned that pushing John didn't help.

He said, 'Of course Sarah might say no.'

'She might,' Carla agreed.

'It would be stupid. The kids enjoy their time with us in Maine.'

'Yes, of course,' Carla agreed.

'And Sarah's not stupid.'

'No,' Carla agreed again, sighing not quite audibly. Did they really have to talk so often about Sarah?

'You're sure you don't mind having the kids?'

'John, I've told you I don't mind. I've told you I'd enjoy it. Tim and Peg are your children. You have a right, a duty, to spend time with them. Would I interfere with that?'

He pulled her into his arms. 'I'm sorry, Carla. I guess I just don't feel comfortable with the situation.'

She pressed against him. 'You're not sorry, are you? You wouldn't want to go back, would you?'

'Christ, no!' he said, horrified. 'Live with Sarah? Is that what you think?'

'Then it's all right,' Carla purred. 'Just ask her if we can have the kids for the summer. If we can, good. If not, we'll be on our own.'

'And that's not so bad either,' he told her, suddenly smiling.

She smiled back at him. One of these days he'd become accustomed to being a divorced father, she thought. And then everything would be all right.

In mid June Tim's school closed down for the summer.

Sarah and Peg, with Rob's help, moved Tim, and his belongings, back to New York.

But while they were in Washington Sarah went to see her mother. It turned into an exciting visit. Katy looked beautiful. Her neighbour, Bennett Ames, was there too. He and Katy exchanged long meaningful glances. So Sarah wasn't totally surprised when the small dapper man took her aside and said, 'I've asked your mother to do me the honour of being my wife.' Sarah hugged him, congratulated him. When she went to kiss her mother, Katy looked at her earnestly, 'Is it all right, Sarah?' Thinking of Mike, Sarah knew. Of a long-ago life.

'Of course it's all right,' Sarah said. 'You've been alone too long.'

After some discussion the couple decided to be married the day after Christmas. Sarah promised that she and the children would be there.

The following weekend both Tim and Peg went to

John's summer house in Maine for six weeks. Sarah wasn't too happy about that but she couldn't deny them the chance to get away from the city.

It was in the early part of July when Bonnie called. 'I've heard from California Television, Sarah.' Her voice was hoarse, shaking. 'It's all off. I really thought we had a deal on *Shining Star*. They'd shaken on it and everything. And now, now they've gone under. Just like that. No money.'

A handshake could lead to a brush-off. A kiss on both cheeks could lead to a kiss-off. That was the business. She told Bonnie. She told herself. And she told Bonnie too, 'Be glad you hadn't signed yet. If you had, your book might have ended up being part of their assets. At least this way it still belongs to you.'

She went directly from the phone to the refrigerator. She took a big bowl of ice cream. Even that didn't help. She'd hoped more than she realized that *Shining Star* would sell.

She thought about calling Glory Ann. Maybe there was something going on. Something she didn't know about. She kept herself from calling by going to bed.

She dreamed of flying to Los Angeles. She went first class. The flight attendant looked familiar. She stepped from the plane. There were crowds all around. The sunlight on chrome and steel was blinding. A tall man carrying flowers came to meet her. She didn't get his name, nor whom he represented. When he led her to a long grey limousine, he turned into Marko, Glory Ann's driver and bodyguard. He handed her into the limo and drove off. They sped through miles of empty freeway. Hours later he pulled up before a shack of corrugated tin. He opened the door for her, and now he was Tony Statler. Inside the shack Roy Carmack was waiting for her. He said, 'Surprise, Sarah!' And that was when she woke up, sweat-covered and shivering.

241

She got up, showered, dressed. Whatever the dream meant, she wasn't going to pay any attention to it.

But over the next few weeks it kept coming back to her. Roy Carmack. Tri-National.

She waited, hoping to hear from Glory Ann. But it was against her nature to wait while someone else did all the work. It was against her nature to do nothing.

Tony had said Roy Carmack never changed his mind. Once he was rebuffed, that was it for ever. Those were Tony's words. How did she know he was right? Why couldn't she go to Roy Carmack, talk to him. But where was he now? Andrew Reynolds had written something about Carmack's being in Toronto. He wouldn't still be there. Or would he? And what about Tri-National?

She decided it wouldn't hurt to know how to reach Carmack. In case she wanted to.

But there were Glory Ann and Ralph . . . If they were setting something up . . .

She looked in the Manhattan phone book. There was no Roy Carmack listed. She called the Pierre. He wasn't there, and wasn't expected. She checked the business directory. Tri-National. East 62nd Street. She wrote down the phone number.

That night when she came home from the office, Laylie said, 'Glory Ann called you.' And shaking her head: 'I tell you, that one, she's something.'

Sarah's heart began to beat quickly. 'When? What time? What did she say?'

'A little while ago is when.' Laylie laughed. 'And what she said was so much I didn't get it all. Mostly about her, and her Ralph . . .'

Sarah looked at her watch. Ten past seven. Ten past four in Los Angeles. She punched out Glory Ann's private number, and soon heard, 'Sarah, is that you?'

'It's I,' Sarah said.

'Oh, my, "It is I!" ' Glory Ann mocked her.

Sarah told herself, Don't count on anything and then you won't be disappointed.

Glory Ann said, 'It's taking so long, Sarah. I thought

Ralph would get it all done in a couple of weeks. But I'm finding out that that's not how it works.'

'No,' Sarah agreed, feeling a vast sinking letdown in spite of her warning to herself. 'No, Glory Ann, that's not how it works. We both know that.'

'Ralph says he can do it. He's not discouraged.'

'Maybe he can.' Sarah took a long slow breath. 'Listen, Glory Ann, would he mind if I followed up on a lead of my own?'

'I don't know. Why would he?'

'I wouldn't cut him out. You know that.'

'If you're going to talk business, then talk to him. I'll just screw it up if I try to be go-between.' There was an instant's pause. Then Glory Ann said, 'There's something else . . . I don't know if you care, or want to know, or anything . . . but just in case . . . Tony Statler's left LA.'

'He has?' Sarah said coolly.

'He hooked up with some Ms Rich Bitch on the south-western circuit. I think she's going to buy him a TV station in New Mexico.'

Leave it to Tony, Sarah thought. Still doing the same old thing.

Then Ralph was on the line, saying, 'Hi. What's doing?'

Sarah asked if Glory Ann had ever mentioned Roy Carmack to him. He said he didn't think so. Sarah went on, explained her previous contact with the CEO of Tri-National. Then said, 'If it won't interfere with what you're doing, would it be okay if I contact him again?'

'Glory Ann really wants to do that show. And I think she should. So sure. Go ahead. If you think you've got a lead.'

'I'm not sure of what I've got. Maybe nothing. But it's something I want to try.'

'So try,' he said.

The next morning she called the office of Tri-National. Roy Carmack wasn't in. He wasn't expected. Sarah left her name, her number.

It was ten days before he called her. 'Miss Morehouse? What can I do for you?'

243

'You can see me. At your convenience,' she said.

'And why should I?'

'I'd like to talk to you.'

'Have you changed your mind?' he demanded.

'I'd like to talk to you,' she repeated.

He told her to be at the Pierre, at seven. He could give her half an hour. He rang off.

She was in the lobby of the Pierre at six forty-five. She wore blue silk, high-heeled blue kid shoes, pearls at her throat. At seven she knocked at Carmack's door, a copy of the AIDS proposal under her arm.

He opened the door, leaning on his ebony crutches. 'Miss Morehouse.'

When she had seated herself, she said, 'Thank you for seeing me.'

'I'd have returned your call sooner. But I was in England,' he told her. He sank heavily into the sofa. 'Now, you have half an hour. Let's get to it.'

'Are you still interested in my proposal?'

'I might be.' He studied her. 'I'm curious to know why you've changed your mind,' he added.

'I want to do this show, Mr Carmack.'

'And what about Tony Statler?'

'You were right about him,' she said coolly.

'I like your style.'

'Thank you. What I'd like to know is if you would be willing to go ahead under certain new circumstances.'

'What are they?'

She described what Ralph Champion was doing. Carmack knew Ralph's work. Sarah explained that Ralph was married to Glory Ann. Carmack knew that too. Sarah told him that Glory Ann wanted to be in the movie.

Sarah thought she saw a glint appear in Carmack's eyes at that, but he listened without comment, frowning. Finally he said, 'I don't understand. What do you need Ralph Champion for? I offered you a perfectly good deal, and you turned me down. Now you're back. Not asking for the same deal, without that hustler. But asking for somebody else to be cut in.'

244

'I promised the script to them,' she said simply. 'If Ralph could get the money together . . .'

Carmack rose. 'It's seven-thirty.'

She got up, took the proposal, started for the door. 'Thank you for seeing me,' she said.

He smiled. 'My pleasure.' And then: 'Call the office tomorrow. Give my secretary Ralph Champion's number and whatever. You've got the money.'

'Mr Carmack!'

He took the proposal from under her arm. 'I'd better have this. Goodnight, Miss Morehouse.' The door closed in her face.

She sparkled. She glittered and glowed.

She was finished making soaps for good. By next winter her name, Sarah Morehouse, would flash on screens across the country. Flash in prime time. A night-time movie. Sarah Morehouse, Executive Producer.

Sarah Morehouse. She doodled it on the edges of the paper. She wrote it, printed it, drew it. Sarah Morehouse.

There was only one person she wanted to tell.

But first she had to let Ralph know that he would be getting a call from Tri-National.

Then she had to speak to Bonnie.

Finally she was ready to telephone Rob.

But even as she reached for the phone, she hesitated. It was going to be difficult. He'd reacted so strangely when she first mentioned the possibility of her moving on. She would have to convince him that he had to move on with her. And certainly she'd find a way to name him associate producer. They would work together. It would be the same as before.

Then she wavered. How would that sound to him? Would he feel that she was trying to bribe him? Would he resent that? Perhaps, even though she wanted so much to see him now, she should wait.

She paced the room restlessly, the blue silk of her dress flaring against her knees. She went out to the terrace. A distant plane seemed to be blinking its lights at her. She was so excited that she could hardly contain herself. But there was no one to share her triumph with. No one. She remembered telling her mother, *You've been alone too long*, and thought now that she herself had been alone too long. There'd been Daniel, then Tony. But still she was alone.

A slim crescent of moon hung like a silver ornament from the roof of a distant building. A warm breeze tugged at her skirt. Faint sounds of traffic rose from the streets below. She was in one of the world's biggest cities, and yet she had no one to talk to. No one that she wanted to talk to. Except Rob.

The doorbell chimed. She heard Laylie go to answer it. Moments later Rob was beside her, saying, 'Bonnie told me, Sarah.'

Bonnie, having sworn not to tell anyone, had immediately phoned Rob. But Sarah laughed. She ought to have known. That was Bonnie for you.

'You must feel wonderful,' he said, smiling.

Elation swept her in a quick hot wave. 'Oh Rob, I can't tell you . . . it's so . . . just what I've always wanted . . .'

'When do you go?' he asked, and now his voice was heavy.

'I don't know. Nothing's signed yet of course. It just happened. I'd expect to be around for several more months.' She paused. 'And you'll be coming with me, Rob. I mentioned it before, I know. I'm going to get you the associate producer slot. It'll be a great opportunity for you. And . . .' she rushed on, 'We'll be together, working just as we always have.'

He said, 'Sorry, Sarah. But no thanks.'

She looked stunned, wounded. He wanted to hug her, comfort her, take back his refusal. But he knew it was no good. He'd gone as far as he could go.

'No thanks!' she cried. 'How can you say that? It's a wonderful chance for you.'

'I know,' he said.

'Then?' When he didn't reply, she went on, 'Rob, please tell me what's wrong? Why won't you come to the

Coast with me? Why are you giving up what is a great chance for you to do what you want to do?'

There were shadows on his face. His eyes looked dark, almost black. He said, 'I don't want to go on like this any more. I'm glad you're going to the Coast. I'm glad I won't have to see you every day. See you, want you. I know I should be congratulating you, and telling you how great it is. And it is great. And I do congratulate you. But the truth is, I'm thinking about myself. I know that's awful. But I can't help it. I'm thinking about me.'

'Robin . . .' She controlled a sudden impulse to touch him. Just to stroke his hand. To run her fingers through his hair.

But he stepped close to her, grabbed her by both arms. His eyes burned in his sudden-white face. 'Don't you understand? Don't you want to?' He shook her so hard that her head snapped back. 'What do I have to do to get your attention? There was Daniel, and I waited, knowing he wasn't for you. And then Tony came along. Okay. I figured you'd see through him, and you did. Damn it, Sarah. I'm in love with you. And I want you. I've wanted you for so long that I'm beginning to think it's for ever.'

Her throat was suddenly dry, her breath uneven. This was what she had been afraid of. Hearing these words from him. Knowing she wouldn't know how to deal with them, with him. 'Robbie,' she said, 'don't spoil everything. You're my right hand. I can't do without you. I wouldn't want to. We're a perfect team. But that's it. Don't imagine there's something else between us.' And even as she said the words she remembered being in his arms, remembered the something else that had briefly been between them, and yearned for it again.

'I'm not imagining what I feel, Sarah.'

She tried to draw back from him, but he held her firmly. There was a heat where he touched her, a warmth that spread slowly through her body. She saw the curve in his lips when he was silent, and remembered how they looked when he smiled.

But she said, 'We've worked closely together for several

247

years, Rob. Sharing the good times and the bad. And there have been plenty of both. Laughing together and cursing together. Don't make more of your feelings than you should. Believe me. I understand.' Her voice had assumed the soothing croon that she sometimes used with Tim when he was being difficult.

Rob heard it, recognized it. Now his white face reddened. He said, 'I hate that motherly tone. Don't use it to me. I'm not your child. There's just barely ten years between us. You can pretend you're ancient if you want to, if you feel comfortable that way, but you're not going to make me believe that's how you feel.'

'Robbie, we're good friends,' she said firmly. 'We've always been good friends.'

'And that's all?'

She swallowed hard. 'That's all.'

'Okay. Then I quit,' he told her. 'I'm finished. I don't work for you any more, Sarah.'

She hadn't expected that. She'd thought they would go on as always. Together.

'You can't quit,' she said. A void was opening up. She saw darkness spreading at her feet. She blurted, 'Rob, please, I can't do this alone. Not this. I really can't.'

'You can. Any smart, fast-moving person can be your assistant or your associate. There's half a dozen at least that you can have in your office by nine o'clock tomorrow morning.'

She shook her head. 'No, Rob. No. Not just any person will do. It has to be you.' All the times he had been there when trouble came up. All the times he had dropped everything and come the moment she called him. Who else was there, who else had there ever been, that she could depend on? Not just in the studio, not just for the show, but in her life.

He said slowly, 'I thought I could visit with Tim, and find some crumbs that way. I thought I'd be near you, playing games with Peg. But, as great as the kids are, they're no substitute for you. I thought I could be satisfied just working with you. Being part of that side of your life.

248

I tried to tell myself that I could go on, just remembering the one time we were together. The time you pretend you've forgotten. When we were honest with each other, and loving, and it was wonderful for both of us. But remembering isn't enough either. I can't go on with that. It makes me somebody I don't want to be. Watching you, but not able to touch again. Wanting you. Loving you, Sarah.'

It was hard, so hard, but she drew away from him gently. She gave the glittering lights below the terrace a single absent look, then went inside. Robin followed her.

She looked around the familiar room. It had seemed so empty only a little while ago. Now, with Rob here, it had recovered itself, had become her home again.

He said, 'Since I've quit, I might as well tell you what I'm going to do.'

'Do?'

'I've got an offer. A good one. Producing, Sarah. I'm going to take it.'

'Producing. Oh Rob. I'm glad for you.' Her voice shook. 'So that's the end of us.'

'It's the end of you being my boss. But not the end of us. Unless you want it to be.'

It was no use arguing. She knew he wasn't going to change his mind. They wouldn't be working together any more.

But she yearned for him. For him, as a man, as a lover. For him. She yearned for him as every reason against it whipped through her mind.

He was too young. Too young for what? He wasn't eighteen after all. He was a grown man, mature, knowing, sensitive. He had proven what he was minute by minute, hour by hour, being with her.

People would laugh. So what? People could laugh at anything they didn't understand. That had never stopped her before. Why should it stop her now? If it was right, then it was right. No one else could judge that. Only she could. He could.

Perhaps it wouldn't last. Well, what did last? And how

did you know ahead of time anyway? Who gave you an unbreakable contract for anything in this life?

She hungered for him. They fitted together and suited each other as if both had been cut from the same pattern, designed to be that perfect match always searched for, rarely found. Always, when she needed him, he was there. She remembered how he had come to stay with Peg when she herself had to go to Glory Ann in Washington. No questions, no discussion. He had come because she needed him. Always, always, when she needed him he was there. She saw him walking beside Tim, with Tim's smiling face turned to him, and saw him with his head bent close to Peg's while they played cards. He'd be a young father to both kids. A young lover to her.

She remembered him loosening her skirt, unbuttoning her blouse, sliding a pillow under her head, to make her comfortable. And then holding her protectively until they came together in passion.

Loving you, he'd said. That was what it was all about. No matter what, she was a woman. She needed love. She had love to give. It wasn't a word she'd used with Daniel, with Tony. It wasn't what she had had with them.

And she knew now that was why she'd been afraid. Why she couldn't let herself understand what Rob felt for her, and what she felt for him.

Rob said, 'I guess I'd better go, Sarah. I'm glad you're getting what you want. If you need me, let me know. And I'll be there.'

She'd never let fear run her life before. She wouldn't this time. She drew a deep shaky breath, and smiled, and put her arms around him. 'Rob,' she said. 'Oh Robbie. I need you now.' She looked into his eyes. 'I've been afraid to face it, afraid of loving you. But that's over. I love you. I don't want you to go.'

And, as he bent his head to kiss her, she thought with triumphant joy, that she had the job she wanted, and Robin, too, so with good luck, maybe this time . . .